BURNING BRIDGES IN NOWHERE

GOING NOWHERE #2

DONNA AUGUSTINE

ONE

When I'd opened the birthday gift Kaden had given me and found a key, I hadn't expected *this*. I thought it was for the outpost—not that I'd ever seen one used. Or a key for a studio, or maybe a small apartment at most. But no. That wasn't how Kaden worked.

I gazed around the town house, *my* town house, at least for the time being. It was nearly as large as his. The architecture and design was clean and simple, as if he'd somehow known exactly what I'd like. The colors were neutral and calming. It wasn't furnished, as if he'd known I'd prefer to do that myself. There was only one huge, glaring problem. This town house was right next to his.

It would almost be like living *with* him. He'd know every single person who came and went. Every. Single. One. Gram wouldn't stand a chance of slipping past him to get to me here. It had to be the reason he'd gotten me this place. Why else?

I'd given my word that I wouldn't act against him, but

he'd taken out an insurance policy on me for the price tag of a town house. It appeared as if he trusted me about as much as I trusted him. Was there a chance he'd done it because I was wholly unprepared for all that dwelled in Nowhere? Maybe, but taking one glance over at him gave me the distinct impression that was not the case.

Kaden was leaning against the counter, watching me. His dark hair was pushed back and his light eyes nearly glowing as they watched me. The angle of his body, the slight arrogance of his expression, was of someone who thought they had it all under control, the writer of the play we were all acting out per his direction. Yep. There was a reason he was keeping me close, and it had nothing to do with benefiting me. This was nothing but a potential trap.

When certain things came to light, certain *relations*, this wasn't the place I'd be able to hole up. Only a lunatic would hide in plain sight of the person who was hunting them. I hadn't needed to know Kaden long to know that hell might be preferable to his wrong side.

"What's wrong? You said you wanted to live in Nowhere, and yet you don't appear happy about this?" he asked.

"I am. I'm definitely happy." I smiled so hard my cheeks wanted to break. I made a show of looking around the place before my face cramped from strain. "It's very generous, but...maybe too much? I did only just start with the company, after all. I'm not sure this is appropriate?" I laid a hand on the railing that led upstairs, keeping my gaze on anything but him.

It really wasn't fair that I had to perfect my lies with someone who'd surely lived for centuries. I'd barely made it two and half decades and hadn't started practicing deception until much more recently.

"I'm sure it'll all work out in the end. Not to mention there wasn't that much available, so it'll have to." He was leaning and smiling, plotting and maneuvering—it was all working out exactly as he wanted.

We'd see about that.

"Is there a realtor or someone who handles these things? Maybe something else will open up?" I stared down at the wood flooring, admiring the grain as if the finish were my biggest concern in life at the moment.

"Sure. I'll get you his number. He should be back in a few months or so." He strolled over, stopping not far from where I stood at the bottom of the stairs. "I'd get settled in while you wait. No rush, right?" He dug into his pocket, pulling out a key. "A spare, not that you need to lock it. No one would dare break in here."

Just as I figured. This place was literally an extension of his town house. I nodded, taking the key, too aware of even the most casual brush of hands.

I needed to start dating. If my life weren't in complete upheaval, it would be easier to do so, but my hormones didn't care that I was in a mess. They seemed to want to fixate on the closest source of testosterone around, and that was Kaden. It didn't help that he had so damned much of it.

He watched me as if he could sense my thoughts. He couldn't, but even the possibility warmed my cheeks. I took a step back, taking a spin around the living room and putting a healthy buffer in between us.

The door swung open, and Cookie, the biggest mood killer and my savior, barged in.

Kaden nodded to us both and left, swaggering out. Of course he'd be feeling his oats. He'd worked me into a corner, gotten his way, and we were both well aware of it.

Cookie walked in and spun around, curling up her lip. "Man, this place is sterile. It's going to need a lot of work to make it livable." She patted the air in my direction. "Don't worry, though. I know a guy. He owns the place I got the furnishings for the outpost. He'll hook you up."

Oh no, not that. This place would look like a seventies sitcom set after its twentieth season of use.

"Yeah, that's really nice of you, but I can't put you out like that. I can manage." *For once in Cookie's life, please let her be easy about something and not dig in.* It was bad enough I was going to be stuck here under surveillance. Couldn't it at least look pretty?

"You're my girl. I can't let you live like this." She was shaking her head, throwing her hands in the air and circling. "You'll die of depression coming back here night after night. I know no one likes my taste that much, but I'm telling you, you'll come to see the wisdom of my design aesthetic. You just need to give it a few decades to grow on you. You don't like it after that, do whatever you want and I won't say a thing." She made a motion of zipping her lips.

A few decades? She was staring at me, waiting for

some acknowledgment. Hopefully I wouldn't be here more than a few weeks, so it wouldn't matter. I gave a nod and the best smile I had left, which didn't say much.

Connor walked in, glanced around, and shrugged. Having given his stamp of approval, he headed over to the kitchen, opening up the empty fridge. "Any food in this place?"

Connor had to eat constantly to feed all those muscles.

"Not yet," I said.

Cookie was walking toe to heel across the living room area counting, but stopped long enough to say, "Dice is bringing some."

How much time did I have? Would she go shopping without me? It didn't matter. I had to keep remembering that this was temporary.

Dice walked in a minute later with bags and boxes in hand, following Connor's earlier path.

"Nice place," he said, dropping all his goods on the kitchen island. "But I can't believe you want to live right next door to Kaden. He's going to know every single thing you do. You know that, right?"

"Yeah, I kind of figured." Which was why instead of grabbing a slice of the weird-looking pizza he was pulling out of the box, I wanted to slam my head into the stone counter. It wasn't as if I didn't want the town house. It just wasn't compatible with my long-term survival.

Cookie grabbed a slice of the black dough coated with what appeared to be some sort of melted cheese.

"It's got decent bones, but I've got to help her make it livable."

Both of the guys laughed, Connor looking like he was choking on his pizza.

"Screw you both. I have good taste." Cookie pointed at Dice. "You think black tie means to polish all your guns for the affair." She turned to Connor. "And you. I don't know what shit you're taking, but you can't even put those arms down anymore. You won't have any shirts that fit soon. Time to quit it."

Connor, usually either silent or nodding, actually looked offended for the first time. "Hey! I'm in good shape. *I* care about my body."

Cookie planted both hands on the island and leaned toward him. "Why? We. Don't. Die. At least not from poor health. You're the only tinker I know who morphs and still has the same crazy body. Take a day off once in a while."

She spun to go at Dice again, but he cut her off first.

"Oh no, you ain't talking more shit about my guns after how many times they saved your ass."

She shrugged. "Fine." The room fell silent before she looked at the food. "I'll leave the guns alone, but a little stingy with the food, no? What, Kaden cut your pay or something? Too many hookers this week?"

"Considering she doesn't even have a plate or napkin for us, I'd be happy there's anything," Dice said.

They all turned to me.

"He's right," Cookie said. "If you're going to have us over, at least have a couple plates, and maybe a chair wouldn't kill you." She was already chowing down on another slice of pizza.

Oh no, they weren't turning this on me.

"I don't remember inviting any of you," I said.

"You had to know we'd be showing up," Dice said, as if that had been the lamest excuse ever.

"Fine. It's my fault," I said with the tone of someone saying *shut the hell up*. I took a slice before I didn't get one. There weren't that many left, and it wasn't looking as if they were going to save me one. "Where do you get this stuff?" The flavor was a little strange, but in an oddly intriguing way.

"Place a couple blocks away. I'll show it to you tomorrow on the way to the furniture store," Cookie said, and then took her pizza back to the living area and started doing her heel-to-toe measurements again.

Connor and Dice were looking at each other, choking on laughter. They looked my way as if this were the funniest thing they'd seen in a year.

"By the way, you are stingy with the food," I said.

It didn't so much as ding their smiles.

TWO

"The surprise is here?" I asked, following Cookie upstairs in my town house.

She stopped in front of the door to the master bedroom and flung it open. "Ta da!" she said.

I braced myself for what I was about to see and then stepped into the room. I should've taken a few more minutes to prepare. There was a black dresser on the side that looked shiny enough to see my reflection in. The patchwork quilt on the bed had colors that never should've touched each other, ever. Then there was the pompom rainbow fringe.

"Is the bed..." I moved closer to make sure the strange color combination wasn't creating an illusion of a dent in the center. I reached down to touch it but stopped short. It might be wise to put on a pair of gloves before touching anything.

"Amazing? Yes. It's already got a dent to roll right

into." She followed me into the room, looking around and nodding. "Now this is comfy. No throw pillows to fuss with. If you come home drunk, you won't care if you leave your boots on with this cover." She dropped onto the bed, kicking up her feet to demonstrate.

"You're definitely right about that." I wouldn't care one bit if this stuff fell apart. If it got stained, it would blend in with the other ones it had.

"Give it a couple of decades. I'm telling you, it's going to grow on you." Her smile was exploding with pride, almost to the point of supernova. She was so pleased with herself that I couldn't summon up a rain cloud. "You're shocked at how quick I can pull a place together, right? I have had centuries of practice, though."

"You do work quickly." It had been one day. I'd planned on dragging out my move from the outpost, but it wasn't going to work out well if she kept this up. Although it might offer me cover. No one would wonder why I didn't want to move in. They'd be more surprised if I rushed.

"Are you busy right now? We can go get some more shit." She jumped off the bed a little too quickly to be bluffing.

No way was I going to the origin of this stuff. This room had been more than enough for one day.

"Actually, I wanted to head back to the outpost and start packing a few things." And it was going to take me a very long time to do so.

"That's fine. I've got a couple more things to do

around here anyway," she said as she followed me out of the room and downstairs.

She headed toward a box in the living room and pulled out a pillow with moth holes and a ripped throw blanket. "I know you don't have a couch yet, but I couldn't resist. It was such a good deal. Ninety percent off. Can you even imagine? They were practically giving this stuff away."

Unfortunately, I could. I didn't want to see what else was in that box.

"See you in a bit."

I didn't bother telling her to lock up on her way out. I'd consider myself lucky if I got robbed.

I headed out, not sure where I was going, but anywhere was better than getting dragged to the scary place she bought these items. I headed down the streets of Nowhere, still feeling out of sorts roaming this place, let alone having a home here. The eternal night, even with a sky full of swirling stars, didn't offset the strange feeling of the darkness at noon. But the night fit this place. Its shiny black streets reflected the glowing lights from the establishments, some of which seemed to be created right from stardust. Everything felt alive, even the signs that would twist and turn or twinkle. The people were even odder, almost as if this place was composed of carnies.

I tried to keep my gaze straight ahead, not meeting eyes with any of them as I passed. I'd been warned by Cookie, Dice, and Connor to stay on the main roads, not to engage. They said if I minded my own business, I'd probably be okay.

Kaden hadn't given me a warning of any kind. Cookie said he'd warned all of Nowhere that I was officially part of his crew. Apparently that carried more weight than anything else. As long as I didn't look for trouble, it most likely wouldn't find me.

Or he'd find them.

Still, everyone else's warning had me ready to launch into an attack when a pair of hands landed on my back.

"Turn here," Gram said before I could get my bearings and swing.

"Gram?" I would've turned and hugged her, but she kept steering me into the nearest dark alley.

The second she stopped, I threw my arms around her, squeezing her tighter than her old bones could probably take. In this new world, my closest friends were people I'd only known for a couple of months. But she was a piece of me, my life, a person who knew me better than anyone. My throat swelled and I dragged in a shuddering breath.

I held on to her as if she'd get taken away at any second, but the longer we hugged, the more I noticed something odd. I'd hugged her more times than I could count. I knew her hugs the way I recognized my own face. The body I was holding didn't feel like Gram, unless she'd gotten a grammy makeover, and even then it was iffy.

I backed up and took in her frame. She still *looked*

like Gram, but there was something altogether different lurking underneath.

"Why do you feel...different?" I took another step back. Was this Gram at all? My gut said yes. I could even smell an aroma of lingering marigolds. But something wasn't lining up.

"I didn't want to alarm you, but I've upgraded a bit since the last time I saw you. You want to see?" she asked, her voice shifting into a higher and younger version as she spoke. She took a step back, smiling as she put her hands on her waist as if posing her new look.

Did I? It wasn't like I could say no even if I didn't, the way she was waiting.

"Yeah, sure."

Gram melted away, and all of a sudden there was a drop-dead gorgeous creature in front of me. She looked like a bombshell from the fifties with bright red hair and curves that were high and round. This wasn't the Gram I craved when I was feeling lonely and down. This looked like a party friend. I'd never been much of a partier, but it looked like I'd have to adjust.

"How exactly did you upgrade?" I asked.

"Don't look at me that way. It's completely normal. That old lady's body was dead and lying in a box back on Earth. I had to do it. Plus it's a bit of a perk from having the friends I have."

"Where did you get a new one?"

"Had it ordered. They grow them on Omega Nine. I've got some pull over there. But we've got more important things to talk about. I need—"

"We do. How do I get in touch with you if I need to talk to you? Where are you staying? I have no way of getting to you." There was no way I was letting her disappear again with no option of getting in touch with her.

"You can't. I'm not staying in Nowhere. This place is too hot until we get some things settled."

She spoke as if it weren't a big deal I couldn't get to her, so I tamped down how jumbled up it made me feel. It wasn't as if it made a difference if I complained. If there was a way to get in touch, she would've told me.

"Because of Kaden? What is the problem with you two?" I asked.

"It's a long story and I don't have time to get into it. I don't want to stay too long. I can't risk being spotted. I just wanted to let you know I was around and that I'll be back."

She took my hands in hers. Even her grasp felt alien, her bony hands gone and replaced with a young woman's, complete with long, pointy nails that sparkled.

I was staring at those hands as she asked, "I can depend on you, can't I?"

I glanced up. How could she even ask such a question? My entire life, it had been Gram and me.

"You know you can," I said, searching this new face for a sign of why she'd even doubt that.

"No, I mean *really* depend on you." She moved her grip to my shoulders. "This isn't Earth. The stakes are a lot higher. I have to know that you'll step up if the time comes."

Step up? A question I'd taken as innocent before was

suddenly feeling a little messier and more sordid. This wasn't my older grandmother asking if I'd be there to drive her to the doctor.

Was she... She didn't mean to act against Kaden, did she? Maybe not. Either way, I'd made a promise to him as well, and I'd meant it. Unless he was actively trying to hurt her, I couldn't imagine a way to justify going against my promise. How to explain that to her, though? She'd never been a fan of *but*s.

"You know that I would always be there for you in any way you needed—"

"Shh." She held a finger up to her lips as she turned her head, listening for something. Her attention focused on a little mouse that was standing on its hind legs at the edge of the shadows. "Gotta go. I'll be in touch soon." She took off down the alley.

"Gram? What the hell? It's just a mouse."

She was already gone.

Gram 2.0 moved a lot quicker than the previous version, and I was yelling at an empty alley. No wonder I'd been hanging on to her for dear life. This was becoming a serious issue with her. Now when would I see her? I hadn't had a chance to warn her about the town house, although she probably knew.

I stared in the direction of where she'd disappeared, not finding any trace of her, just inky darkness. I continued to stare for another few minutes as I replayed what she'd said, and everything about it made me want to shudder.

We needed to have a long talk. Enough with these

short meetings. I needed to know what was going on between her and Kaden. I'd given my word, and I hadn't done that lightly.

I should probably get out of this alleyway, though. This was exactly the thing the guys and Cookie had warned me about. If standing in a dark alley wasn't asking for trouble, nothing was.

I spun to leave and then stopped. Kaden was there at the opening of the alley. He was standing so still that I wasn't sure he was breathing.

The look on his face made my lungs stop working. My heart seized and a tremor ran down my spine. Had he been somewhere close? Had he heard me talking to Gram? How much had he heard? What had I said? I replayed every word in my mind. If he'd heard only that last bit? It wasn't good. No, it was worse than not good. It was horrific. The more of the tail end of the conversation he'd witnessed, the worse it all appeared.

Knowing him, that was where his mind would go. He wasn't the trusting sort. He'd think I was colluding with my grandmother and not just reassuring the one I loved I'd always be there for them. If he wanted to, he could twist that conversation into all sorts of horrible things— and from the look in his eyes, he was already hard at work.

This was it. *This* was what had kept me up at night, made me fear getting too close, too settled. From his expression, it was going to be every bit as bad as I'd expected it to be. Every time I thought of this moment, I'd gotten a knot in my stomach, and the reality felt a million times worse.

If he'd hear me out, give me the benefit of the doubt... I had to try, and I had to do it now, because he wasn't going to give me another opportunity from the looks of it.

I took a few steps toward him but then paused as his gaze hardened even more on my approach.

"Kaden, I don't know what you heard, but that conversation—"

"Do you realize who your gram is? That the one you assured your loyalty to is the infamous Rathia?"

I wanted to declare that whoever he was talking about wasn't my grandmother, that he was mistaken. Except I'd heard that name before. Grandpa used to call her that. I remembered asking him why he had, since it wasn't her given name. He'd said he didn't know himself, other than it made her happy.

"I don't know what your issues are, but she's not the monster you think."

"I guess that depends on what side of the line you're on, and you've made it very clear where you're standing." His voice was chillingly cold.

"Don't accuse me after what you've done. Why did you want me at the town house if not to keep tabs on me? What are you doing now if not spying on me?" Instead of keeping it cool, trying to talk to him, I was yelling and throwing accusations back.

He stared my way, his anger filling the alley. "You need to leave Nowhere tonight."

That was it. I'd been judged and sentenced in all of a few minutes. Why had I ever imagined anything else?

It didn't matter. He could say whatever he wanted. It was my life, and I was done taking orders.

"I'm not leaving," I said.

"Nowhere is mine, and I want you out. You won't have anywhere to stay unless I allow it."

He said that Nowhere was his. But it wasn't. No one owned Nowhere. Not even the *king* himself.

"I'll figure it out on—"

He turned his back on me mid-sentence, not willing to hear another word. That was it. We were finished.

I didn't think we'd be *best* friends, but I'd thought we'd formed some kind of relationship that would merit at least his hearing me out. But this was it. I didn't even get to attempt an explanation of what happened. He just cut me off. Just tossed me out like last night's leftovers.

I stood there, debating my options until a fine drizzle turned into rain. I was standing in a puddle as I sorted through what my options were.

Gram hadn't given me a way to contact her, so she wasn't an option. Did I pack a bag and go Topside? I still had money. I could find somewhere to stay.

The clerk at whatever hotel I found might not remember me for more than five minutes, but I wouldn't be without shelter. It would just be a miserable existence of no one ever knowing me. If I left here, I'd be doomed to a life of invisibility. Every meeting would be a one-off. A life filled with elevator conversations.

If my prospects Topside were bad, Nowhere was

worse. I wouldn't even have a roof over my head in Nowhere because Kaden would surely lock me out of the town house.

Unless I had a job, and a new position. I did have options. There was always Alaric, but I didn't want to show up there, wherever he was, in the middle of the night, drenched and desperate.

So where did that leave me? With one option.

THREE

I stood on the stoop to Cookie's place. She was as loyal as they came, but she was also independent. Would she hear me out, or would she immediately side with Kaden? I'd spent the entire walk envisioning her kicking me down the front steps with her steel-toed boots. Even if Kaden had already told her I was to be banished from Nowhere, maybe she'd at least listen to my side, try to understand where I was coming from. She was my best bet—and also my only option at the moment.

I was mid-knock when she flung open the door and looked at me for a half-second. That was all it took for her forehead to bunch up like a used accordion and her jaw to drop.

"You look like shit. What happened?" She waved me in.

Cookie didn't care for upscale furnishings, and she also didn't care if you dripped all over her floor. There was something very endearing about that when you were down and out, and forming puddles wasn't even on your radar.

"Before I tell you, I need you to promise to hear me out."

She sucked air in between her teeth. "That bad, eh?"

It wasn't bad if she'd listen. If she heard the story from Kaden, though...

"On the surface, it might appear that way. I swear, though, it wasn't what it sounded like. Will you hear me out?" If I couldn't get Cookie to listen, it would be downhill from here. Without her help, I'd be doomed to live a nameless life in Topside. The guys might not condemn me, but my hunch was they'd ultimately follow Kaden's lead. Gram was as dependable a shelter as a tent in a hurricane.

"Of course. I'd probably say almost anything at this point to hear what happened." She walked toward her living room, motioning me farther in.

Dice and Connor were lounging on her couch, and my brain skipped. It was going to be bad enough telling her, but I was going to have to tell all of them? At the same time?

I'd have to. If I didn't, Kaden would.

"Damn, you look almost as shitty as that first day you showed up at the outpost. Remember? You thought you were going to get tossed off the bridge," Dice said, and then laughed.

That had to be the worst memory he could've recalled. They didn't know how close their boss was to throwing me into the river himself right now.

"Well? Out with it," Cookie said. "You can't make an entrance like this and then leave everyone hanging."

I glanced down at Cookie's feet. At least she didn't have her steel-toed boots on. Dice had his guns, but they were holstered. Connor was slumped, muscles looking lax. None of this guaranteed my safety, but I'd have a better shot.

"I'm guessing you all remember there were some questions around who my grandmother was."

"Shit. I'm not sure I want to hear this," Dice said, then leaned forward, making sure he wouldn't miss a word of it.

Connor rolled his eyes and let out a low groan.

Cookie dropped onto her couch, still looking unaggressive. "Oh no, this ain't going to be good. I mean, I knew it would be bad, but I thought there'd be some entertainment value in it. This isn't going to just be bad—it's going to be *bad* bad, isn't it?" she asked.

I nodded.

"Just get it out," Dice said.

I nodded again and then began to pace the room in front of them. "I didn't know who my grandmother was initially, but I'd come to suspect in the last few weeks that she wasn't just the little old lady I loved. She was also someone Kaden didn't particularly like. Tonight, he found out who she was, and it didn't go well." I ran through the entire story, knowing at this point that there was no holding back.

I finally stopped pacing and looked at my audience. All three of them were gaping at me.

"Wait, who did you say your grandmother was?" Dice asked.

"You heard her. It's Rathia," Connor said, and then groaned again.

"That's pretty bad. But you know that, right?" Cookie asked, looking subdued for the first time since I'd known her.

I nodded.

She shrugged but didn't stand up, or scream that I needed to get out of her house right then and there. Dice wasn't pulling out his guns, and Connor wasn't flexing. They didn't instantaneously hate me, and I was finally feeling like I might not have to make a mad dash for the door and run for my life. They were doing what I'd hoped Kaden would've done, but hadn't—they'd given me a chance to explain. They'd trusted that I wasn't a monster. They'd heard me out and understood.

"Oh, what a shit pile this is. And Kaden only heard the end of the conversation?" Dice asked.

"I don't know, but I think so. I just don't know..." I began to pace again. It was better than watching Connor hide his face in his palm, Dice shake his head, and Cookie frozen in her cringe face.

"I can't even imagine how pissed he was," Dice said.

"He told me I have to leave Nowhere." Kaden had kicked me out. Not just of the house, the outpost, or his life. He found me so detestable that he'd booted me from an entire place.

"Well, that's a little severe. It's not like you were

working with her," Cookie said, but still looked a bit dazed.

"I've barely seen her. How could I have been plotting with someone I haven't talked to for more than a handful of minutes in months?" I threw my hands up, feeling like I was spinning out of control. Why couldn't Kaden have listened to me? Just heard me out?

"We all know she's too shitty a liar to have pulled that off," Dice said, and then looked over at me. "No offense. It's working in your favor, and right now, you need all you can get."

"None taken." I walked over and dropped onto the chair. "The only reason I didn't say anything when I first suspected there was a problem was that I was afraid of this very thing happening. And now it's as bad as I feared."

"When did you suspect that your grandmother was working for the other side?" Dice asked.

"The first time was when she sent me a message asking for a meeting at that bar in Nowhere. Kaden showed up instead, saying he was looking for someone he didn't exactly get along with. It might've been a coincidence, but then I saw Gram again and questioned her. She said there was some bad blood but didn't say anything else. I still don't know what the problem is. I only know they're on opposite sides of a fight." Whatever the cause, it was bad enough that I was getting hit with shrapnel because of proximity.

"It's a pretty big divide. The people she's with have done some bad things," Dice said.

I waited to see if he'd continue. It would be nice to know why I was getting excommunicated.

He shook his head. "Kaden should really be the one to tell you."

"Sure." Didn't look like I'd ever know, because Kaden might never speak to me again.

Cookie kicked my foot with hers. "Look. He'll get over it. I'm not saying that it won't be awkward for a bit, but he'll realize you weren't trying to screw him over. It'll get better. He doesn't like surprises."

"You really think he'll get over it?" I tried to focus solely on Cookie and ignore the looks flying between Connor and Dice.

"Of course." She flipped her hand, as if this wasn't the end of the world. "It throws you when you first hear it, but I'm already adjusting to Rath"—she took a deep breath—"*Rathia* being your distant relation. He'll adjust."

Distant relation? I swallowed. Even Cookie had to pretend to get past it.

"So what do I do now?" I asked, glancing around.

The three of them looked at each other, no one saying anything. In spite of what Cookie said, this was bad. Nothing would make me think anything else.

"You come to the outpost tomorrow like nothing happened," Cookie said, breaking the silence.

"He doesn't even want me in Nowhere. I'm not sure the outpost is the way to go. Maybe he needs a cooling-off period?"

She shook her head immediately. "Kaden is like forged steel. Once he cools down, he hardens more. He'll be set in his ways. Better to get him while he's still malleable, or as much as he can be. You'll stay here tonight and go in with me tomorrow. It'll be fine."

"That's a solid plan. Yeah, it'll be good." Dice gave me a thumbs-up.

I glanced over at Connor, who was quiet. He opted for a noncommittal shrug. It wasn't confidence inspiring. In fact, it gave the impression that he thought this was going to go down in flames. That made two of us.

FOUR

I was on my spot on the couch in the outpost, going through lollipops like an alcoholic throwing back shots on a wicked bender. I'd had five in this last episode of *Seinfeld* alone. It was a particularly funny one, and it still couldn't keep my attention. All I could do was watch the door, waiting for Kaden to walk through it.

It felt like we were all waiting. Dice had cleaned the same gun barrel three times. Cookie was putting back almost as many lollipops as I was. Connor, who was always quietest, had been pretty much mute the whole morning. It's as if we were all expecting a storm to touch down and none of us knew if it would come in as a breeze or take out the entire town.

Kaden would be walking through that door any second, and my gut was saying no amount of lollipops was getting me through this unscathed. Cookie had thought this was the way to go—just show up like I should be here. She hadn't heard him last night, seen the way he'd looked at me. Dice had sought him out earlier today, but no one had been able to reach him, which was unusual. He'd been so angry at me he hadn't wanted to speak to anyone.

Cookie nudged my leg with her foot. "Calm down. It'll be fine."

"I'm good." I took a deep breath and then another, but no amount of breathing seemed to unclench the tightness around my chest or the ache in my gut. I wiped my palms on my jeans.

She'd known him much longer than I had, by a measure of decades. She thought this would work, and I should believe her. Who was I to say she was wrong? I was some Johnny Come Lately, a newbie without a clue. But no matter how I tried to convince myself, I still couldn't seem to unclench my muscles or stop staring at that door, almost wishing I could get this over with one way or another.

It turned out I didn't have to wait much longer. The man of the hour walked in fifteen minutes later. His gaze met mine the second the door swung open and didn't leave it.

The room went still. Or *stiller*. Even *Seinfeld* seemed to shut up, but it might've been the blood pounding in my ears, dulling the noise coming from the television. My lungs burned because I'd stopped breathing at the same time my heart decided it was running a marathon.

He stopped at the edge of the sofa where I sat. His expression was closed off, giving me no idea if he was going to tell me I had an assignment or point at the door and tell me to get the hell out.

"Why are you here?" he asked, his voice cutting through the ringing that had filled my ears.

"I..." I swallowed, suddenly losing the ability to speak. This hadn't been the right move. In fact, it couldn't have been more wrong. He hated me, and this would not end well. "I, uh..."

His gaze skimmed me before returning to my face. "I thought I made myself clear last night that you aren't to come here anymore. You're. Not. Wanted. Here."

Kaden had never looked at me so coldly, not even the first time I met him. I felt like I was six years old again, abandoned and unwanted.

"We told her to come," Cookie said, getting to her feet. Dice stood as well, along with Connor, gathering around me.

I was the only one sitting, feeling like I was almost cowering, but it took everything I had not to crumble. My eyes were burning; the tears wanted to come and shame me even more. My bottom lip trembled until I pressed my lips tightly closed.

Cookie moved forward until she was standing in front of me, placing herself in between us. I wanted to take back every horrible thing I'd ever thought of her when we first met. She might be the best person I'd ever known, and as soon as I could talk, I'd tell her.

Kaden turned his icy gaze on her. "You shouldn't have. She needs to leave. Now." He took one last glance at me, and then I was dismissed as he turned and walked away.

Silence followed. Dice and Connor might've been whispering something to each other, but I couldn't hear it. Couldn't compute anything past the humiliation I was feeling. I leaned forward, resting my arms on my legs and letting my head drop forward.

I'd lost my human life months ago. I was supposed to be an accountant, but that future was gone. Then I was going to be a tinker, but now I wasn't that either. I'd barely been clinging on to this new world, hardly had my feet underneath me, and now this life was gone as well.

I had nothing. I was nothing.

No. That wasn't totally true. I could get other work. Alaric might still want me. I'd go to his organization and pray he never figured out my weird link with Chaos. Would Kaden tell my secret? I hadn't believed he ever would, but I'd also hoped this wouldn't come to such a dire end.

I dragged myself from the shock of what was happening to hear Cookie chasing Kaden down like a pit bull.

"Kaden, she didn't do anything wrong," she said.

"She's out of here. *Now.*" His tone reverberated down the hall, as if his wrath could shake the building.

The sound of his footsteps faded.

Cookie was back, one hand on her hip, another pointing in the direction of Kaden's office, as she stared at Dice and Connor. "Are you two going to do something? Get in there and help me try to fix this."

"I'll go try to talk to him," Dice said, but he sounded already defeated. He knew it wasn't going to work, just the way I did.

Connor nodded, not looking any more optimistic, but following Dice anyway.

I sat there, not moving. I *had* to move. Dice and Connor were only going to make this worse. Cookie might've known Kaden longer, but my instincts about this had turned out to be more accurate. If I didn't move, Kaden might come back and drag me out of here. It would be a final blow I couldn't handle. I had to get to my feet and get out of here, but I was paralyzed.

I finally looked up and saw Cookie staring at me with pity. I'd cut my teeth on pity and had never acquired a taste for it. It was bitter and salty and all-around crap, and I'd never wanted to see that look again. The only thing it did was force me to my feet so I wasn't so pathetic looking.

"I'm fine," I said, even though that was ridiculous and we both knew it. I glanced at both exit doors: one that would lead to Nowhere and one that would lead to Topside. There was nothing left for me Topside. I couldn't work, have friends, or a life at all because no one would remember me.

But my options in Nowhere were bleak as well. I had no place to go, and Kaden would try to drive me out.

"What's wrong? Come on, you're going to come with me," Cookie said, as if she could hear the mental debate in my head. She grabbed my arm, tugging me toward the door to Nowhere. "You're one of us, and you belong in

Nowhere." She motioned to the door to Topside. "There's nothing for you there."

I nodded, moving in her direction before she decided to drag me across the room.

She went to open the door, and I pulled back. There was one final thing I needed. I couldn't be a coward and leave without it.

"I need to talk to him one last time before we go. Can you give me a minute?"

"You sure?" She didn't have any of the hope she'd clung to yesterday, or even a couple hours ago.

"Yes. It has to be done before I leave."

She nodded, seeming more at ease. This wasn't going to be some sort of last-ditch begging affair where she'd have to come drag me out.

I took a deep breath and headed toward Kaden's office, now expecting things to be as ugly as I'd feared. I kept walking, praying my knees wouldn't give out, steeling my spine as I did. All I wanted was to leave this place, but I couldn't. Not yet.

Connor and Dice were walking out of the office as I approached.

Dice opened his mouth and shook his head.

"I've got to," I said, moving around them as they both stood there, stumped at why I'd subject myself to anything further.

The door was ajar and Kaden was standing behind his desk, looking down as he sorted through papers. I shut the door to the office, not wanting an audience to any further humiliation I'd endure.

He wouldn't look up, even as I neared.

Each further insult from him battered against the steel I was trying to keep erected, making it look more and more impossible that we'd ever speak again. Every step closer was further confirmation he was turning his back on me for good. I'd started to believe Kaden would be someone I could rely on. I'd expected him to be mad, but not to cut me out like this.

Yes, I hadn't told him that Gram might be someone from his past, but it wasn't as if I'd conspired against him. Was I expected to give him blind loyalty? For what reason? He'd never given it to me. We'd never signed some mutual pact that said we had to tell each other every detail of our lives. I'd sworn I wouldn't act against him, and I hadn't.

I stopped right in front of his desk, refusing to say a word until he acknowledged me, as my own rage rose to meet his.

He finally looked at me. "What?" The word was short, clipped, and cold, and that was nothing compared to the hoarfrost generated by his stare.

In this moment, I hated him. Hated that he could turn against me so easily. Hated that I'd trusted him even a little. Hated that I might've started to care for him. It had been a one-way street. No one who cared for me could turn their back like this without hearing me out.

"I need one thing from you. That's it, and you'll never have to deal with me again."

If he cared, he didn't show it. His face was stone cold.

"Then get on with it," he said, having already

dismissed me and going back to shuffling through some papers.

"I want your word you won't tell anyone about Chaos."

His hands stilled for a second. "I told you I wouldn't."

"You've told me a lot of things." Things I'd believed. Not anymore.

His hand stilled for a fraction of a second. I wasn't delusional enough to believe it revealed some softer emotion. He was heartless.

"I won't. Now if that's it, get out."

I turned and left, swearing I'd never come here again, not even if he begged me on his hands and knees. I'd swallow a bullet first.

FIVE

I didn't turn around and look at the outpost. I refused to, even as it felt like another chunk of who I used to be was being torn from me. It was done and gone, and so was Kaden. Another chapter closed, but I'd find my way, because I had to. Failing wasn't acceptable. Leaving Nowhere wasn't either. He wouldn't drive me from here.

We walked back to Cookie's in silence. One of her better traits was knowing when to let a subject be. Unless she was being quiet because she didn't know what to say, which was a definite possibility. The last pep talk and plan didn't pan out so well.

She opened the door to her home and then waved me to follow her. She swung open the door to the room I'd stayed in last night.

"You can stay here as long as you need. It's not like having your own town house, but it's comfy."

The room looked like the rest of her place, which was a lot like the lounge. It was the perfect place to hide and lick your wounds, and right now I felt like I was on the verge of bleeding out.

"You're really offering me your spare room? Because I don't know how long it's going to take me to figure things out." She owed me nothing, and this was a favor that would cost her. When Kaden found out...

"Why wouldn't I? It's just sitting here gathering dust."

Some people meant that metaphorically, but it didn't seem to be the case here. It was still the best thing anyone had ever done for me by a mile.

Did she not realize what this could cost her? She had to, right? Cookie was brash, gruff, and many other things, but she wasn't an idiot.

"This could cause you a lot of grief. He's going to be mad. Maybe even furious."

"Let him. He's acting like a dick. When he eventually figures that out, he'll thank me." She shrugged off the coming rage as if it were nothing.

"What if he doesn't?" She'd known him so much longer. Did she not realize how bad this could get?

She paused for a moment as she looked at me, no bluster in her expression as she calmly said, "If someone is going to be an ass because I did the right thing, that's their problem. I'm doing this, and you're staying here." She put out her hand, her swagger coming back. "Now give me the keys to the town house. I'm going to get the guys and pack up your shit and bring it here. Might as well lay it all out for him now. I've never been a fan of hiding."

I hugged her before she knew what was coming.

"Oh no," she groaned. "How long is this going to last?" She stood there, arms still at her sides, accepting the hug like a twelve-year-old being forced by their parent.

I gave her one last extra squeeze and then let her go. "I'm sorry, but I had to."

"You know, Hank did warn me about the touching problem when you first started. Is this whole hugging thing going to happen a lot?"

"Only when you save my ass repeatedly. Other than that, I'll try to hold back." I crossed my arms in front of me so I didn't break down and hug her again.

She threw a hand up. "It is what it is. Now hand over the keys so we can go get you some stuff."

"The door is open, but I'm still not feeling good about this."

"You act like you just met me or something. You know I do what I want." She lifted her eyes skyward and sighed.

"Just don't get into a fight for me, okay? Promise?"

"Chickie, I get into fights because that's the way I roll. I came out kicking and screaming, and nothing's going to change that," she said, laughing to herself as she headed to the door. "There's stuff in the fridge and a hidden stash of lollipops in the oatmeal box that I don't let the guys know about. They're for emergencies, but those pigs will eat them all."

· · ·

I MADE it two hours before I was digging into the emergency stash, staring at the door, watching, waiting.

By the time she finally showed up, I was sick. I wasn't sure if it was nausea from all the sugar, nerves, or that Kaden had somehow known I was going to eat those lollipops and poisoned them.

Cookie walked in, Connor and Dice on her heels. They had bags of my things they dumped on the floor, on their way to collapse onto the couches. No one spoke as they slumped in their spots and groaned.

"What happened? Was it that bad?" I asked.

"It could've gone better." Dice ran a hand through his hair.

"Because it couldn't have gone worse. That's for damn sure," Connor said, looking at him.

"He's mad I'm here at Cookie's?" Probably the stupidest question of the century. What else could it be? Kaden wanted me out of Nowhere, and instead I'd moved a couple blocks away. I was slumping back and groaning with them.

"Mad might be an understatement," Cookie said.

"What did he say?" I covered my eyes with my arm, afraid of what I was going to hear.

Cookie kicked her boots up on the table. "That he doesn't want you in Nowhere. He wants you completely gone. Pretty much what we expected."

I nodded. I might have to leave in the middle of the night so I didn't take her down with me. She wasn't going to give in and do what was best for her. I'd pack tonight. At least I'd be Topside with a clean conscience.

"Oh no, I can see it written all over your face. You aren't leaving. He's acting crazy, and we aren't giving int o this."

She was digging in, just as I'd feared.

Connor and Dice were looking at her with expressions that said they were glad she was taking that risk because they didn't want to. I didn't blame them.

I didn't say anything. If she insisted I stay, I'd stay for the least amount of time I could. There were other options, and I'd be pursuing them as soon as possible. I wasn't taking her down with me if I could help it.

"I don't know why he wants me out of here so badly. I'll gladly avoid all the places he goes. Can't he just ignore me?" I slumped back into the chair, staring at the ceiling. Why did he have to make this so difficult? There were plenty of people I didn't like. I'd never try to evict them from a city, even if I could. I'd ignored plenty of things in life. It was what you did when you didn't like something. He should act like a sane person and ignore me.

"No. You don't understand. He *can't*. I mean, I really think he *can't*, and that's the issue." Cookie threw her hands up in the air as if I were being obtuse.

"Of course he can. What do you mean?"

"Just a hunch." She shook her head, like it wasn't worth explaining.

I caught a glance passing between Cookie and Dice. "Do you all know something I don't?"

"No, of course not." Cookie shrugged.

"He seems to be overly sensitive about the situation.

Probably because you're new or something." Dice mirrored Cookie's shrug.

Connor kept his head down.

"Either way, I don't think he's going to force the issue of your leaving," Cookie said. "Him being mad wasn't the worst of the trip anyway."

"What was worse?" What had happened over there?

"Okay, well, I got a thing I have get to." Dice stood, suddenly in a rush to leave.

Connor jumped to his feet, finding a burst of energy. "Yeah, I'll come. Remember? I promised to help you with that thing."

Dice and Connor were looking at each other, nodding.

"Yeah, go run to this *thing* of yours." Cookie rolled her eyes.

I barely got a thank you out before I saw their backs and they were gone.

"What else happened there?" I asked.

Cookie's chest rose and fell before she spat out, "The twat was there."

"Antoinette was at my... She was at the town house?" The town house wasn't mine. It was never really mine. But oh did that burn in a special sort of way.

Cookie nodded.

Had Kaden made up with her? Was he going to give her the town house now that he'd booted me?

Someone could've picked up a rusty butter knife and stabbed me in the kidney and it would've been less painful. Of all people, she hated me the most. Wanted nothing but the worst for me and was probably skipping all over that place.

"She saw us and followed us in. Then? She. Wouldn't. Leave." Cookie dropped her head back, as if her neck couldn't sustain the weight of the thoughts running around her mind. "If I was sure they weren't getting back together, I would've beaten her right there and then. But even I know we gotta pick our battles right now."

She didn't say anything else, and I didn't ask. I'd heard too much already. If I got another detail about what that woman was doing in my—*the* town house, I might have to burn it to the ground.

Cookie turned on the TV to some eighties movie and then went to the kitchen. She returned with a basket heaped full of taffy, and other wrapped candies she put in between us.

"This is the emergency-of-all-emergencies stash," she said.

I grabbed a handful and settled in, trying to forget everything else that had happened today.

COOKIE WAS LOUNGED out on the couch, yawning and looking like she was ready to go to sleep, when I asked, "Do you know where Alaric's outpost is?"

"Why? You want to egg it or something?" She yawned again.

"No. I was thinking of going over and talking to him tomorrow."

It was the only way forward. I'd get a job with him, get out of Cookie's place and remove her from the line of fire, and start to rebuild a life, again. This time I'd be a little pickier in the people I put my faith in. I'd do a lot of things differently.

"Why would you want to talk to him? He's so damned boring it makes my head hurt."

"Because he offered me a job once," I said, knowing it was going to go over as well as a brick through a plate-glass window.

She shot straight up, wide awake. "You're going to go work for him?"

"If he'll still take me, yes."

This was going to go as well as I'd expected. The look on her face was that of a B-list actress in a horror flick.

She was on her feet, shaking her head. "You can't do that."

"I have to do it." I'd thought about it all day. He was the only option left. There was no other choice, and she'd come to see it too.

"You can stay here until things are smoothed out," she said. "He's going to come around. I know it."

"This isn't going to get smoothed out. Even if he does come around, I won't. Not after he turned his back on me the way he did. This isn't just about whether he *wants* to take me back. *I* don't want to go back. You can't say you would either." No one with a shred of pride would, not after the scene he'd made at the outpost. He'd humiliated me enough.

She was quiet for a few seconds before she dropped

back onto the couch and nodded. "You're right. I wouldn't."

"Thanks."

I unwrapped another candy, but not even sugar was fixing this day. Hopefully tomorrow would be better.

SIX

Alaric's outpost was a few streets over from Kaden's. I'd prefer a galaxy away, but at least they weren't next door to each other. If I did work here, the notion of waving to Kaden on my way in every day was as appealing as a root canal.

As far as locations, being across from the shoreline with the waves crashing was kind of nice, not that there seemed to be any windows. Just like Kaden's outpost, there wasn't anything to see but a single door. If Cookie hadn't told me about the red bench right outside the entrance, I wasn't sure I would've found the place.

I straightened my sweater, wondering if Alaric would even speak to me. Kaden had said he wouldn't repeat anything about my little Chaos problem, but that didn't mean he hadn't said other things to discredit me. He wanted to run me out of Nowhere, after all. From what I'd witnessed between Kaden and Alaric, Kaden wanting me gone might work to my benefit.

I knocked, wondering if anyone would answer. If his crew was anything like ours... Not *ours*. *Kaden's*. They might be too busy watching reruns or out to lunch. This could take several tries and several days. The longer it took, the longer I'd be a burden. My life might not have turned out the way I intended, I might not be an accountant, but I was still going to be a self-sufficient adult.

The door swung open, and a young man in a suit stood there.

"Alaric's outpost. May I help you?" His smile appeared to be bought and paid for.

"Is Alaric available?"

"May I have your name?" He waited, finger poised over a tablet.

Tablet. Would they try to aptitude-test me? That hadn't gone very well the first time. I'd have to stall. Maybe I could say I was allergic to testing or something.

"Name?" he asked again.

"I'm sorry. Billie Hendrick."

"Let me check and see if he has an opening. You can come in and have a seat while I inquire." He waved me into the building. It was fresh and bright, with abstract paintings on white walls. I could've been in the waiting room of a Beverly Hills plastic surgeon, not that I'd ever seen one of those in real life. But this was what the TV shows made them all look like.

I took a seat, wishing I hadn't worn jeans and the ass-kicker boots Cookie had given me. I'd thought badass was the look to shoot for, but corporate attorney might've been closer to the mark. Even my nail polish was chipped, which had been an oversight. I folded my hands strategically.

"Can I get you something to drink while you wait?" he asked, smiling as if he hadn't been checking out my boots.

"No, I'm fine. Thank you."

He smiled again, like his jaw was greased regularly, and then walked down the hall out of sight. I sat, checking out the fish tank, listening to instrumental music that wasn't too moody or too frivolous.

Alaric appeared a few minutes later, in a crisp blue suit, with his thick, tawny hair brushed back. I'd forgotten how attractive he was, or maybe I hadn't noticed because of everything else going on. Maybe it was because Kaden had been close by and it was hard to notice anyone else.

That was before Kaden turned his back on me. I had a new appreciation for Alaric. Raw charisma couldn't hold a candle to someone who might be kind enough to hear a person out.

I got to my feet as he stopped in front of me. His smile was genuine, and he didn't so much as glance at my outfit. No, he met my eyes with his warm stare, as if my visit were truly a nice surprise.

"Billie. It's great to see you. Want to talk for a bit?" He motioned toward where he'd come from.

"That would be great."

His office was as pristine as the rest of the place. And as white. What was with all the white? I was starting to understand what Cookie was talking about, at least in this instance. It was nice to have a place where you weren't afraid to kick up your feet.

Alaric opted not to sit at the formal desk and walked over to a seating area along the far side of the office. He took the chair, leaving me the couch to myself. I settled in, feeling more comfortable than I'd thought I could, considering.

"I'm going to make this as easy as possible. If you came here to find out if I'm still interested in bringing you on to the team, I am. Name your price." He crossed his legs, looking like he was having a great day.

Those words were like mainlining Valium. Maybe I hadn't given him the credit he was due? I hadn't expected him to make me get on my knees and beg, but *this* simple?

Was he making it easy because he still thought Kaden wanted me? If I was going to work here, the subject would be addressed eventually. It seemed unlikely, though. Odds were someone had seen Cookie and the guys carrying my bags out of the town house. That trio wasn't exactly subtle in their movements. Then there was Antoinette. She would've been blasting the news.

"I'm guessing you've heard the gossip?"

He nodded. "There were some murmurs about a break."

"Well, they're true. I..." I'd rehearsed all possible excuses, and none of them had sounded any better on the fourth or fifth time I repeated them.

He waved a hand and shook his head. "I don't need to know what happened. What I do hope is that you don't go back. You deserve better than that. There are very few people that remain unscathed around that man."

"It wasn't like that. We were never together." It was bad enough I'd gotten kicked to the curb with work. I didn't need it spreading that I was a scorned lover, too. There were probably enough rumors about me.

"I don't know what happened, but I'd bet he'll be back. He was too interested to walk away."

Was Alaric hiring me simply because he believed Kaden still wanted me? It wasn't as if I were misleading him, and I was too desperate not to take the job. This was my lifeline, an avenue to rebuild. I'd run with it for as long as it lasted.

"I don't want to rehash all the details, but trust me when I tell you our situation is completely closed. I do feel obligated to tell you that this might not go over well with Kaden, even though we are done." I'd said it. Maybe I played it down, but I'd gotten it out. Alaric was forewarned. If he misinterpreted that too? It was on him.

He smiled like a pageant girl with a mouthful of Vaseline. "I'm sure it won't. That's fine, though. I'll deal with any fallout. When can you start?"

"When do you want me?"

"How about this? I've heard you lost the town house. I've got a few places that I keep for exactly these instances. We can tour them tomorrow, and you can have your pick until you decide on something more permanent. Take a week to get settled in, and then you can start taking assignments when you're ready." He was literally sitting on the edge of his seat, waiting for my response.

"That sounds wonderful, but if you don't mind, I'd rather start right away. And I'll find my own lodgings." I'd never be beholden to anyone again for where I laid my head.

I WALKED out of Alaric's outpost like I'd just been given another lifeline. I had options. I had a job. I looked up at the swirling universes above, wanting to let out a loud yippee and do a couple of cartwheels. I wouldn't, just in case someone was watching. I'd wait until I got a block or two over.

I turned, and all my relief crashed into a brick wall. Kaden was standing not ten feet in front of me. He pointedly looked at the door to Alaric's outpost and then back to me.

"This was the best you could do?" he asked.

"Alaric has a lot to offer. More than I gave him credit for. From where I'm looking, I just climbed a rung up."

In the distance, I saw Antoinette heading toward us. If I tried to leave now, it would look like I was running from her. Technically it would be running, or at minimum a very fast walk.

She closed the distance and looped her arm around Kaden's. Cookie was right. So much for the breakup sticking. How long had it lasted? Right up until my bags were packed? He'd gotten rid of me nice and neat, and she'd swooped right in.

"Ah, so I heard you're leaving? Going Topside?" She

smiled, as if we were sharing pleasantries and her boyfriend wasn't trying to drag me out by my hair.

"No. I'll be staying in Nowhere." My tone was barely civil.

"Are you sure that's the best idea?" she asked with mock horror, as if she had any concern.

"I don't care what people figure out or if they don't want me. You want me out? You'll have to drag me out of here and then kill me afterward, because I'll just come back, again and again." I turned my gaze to Kaden, making sure he knew this last part was solely for him. "I don't need you. I don't need anyone."

I left him standing there, but not before I caught a glimmer of admiration in his eyes. He might not like me, might even hate me, but he respected me. For once, I was starting to respect myself. No one was going to tell me who I should be, what I should be, or what I deserved.

SEVEN

Three months later...

JIM, one of the other tinkers that worked for Alaric, walked into the lounge area. He smiled my way as he headed over to the cappuccino machine. "Billie, would you like a chai latte?" he asked. "We've got that new blend in for you." He plucked a piece of lint off his pristine polo shirt and smoothed his hands over his pleated khakis.

"No, thank you. I'll try it tomorrow." I'd actually tried it this morning, and it lacked spice as much as this place did. I was drowning in bland.

"Too much caffeine, too late?" He nodded, as if overconsumption was a sin worse than murder. "I usually avoid it too, but I have a late-night assignment and need a little more pep in my step tonight."

"Do you need any help?" I asked as I stood, knowing

he'd refuse. I pushed my chair in so the place looked just so, not a thing out of place. Wouldn't want anything out of order, not even for a couple of hours, because that really ruffled feathers.

"No. It shouldn't take me long. It's a teenage setup. She's had a crush on this boy for a long time, and some power that be feels it's a good idea for them to fall in love. I love *love*. Don't you love love?" He gave a little shimmy, as if he couldn't contain his joy.

"Yeah, *love*. It's just great." I wish I could actually drown from blandness. It might be easier than hearing about his newest assignment.

We got a lot of those jobs. Easy jobs. Frilly jobs. Crushes and college admittances. I wasn't sure who bothered to pay for most of them, because they were so idiotic, not that we'd ever find out. Just like with Kaden's company, everything went through IBA, the Independent Board of Adjusting. Difference was, when I worked for Kaden, the need for secrecy made sense. I guessed people liked their privacy, no matter how stupid or petty or idiotic the job might be.

"Nice pants," he said, looking at my jeans for a little too long and not in an *eyeing up my ass* kind of way.

"I just changed. I'm done for the day."

Alaric's had a corporate-casual dress code while in the outpost. After all, it was important to keep up appearances for any guests that might wander in once in a decade.

"Well, I'll see you tomorrow," I said, waving as I headed out.

He waved, and gave me a mock pout, as if he were actually sad I was leaving.

Sarah was walking in as I was departing. "Oh, Billie, I was hoping I'd see you."

"Hey, what's up?" I asked.

She smoothed a hand over the already perfect bob. "I didn't want to leave a message where everyone could see, but you left your coffee cup on the table yesterday. Not that it was a big deal, but if you could try to remember in the future?" She kept her expression friendly even as she held her hands in a white-knuckled grip in front of her.

"I'm sorry. I got a call last minute and was running late." I tried to step around her.

Her eyes went wide as she moved with me. "Late? Oh, was the job not properly marked on the schedule? If so, I'll have to talk to Maria about that." Her eyebrows were about to knit together.

I shook my head quickly. "No, it was there. It just slipped my mind."

"Oh. Okay. I understand," she said, smiling, as if everything was exactly as she expected.

"Well, I'll be heading out now." Because talking to her for another minute might kill whatever brain cells I had left.

"See you tomorrow. Don't forget we have movie night. I told Jim not to pick out anything too scary this time." She giggled.

I nodded, as if I'd be there. As if I hadn't missed last movie night, and the movie night before that. As if we weren't all happy that I missed every movie night.

I walked out of there as fast as I could, not that she'd care. She was probably busy looking for any scuff marks my boots left on the perfect white floor.

It typically took me a half a block to be able to breathe easily again. As I walked, I went through my usual litany of why Alaric's wasn't bad. For instance, most of the jobs were conveniently scheduled. Not many late nights there.

They also tended to not be taxing or draining. The chances of the balance of things getting thrown off and Chaos arising was pretty much zero. Most of Alaric's crew had never even seen Chaos from afar. That was definitely a plus for me, considering my history with it. I never knew how long my grandmother's fix would last, but it wasn't a problem here. So there were definitely good things about Alaric's. Yes. I would just have to keep reminding myself, over and over.

I turned the corner and wanted to immediately turn back, but it was too late. *They* had already seen me.

Hank, Tank, and Frank, the guys that handled the bridge crossings, were all watching me walk down the street. It had been a long and tedious day, and this was not the ending I'd been hoping for.

"You really disappointed us," Hank said as I got closer. Or was it Frank or Tank? They were impossible to tell apart. They kept their salt-and-pepper beards the same length. Their brown eyes were all the same shade. They even tended to wear the same plaid shirts, so there wasn't a distinctive style I could use.

"Guys, we've talked about this. It's his life. He can do

what he wants." Why they thought I had any control over Kaden's dating life was beyond me. I didn't want to hear about Kaden anymore, let alone actively discuss him.

"This is not acceptable," one of the three said.

"Well, you should tell him that instead of trying to get me to fix something I can't control." How many times would we have this conversation before they accepted it? Why did I keep having this conversation with them? I should just walk away before this continued.

They were already getting into their complaining stances, and like clockwork, they started.

"We put our reputations on the line working things out for you, and now she's back in the picture? Not good. Not good at *all*."

"We put our faith in you and this is not acceptable."

"Not acceptable at all."

"Get rid of her."

I sighed, knowing we were nearing the end. "I'm sorry, but I can't. He is not my problem."

"We want you to know, you've been a great disappointment," one of them said, and the other two nodded.

The first time we'd had this conversation, those words crushed me. The second time, they'd burned. But considering this was the twelfth or thirteenth time? Yeah, I'd come to terms with it, just as I'd accepted the old beaters they supplied me with for jobs and the occasional broken door that forced me to stay in a hotel. Some people couldn't accept the inevitable.

"Again, I'm very sorry," I said, launching into my usual verbal dismount. I finished it off with a shrug.

They gave me their final grunts in unison, and we called it a week.

I walked faster, falling into a rhythm as I headed down the street to get my dinner. I wove in between the *people*, avoiding eye contact with most. This wasn't really a smile-and-wave kind of place. It was more "keep your head down and mind your own business." That was fine by me. I had no desire to talk to anyone else tonight.

I walked into Eli's, the eatery a few blocks from my place. Eli nodded to me from behind the counter, his large bald head looking like it might topple over on his incredibly thin neck.

"Billie, same?" he asked, my name sounding closer to *Bibbi* when he pronounced it.

"Same. Thanks, Eli."

He bagged it up and laid it on the counter less than a minute later.

They didn't call it pizza here, but that was the closest word I had for the black, doughy, cheesy stuff he made. I'd been addicted to it since my first bite when Dice brought it to the town house.

"See you tomorrow?" Eli asked as I went to leave.

"Maybe," I said, telling myself I'd go get something else for dinner. I'd probably be right back here, but I wasn't ready to admit it yet.

It wasn't as if I wanted to eat this pizza constantly. Places in Nowhere didn't always have kitchens. It was really out of my hands until I got a more comfortable apartment.

My rationalizations were cut short as a more pressing

problem presented itself: Tarvan was standing outside his shop, watching me.

"Hey, pretty lady, care to get your fortune read tonight?" he asked as I passed.

"No, thank you." It was the same answer I gave every night—not that it deterred him from stalking me anyway.

"I think you'll find the information enlightening," he said, smiling with pointy black teeth.

"No, thank you. I don't have the money to waste." Actually, I did—even the petty jobs I did for Alaric paid pretty well—but I had no intention of letting Tarvan swindle me out of my earnings. After all, I needed to get a place with a kitchen, and real estate in Nowhere wasn't cheap.

"For you, I do it for free. What's the harm?"

He held out his two-thumbed hand with iridescent palms. I wasn't sure what Tarvan was, but it was pretty far from human. Could he do something to me merely by touching? I didn't rule anything out in Nowhere.

It was one of the first rules Cookie had given me when she realized I was intent on being here on my own: don't take anything for granted, and don't let anyone get me alone—ever. I'd survived the last few months, so it was pretty decent advice.

"Thank you, but I don't want to put you out."

I kept walking, and he snaked his hand out, grabbing me. I spun, speechless. Tarvan was annoying and persistent, but he didn't typically push it further.

"Go with caution." The calm and flirty voice was

gone, replaced by a lower, intent one. "They're coming for you."

I froze for a few seconds before I came to my senses. "You don't know what you're talking about. No one is coming for me." I yanked out of his grasp. "You can try to scare me, but I'm not paying you or buying into your games."

He put his palms up. "You were warned."

I half walked, half ran away. He was trying to get money from me. That was it. He was a scammer. He might've offered his services for free, but it was simply to intimidate me into giving something else.

He reminded me of a psychic I went to see when I was eighteen who had told me I was cursed. They'd demanded fifteen hundred dollars to lift the curse. It didn't matter. I hadn't had the money.

I'd wondered for a while if the psychic had been right. My mother was a drunk, who hadn't been able to care for herself, let alone me. My father had disowned me before birth. Still, I hadn't paid her to remove that curse, and I wouldn't fall prey to this man either, even if I did speed up a little faster.

In spite of my better sense, I glanced back before I turned the corner. He watched me go as he shook his head.

Whatever, scammer. Shake your head at me all you want.

I was so distracted by Tarvan that I didn't see it coming. I was still looking over my shoulder when I heard the sound of a stick swishing, right before it connected with my stomach.

I bent forward, gasping to get the air back into my lungs and staggering from the shock of the blow. Another hit to my back brought me to my hands and knees, and my dinner fell into a puddle beside me.

"Bitch," someone yelled before they kicked me in the ribs.

"Chaos whore," another one called before they spat on me, then kicked me on the other side. "You think you've got the right to fuck everything up? That you're above it all?"

They knew. This wasn't a random attack. I wasn't being mugged. They knew about Chaos, that I was immune to it somehow—or worse, that it had been drawn to me.

"Please, don't do this. I didn't mean—"

Another blow landed on the side of my face. I choked on a mouthful of blood. It didn't matter. They wouldn't stop no matter what I said. I tried to look up, place the faces of my attackers, and took another blow to the face before I could.

Kick after kick, hit after hit—the coppery taste of blood dripped from my lips. I'd been fearing the moment someone would discover my strange connection to Chaos. Now it was here, and it was worse than I'd imagined. They were going to kill me.

I curled up into a ball, wrapping my arms around my head. It was futile as I lay huddled in the center of a horde who wouldn't stop until I was dead. I wasn't sure how many were attacking me. There were too many to count.

Between the legs kicking me, I saw glowing eyes in the distance. I could feel the hunger emanating from the creature who lurked. If the horde didn't finish the job, that thing would.

Blows struck my ribs, my head, my legs, as they closed in around me. I covered my head with broken fingers, wondering why I was prolonging the inevitable. I never really knew how strong my will to live was until I was at the cusp of death. Turned out mine was stronger than I'd imagined.

The blows slowed as they panted. They didn't need to waste too much more energy to finish me off. I was struggling to breathe; my lungs felt like two deflated beach balls in my chest as I sucked down as much blood as air. Running was no longer an option, as at least one leg was broken. It didn't matter. I'd crawl away if given the chance.

I looked around, searching for someone, anyone, who might take pity on me.

That was when I saw Gram. She was standing in the distance, watching. She made eye contact with me and then she was gone.

"Gram," I tried to scream, but I couldn't get her name out past the sounds of grunts coming from my attackers. It didn't matter. She wasn't there anymore. And she'd already seen me anyway.

My arm dropped lower as the strength to block the

strikes faded. My ears rang as more kicks came, and my vision grew fuzzy.

I was barely clinging to consciousness when the ground shook as if a mountain had been dropped beside me. The blows suddenly stopped, and the only sounds left were gasps and feet scuffling away.

A deafening roar split the air. The gasps turned to screams. I couldn't run. I couldn't even crawl anymore. Even if I could, my eyes were swelling shut. It was hard to see what new evil had come to finish me off. Was it that thing with the glowing eyes, or worse? I could do nothing but wait for the killing blow and hope it came fast. If I was going to die, I wanted it done.

"That's right. Run. But it won't make any difference." Kaden's voice was low and menacing. Was I dreaming? Was it really him? I tried to open my eyes, managing a single slit. Kaden was standing there, in between me and the horde that was running away.

He turned and knelt beside me. "Billie, it's me. I'm taking you home."

Warm air swirled around me, lifting me from the ground, but even that touch was too much. I felt consciousness being pulled away, my brain shutting down from the pain my body could no longer handle. Tears ran down my cheek, and something soft wiped them away before the world faded to black.

EIGHT

I woke as the wind burned my cheeks and I could hear waves crashing. I could smell Kaden all around me as he carried me.

A door opened and an older woman asked, "What happened?"

"She was attacked. Bring supplies and meet me in the tower bedroom," Kaden replied as he continued to walk and then was climbing stairs.

"Where..." I tried to catch my breath enough to get a full sentence out, but it was as likely as being able to run a marathon.

"My estate," he answered. "It's out of the city. No one would dare come here."

I turned my head slightly, taking in as much as I could through eyes nearly swollen shut. He carried me into a large bedroom—the walls, the floors, all looked like the same dark stone that the city streets of Nowhere were made from.

He placed me on a large bed, barely glancing at my face before examining my body. I did a mental assessment as well. Trouble breathing: partially collapsed lung? Definitely broken bones and throbbing pain too many places to take stock of. The only parts that weren't excruciating were numb. It might be easier to determine what parts were okay, and I wasn't sure there were any. If I were a doctor, my diagnosis would've been gloomy.

The physical pain wasn't the worst of it. Had I really seen my grandmother? Had the only person I'd ever counted on betrayed me? Or had I been out of my mind and delusional? I'd lost count of how many kicks to the head the horde had delivered.

No. I couldn't have seen her. She would've helped me.

I had worries right now other than conjured illusions. I tried to lift my head.

"Don't move," Kaden said.

It was easier to obey. What I could see was bad, and what I felt was worse. My fingers were no longer shaped normally. My clothes felt wet and sticky with my blood.

The older woman entered the room. "Is she..." Her question hung in the air as she realized I was awake.

Kaden finally met my gaze for more than a second. "Of course she is, because I'm going to make sure of it. But she's going to sleep now."

There was no fighting the urge. Even if I could, I didn't want to. I craved oblivion.

. . .

VOICES PULLED me from my sleep, or maybe it was the pain that wouldn't let me be.

"Do you need help?" a man asked.

"No. I can handle it," Kaden said. "Go back to the city and see what you can find out."

My eyes opened a little easier, but I wasn't sure if it was because some of the swelling had gone down or because they were covered in some sort of grease. A strip of sheet covered my hips and another covered my breasts, but I was bare besides those. My clothes lay in a shredded heap on the floor, looking as if they'd been ripped from my body.

The man was watching Kaden apply some more salve to my leg, as if there were something incredibly interesting about it. Then I realized why—Kaden wasn't just applying a cream but painting something on me with a blue, greasy paint. He'd apparently been busy, because nearly half of my body was covered in intricate symbols and shapes.

"She's awake," the younger man said, looking at me. I didn't remember ever meeting him, but something about his youthful face and shaggy blond hair seemed oddly familiar.

"She's exceptionally stubborn like that," Kaden said, keeping his eyes on what he was doing.

"You didn't put her to sleep?" the man asked.

They spoke as if I weren't lying there listening to every word.

"I did. She keeps pulling herself out."

How many times had I woken? I couldn't remember. How many times had he put me back under?

"That's surprising," the young man said.

"Not for her. Now go. I need you there more than here," Kaden said.

The young man nodded in my direction, as if we knew each other, and then left the room.

I took a breath, realizing I could fill my lungs if I ignored the sharp, stabbing pain, and it felt like an absolute miracle. I didn't know what Kaden was doing, but it was working. My self-diagnosis was shifting from "brink of death" to "banged up but going to make it."

When it seemed as if death were inevitable, it had been an eyeopener how strong my will to live really was. I didn't care if I had nothing, if I was starting over yet again, and had to rebuild an entire life. At least I had the chance.

"Thank you," I said, not sure if he'd acknowledge me as he continued to paint. It wasn't as if we'd left off in a good spot, or even a mediocre one.

He stopped painting for a second and turned slightly toward me. He gave me a nod before going back to work.

"How did we get here?" I asked.

He took a few minutes before answering. "There are ways to get around Nowhere that you're unfamiliar with," he said.

I waited for him to continue, but he didn't. He might've saved my life, but it was clear that bygones weren't going to be bygones. He'd saved me, but I wasn't ready to skip along and hold hands. I had no great need to speak to him.

I let the silence expand for a few minutes as I watched him continue to paint, working his way up my leg. When he was painting the inside curve of my knee, an uncomfortable awareness drove me to awkward chatter in spite of all my tough thoughts.

"Who was that guy that just left?" I asked.

Kaden didn't acknowledge the question.

I got it. The trust was gone.

Unfortunately, his distrust and maybe even hate of me didn't seem to diminish my body's reaction to his closeness. I was just healthy enough for my heart rate to kick up.

"Is this almost done?"

He looked at me as if I were the biggest ingrate ever. Or maybe that was hate shining in his eyes.

"No," he said.

Two decades ago I would've sobbed at the rejection hot on the heels of the beating. A couple of months ago I'd cried when my life was stolen, and cried again when I got stuck at the outpost, when I lost everything. I'd cried as they beat me. And begged. That had been the worst of it.

I didn't cry now because I didn't have any tears left. If Kaden hated me, that was his problem. Not mine.

"Why did you help me? Why are you still helping me?" I asked.

He turned toward me, as if he were trying to forget

there was a head attached to the body he was working on.

"Try not to move. I don't want my work undone," he said, not answering my question.

I didn't bother asking again.

It was hours before he was done, and my body was covered in markings I couldn't begin to fathom. Neither of us spoke again in all those hours.

NINE

Waking up was like trying to swim to the surface in a lake of molasses. My name was being called, and I didn't want to answer. Everything hurt when I woke. But it wouldn't stop pulling me toward it, as if I were being dragged up from the bottom where I was lying, whether I wanted to be or not. The voice grew clearer and more insistent, pulling me along steadily, even as I resisted.

Cutting through the numbness of oblivion, hands gripped my shoulders and then touched my cheek, forehead, ran over my hair. Something cold grazed my lips, a drop of moisture dripping between them, making my tongue quest for the source.

"It's time to wake up." Kaden's voice was clear and insistent.

He was working magic on me, forcing my body to respond, my consciousness to come awake and answer him. I didn't want to see him. I wanted a few more minutes of peace. I wanted to see no one, but it wasn't to be. I opened my eyes, knowing there'd be no escape while he was here.

"It's time to eat," Kaden said as he stood over me.

I didn't want to eat. I wanted to go back into oblivion, forget what had happened. Every movement hurt. My right leg was in a cast, along with my left arm. There was a drip attached to my arm.

"This is Soleil. She's going to help you."

The older woman from before stepped forward with a kind smile that I couldn't return. Even that much movement hurt.

Kaden left without saying anything else, and I was glad. I was in too much pain to handle the situation between us. He'd hurt me more than I'd imagined possible, considering I hadn't known him long. Then, after he'd stepped on me emotionally, kicked me out, he saved me, even though he clearly still hated me.

Soleil came forward and propped up the pillows behind me.

"Thank you, but I'm not hungry."

She took a bowl from the other side and moved it toward me. "You need to eat. It's been days."

Days? Did I ask how many? Did I want to know? My job. My assignments hadn't been earth-shattering, but I couldn't afford to lose another job. Kaden would surely kick me out of here too, and I couldn't start from scratch again.

She was hovering nearby, trying to scoop a spoonful of goop in my mouth.

"I can do it," I said, trying to reach for the spoon with splinted fingers.

"Let me help you," she said, refusing to hand me the spoon. "It'll get easier once your jaw gets better. Kaden worked very hard on you, so it'll heal fast."

"Really, I can do it," I said, trying to grab the spoon again.

The door to the bedroom swung wide.

"You're up!" Cookie said, walking in and taking the bowl from Soleil. "I got this."

"I need to make sure she eats," Soleil said, trying to grab the bowl back.

Cookie held it out of reach. "I got it. I'm not an idiot. Now go. I'm sure you have other things to do."

Soleil looked at the bowl and then the look on Cookie's face. "If that bowl isn't empty—"

"It'll be empty," Cookie said, keeping the bowl out of reach of the much shorter woman.

Soleil scowled in her direction, wiped her hands on her apron, and then, like almost everyone else I'd ever met, gave Cookie her way. She was shooting Cookie warning glances right until the door was shut.

"What the hell are they feeding you? This looks like shit and…" Cookie sniffed it and wrinkled her nose. "The smell alone might set you back a decade."

She walked to the window, opened it, and tossed the contents out, then put the bowl on the table beside me. "There. It's empty." She whipped a bag out of her pocket, retrieving a smushed donut. "It doesn't look good, but trust me, it's better than that slop. Got it from the leprechaun place."

As much as I didn't want to eat, I had to try after she'd smuggled it in. Plus, just seeing Cookie made me feel a little stronger, as if some of her resiliency was already rubbing off on me.

"Thanks. And thanks for coming." I took it, trying to nibble on it without opening my jaw too wide. The insides of my cheeks were raw and cut.

"The guys wanted to as well, but Kaden has us running pretty crazy with..."

"With what?" I asked, finding myself craving to hear about assignments that weren't teenage crushes and college admissions.

"Just things. Busy time." She dropped onto the chair beside my bed and kicked her boots up onto the side rail, looking me over. "I'm not going to lie and say you look good. You look worse than the slop I threw out the window. They did a real job on you, but you'll heal up. Tinkers don't scar."

She was wrong. I was already scarred. It was just in places no one could see. I wasn't going to think of that, though. I was going to focus on good things only, like my smushed donut. It was worth the pain of chewing to taste something this spectacular. And I was alive. That was all that mattered.

"This chair sucks." She shifted, and then shifted again. "Scoot over and give me half that donut."

I shifted as best I could, and then she forced me over

another couple inches as she shoved her way onto the bed. I must've really looked as bad as she said, because she was pushing a little more gently than was her typical nature.

She held out her hand, waiting for her half of the donut.

"You're really going to take half the donut you just gave me?" I wasn't sure why I asked. Of course she would.

"Let's not act like you're going to eat the whole thing. It'll be stale before you finish it."

She was right. But if I had to give her back half the smushed donut, this was the best time to hit her up for something else.

"Can you do me a favor?" I asked.

"Whatever you need," she said before eating almost all of her half donut in one bite.

"Can you get a message to Alaric that I'm sorry I'm missing work? You know, in case he hasn't heard?" He was a decent guy. He wouldn't fire me, would he? He'd hear me out, at least. As long as he knew I hadn't stopped showing up on purpose.

She let out a short laugh. "Trust me, he's heard about what happened. All of Nowhere has. But I'll go make sure if it makes you feel better." She shrugged.

She'd never understood how I was able to keep my sanity in that place, but I couldn't lose that too. I just couldn't. What was before me was already scary enough without my being unemployed as well.

"How's it going with you and Kaden? You two getting along or what?" She was wiping her hands on my blanket as she asked.

"Barely speaking. He might've found me, brought me here, and done some magic healing stuff, but I'm fairly certain he still hates me."

It was alarming when the man who despised me the most was the only one who'd helped me as I was beaten and humiliated. I'd walked out of his outpost clinging to my pride, thinking how I'd never set foot in there again, only for him to find me like that. And now I was stuck here with someone who detested but pitied me. It was the icing on the cake of a bad run.

"Do you hate him? I know you were hurt by his idiotic ways." Cookie's voice was unnaturally soft.

"I don't know how to feel. I can't hate someone who saved me. That being said, I don't trust him and I don't like him. So there you go." I left out the part where even when I was lying in pain, his nearness played my insides like a piano virtuoso without even trying. If he'd known, he would've run out of the room to get away from me. He barely wanted to look at me, let alone touch me.

"Just for the record, he doesn't hate you. He wouldn't save someone he didn't care about."

"Yeah, maybe." She'd also thought going to the outpost was a good idea, and that he'd come around.

"Whatever is meant to be, you'll figure it out," Cookie said. "And I'll be here for you. Or I will next week. Kaden has me running some errands. You won't be getting out of this bed for a little while anyway."

"Where is this place, exactly?"

Cookie laughed. "We call it the fortress. It's literally carved out of the mountainside far away from the city, in the middle of Nowhere's nowhere."

I gazed all around at the gleaming black stone. It looked like polished black granite, with the thinnest veins of crystal here and there that added to its sheen, giving it an almost ethereal glow.

"When things get crazy, this is where we fall back to on occasion. I have a room on the floor above. Home sweet home."

Home sweet home? I definitely couldn't handle this much reality right now.

"You know, I've had some rough patches in my life too. I didn't get to be this fabulous by accident." She took a deep breath in, as if she were still feeling her own scars. "You might not believe this now, but it gets better. You don't forget. You never forget. But you come out of it."

She didn't tell me what happened to her, and I didn't ask. If she'd wanted to, she would've. It was hard to imagine what could've messed her up, how bad it had been. It might be better not knowing. Considering how rough it could get in one mortal life, having centuries left a whole lot of opportunity.

"How long did it take you to bounce back?" I asked.

"I don't know. I'm still working on it," she said, and then giggled. "One of these days I'm really going to be past some of my crap. I'm positive." She laughed a little harder.

"You will," I said, laughing for no reason I could think of. "We'll both be perfect. No problems."

Every laugh hurt, but it still felt so much better than crying. I was banged up and bruised in more ways than I'd ever thought I'd survive, but I had. I was alive.

TEN

Kaden hadn't popped his head in even once as the days piled up. His steps, his voice, had sounded outside the door. I'd smelled his scent on the t-shirts I wore, but he clearly had no interest in me. I was feeling a little like an unwanted prisoner, and it seemed as if I'd been in this room for weeks.

Soleil had brought me some books and whatever type of amusement she could dig up, including some weird tile games, but it wasn't enough. Boredom was becoming like a drug that pumped through my veins, making me lose all fear of repercussions. I was ready to do some pretty stupid things right now, if only to break up the monotony.

Cookie wasn't even around to stir up the doldrums with her antics. She'd gone back to the city, so it was me and Soleil. Every. Single. Day. I might not be ready for a marathon, but damned if I wasn't getting out of this bed, and then this room, today, even if I had to crawl my way to the door.

Soleil walked in, tray in hand, and stopped abruptly. "Are you trying to get up?"

"I'm feeling better."

Everything being relative, my current status *was* better. I'd felt like a warmed-over corpse a week ago. The beating had proven one thing—I definitely wasn't human anymore. Mortals didn't heal this way. Or maybe it had been Kaden's magic? I might've asked him if I'd seen him.

"Is Kaden around?" I asked, gripping the bedpost.

"I believe he's about here somewhere." She suddenly got her motor moving again, putting down the tray. She crossed the room with her hands out, as if she were going to catch a toddler.

Yeah. He'd been around constantly, but not in this room. He'd been avoiding me for months before this. Why would there be a difference now? I was very aware that my welcome had worn out, if I'd had one in the first place. It was past time to leave.

I held up my arm with the cast and pointed down at my matching leg. "Do you know if these can come off? I was going to ask Kaden, but..." He was avoiding me? He hated my guts? He never wanted to see me again, let alone have to speak to me?

It didn't matter how he felt. It meant nothing to me. He might've saved me from death, which I'd thank him for, but I didn't feel any overwhelming urge to be near him. He had nothing to worry about. I'd say what I had to and get out of here.

"You'll have to ask him." Soleil was glancing at the

open door, as if expecting some mayhem to come, because why? I was looking to leave? I was up and about? Uttering his name? It was hard to know what was setting her off. She kept everything so close to the chest it was like trying to read a blank page.

"Do you know where he is?"

"Not sure."

Screw it. If I could walk, I'd saw the casts off myself. A good steak knife and maybe a pair of pliers should do the trick. How hard could it be?

Would it be safe to go back to my place after I left? I'd figure out something, because I wouldn't stay here.

Gripping the post of the bed with my good arm, I tested out the leg in the cast. Soleil hovered, as if afraid I'd break something else. She was probably terrified she'd be feeding me for another...

Was it a week? I'd been here so long that the days had run together.

"How long have I been here?" I asked.

"Close to two weeks." Her hands were out, like she was getting ready to catch me. Except Soleil was tiny, so I'd better not fall. She couldn't be more than five feet. If I did, I might kill her.

"*Two?*"

"You slept a good chunk of the first few days."

It was worse than I'd imagined, and on so many levels. Hopefully Cookie got the message to Alaric.

I had to get moving and figure out a plan. If that horde was still looking for me, I might have to hide out somewhere else for a little while. There had to be somewhere people couldn't find me. A place called Nowhere *should* be easy to get lost in.

"You don't happen to have some pants I could borrow, do you?" I asked.

The coming conversation with Kaden was going to be cringeworthy as it was. It was strange enough to have to thank someone and then tell them you were leaving because you hated each other. Saying it while standing in his borrowed t-shirt? Nope. Couldn't do it.

I'd been standing for a couple of minutes and not falling over, so Soleil finally backed up a little.

She started toward the dresser. "What did you want to wear? There's clothes in here for you. Kaden had them brought."

Should've known. He always did think of everything. Even if he hated me, he was too efficient to leave a detail like that hanging. He hadn't gotten me pajamas, which was strange, but it didn't matter.

I moved with an awkward gait away from the bedpost, venturing into the no man's land of the middle of the room, my leg feeling shaky but taking my weight. Another couple of steps, and another few to go, and I'd be able to take a break. Why did this room have to be so large? It didn't bode well for trying to find Kaden.

"You sure you're ready to be up and about?" Soleil asked, shadowing my steps.

"I'm good." I tried to walk a little faster, feeling like the Tin Man who'd been left out in the elements for a couple decades.

I made it to the dresser and leaned against it, gathering up some strength before I found a sweater. Unless I had a saw, there'd be no getting jeans over this bum leg. Luckily, there were leggings as well.

There were undergarments in the top drawer, all the right sizes. Well, he *had* seen the goods. Wasn't surprising he'd figured out the cup size.

"I'm good. I've got this."

Soleil was hovering nearby, but I wouldn't have her soon. I'd better figure out how to handle this on my own.

She stared at me, her face getting lopsided.

"I swear, I do."

She shook her head. "Yell if you need me," she said as she left.

"Thanks," I hollered back, having no intention of doing any such thing.

There was a long window beside the dresser with a view that seemed almost impossibly high. There were cliffs to the side, and below was all gleaming black stone, the same as the streets in Nowhere and the walls of this room. Cookie hadn't been kidding. This place was part of a mountain. Looking below, I saw it had to be at least a three-hundred-foot drop onto jagged stones and a crashing ocean. There'd be no sneaking out a window, either.

That left one option. Out the front door.

Walking stiffly, I ventured out of my room for the first time in weeks. The hall looked like it was carved from the same dark stone as my room had been, but the polished surfaces reflected the candlelight so well it didn't seem that dark. There were a lot of candles here too, as if there weren't any electricity.

As I passed the many closed doors, I wondered if one of these were his. How close had he been to me, night after night? Yet not having come by once?

I got to the top of a massive staircase, and of course it had to be a double flight down. How tall were these ceilings? I could try to go down on my butt. It wasn't the most dignified way, but it was better than ending up at the bottom in a lump of broken bones.

"You planning on going somewhere?"

I startled at the sound of his voice behind me, and Kaden reached out a hand to my waist, as if he thought I'd fall. As if that wouldn't make things easier for him.

"I was just..."

Standing on top of the stairs like an idiot? Soaking up his scent like he was the first brewed cup of the morning? Why did I seem to crave his presence even when I hated him?

No matter how I felt, he surely didn't have the same dichotomy of emotions. He didn't seem angry or happy. He seemed—distant. I could handle hate. This distance? It wasn't sitting as well. No matter how often I'd told myself that it didn't matter, a tender piece of me that I hadn't managed to quash, or ram into a compartment and lock away, stuck its tongue out at me. It called me a stupid pretender.

"Were you planning on going downstairs?" he asked.

"Yes," I said, all too aware of his hand still burning at my waist.

He picked me up and carried me down the too-long flight in awkward silence.

When we got to the bottom, he didn't put me down but asked, "Where were you heading?"

"I was actually coming to look for you."

"Then the office it is," he said, heading down a very long hall.

"I can walk." But I didn't want to. Being in his arms was the first time in weeks I'd felt truly safe. It was probably because he'd single-handedly scared away the horde. That had to be the only reason.

"The floors are slippery, and the cast will make it worse."

So it wasn't that he wanted to hold me, felt any kind of comfort from being close to me, too. He was afraid I'd injure myself more, and then what would he do? He could end up stuck with me for months.

I turned my head, looking at the floor behind us instead of his profile, wondering why that stung so bad.

The office was exactly what I'd expect to find in this fortress. It was massive, with walls lined with books. There was a sitting area in front of a fireplace and a large desk set in front of massive windows on the other side.

He set me down on the couch and then took more than a few steps away from me. So much for him wanting any kind of closeness. What we were was brutally obvious at even a cursory glance.

"How much longer do these have to stay on?" I asked, motioning to the two casts.

"If you promise to be careful, I'll take them off now."

"Sure." It would be easier for him to take them off, but they'd be coming off either way.

He walked out of the room and came back a minute later with a small saw that he put on the nearby table. He walked over and picked me up as if it were something he did all the time, then placed me on the table as well.

He sawed through them as I tried to figure out what my next move was. Each piece of cast that fell off took with it my last excuse for staying even another day. He'd probably wanted to push me out the door the night he brought me here, but I wouldn't think of that. It brought a fresh round of wounds I couldn't quite deal with on top of all the physical healing.

He finished taking off both casts, and I shifted to get to my feet. He held out his hand, offering assistance that I declined. I knew where we stood and didn't want any further confusion on the matter.

I got to my feet, reaching for a chair. I took a few steps, feeling not totally unsteady but weak. How was I going to walk out of here when I wasn't sure I could make it across the room?

It didn't matter. Somehow I would, because I refused to stay another night in this place with him hating me the way he did. I'd figure it out on my own, and it was time to say my goodbyes.

I edged slightly closer to the fireplace that was large enough to stand in, warming my hands while I recited what I'd been playing in my head.

"I want you to know I'm grateful for what you did for me. I really am, but I should head off now that I'm back on my feet. I'll leave this afternoon. If you could maybe give me a map or something...? I'm not quite sure where I am or how to get back to the city."

I kept my focus on my outstretched hands, waiting for his response as the seconds ticked by.

"No," he said, short, quick, and harsh.

I jerked my gaze back to him. Could he be so cruel that he wouldn't give me directions back? Why had he saved me if his hate was that thick?

"You won't draw a quick thing up for me so I know where I'm going? It doesn't have to be elaborate."

He crossed his arms in front of his chest and had the look of a man who'd made up his mind. "No, I won't, because you can't go."

Leave it to Kaden to make things worse between us. He'd give me a hard time leaving if only because that was what *I* wanted to do. He hated me so much he'd chop off his own nose.

"You don't want me here. I don't want to be here. Going is the only sane thing to do. Now if you can tell me how to get out of this forsaken place, I'll be going."

From what I'd seen from my window view, the place looked like it was going to be a straight shot down a cliff. The map wasn't a luxury but a necessity.

"You don't seem to understand. There isn't anywhere safe for you right now other than here. You can barely walk." He was leaning on the table, making a point to run his gaze up and down the length of me.

"I'll manage," I said.

"Yes. We saw how well that went."

My face burned and my words were choked off for a moment. He'd found me on the street, battered and humiliated, which was enough to make anyone want to forget. Now he was throwing it in my face? It was beyond what I could take. It was one insult too many.

"Forget it. I'll find my own way."

I turned and headed to the door but couldn't get my hand to raise to open it. He wasn't even speaking and he was controlling me. I kept focusing on getting my hand on the doorknob, but the only thing that happened was a trickle of sweat down my brow.

"You're going to hurt yourself," he said, sounding as if he were the one stuck in a room against his will.

I spun on him and then had to grab the wall to stop myself from falling.

"Why are you doing this? You don't want me here, so enough with the tricks and let me out." I was white-knuckling the trim on the wall, trying to keep myself standing. I'd barely made it across the room. I didn't have the energy to fight off his magic.

"Why? Because I let you out and I'll be picking up the pieces an hour from now." He was scowling.

I couldn't deny that I was in weak shape, but it didn't matter. "I'm not asking you to be my savior. You can leave me wherever I fall with a clean conscience."

"It took a lot of work to repair you. I'm not letting it all go for nothing. You're staying until you have a slim chance of surviving." He dropped onto the chair, reclining with his legs stretched out.

"I'm not asking you to protect me." He wasn't even

breaking a sweat to restrain me in this room, and yet I could barely stay standing. The entire situation made me want to beat him.

"I'm aware, and yet I keep finding myself doing it anyway."

"You're insane. Do you know that?"

He shrugged, the name calling not fazing him.

He made no sense. He sounded angry that I was staying, even as he was the one insisting I couldn't leave. As much as I wanted to rant and rave and continue fighting, the bottom line was that all I was capable of doing was gripping the wall for dear life to stay standing.

"I didn't ask for your help." I hadn't called anyone. I hadn't had a chance.

"That is correct. *You* didn't." An elbow on each arm of the chair, he steepled his fingers in front of him as he watched me.

"You're saying someone else did?" I asked. "Who?"

"I'm not sure you want to know."

Kaden wasn't an idiot. Saying that was going to make me insist on knowing.

Or maybe not so idiotic after all.

"Who?"

"Your grandmother."

"Wait, what?" I wavered in my spot for a second as he watched. She had been there. I hadn't imagined her.

"Your grandmother. Instead of going to you herself, she sent word to me." There were a thousand condemnations and I-told-you-sos wrapped up in that last sentence.

He was right—I hadn't wanted to know—but I

wouldn't be so fast to believe that the situation was as black-and-white as he portrayed it. He hated her. Of course he'd try to paint this in the worst possible light. He was in a dark place with her, and that tainted everything he saw. This was the woman who'd kissed my scrapes and bruises, and he'd have to give me something a lot more damning than this. I wasn't such a fickle soul to turn my back on her over some hearsay, no matter what he might think of me.

"She wouldn't have left me. If she called you, it was because, for whatever reason, she couldn't help me."

He stared at me so intensely that I nearly flinched. "I probably should let you go on thinking the best of her, yet I feel some compulsion to help you stay alive. As long as you remain delusional, that's harder to do. I have an eyewitness that put her at the place and time of your beating."

I did flinch this time but refused to back down. "If they were your people and telling the truth, why didn't they step in? Maybe they're lying?"

"They had very specific directions."

That made things clear. They'd been instructed to not interfere in anything, just spy on me.

I wasn't considered one of his anymore. I'd been kicked to the curb, an outcast. It was probably luck that they didn't get a kick in themselves, or maybe they had. This was the man I was supposed to trust over my grandmother? Not likely.

"People like that aren't reliable." Anyone who was on the payroll couldn't be trusted, in my book. "While we're at it, how did anyone even know about Chaos? Did you tell them? Maybe you had spies in place watching because you were waiting for this?"

"And then save you?" he asked, saying nothing else because it was too stupid to argue and we both knew it. "How long do you think she was going to let it continue for? How much longer do you think you had?"

His expression reflected every question I'd thought of myself. What if he hadn't shown? Would she have left me to die?

No. Don't let him get to you. He's trying to twist your mind against her because he hates her.

"She had a reason. She wouldn't have left me to die. If you want to hate me for keeping her a secret, the one person who was decent to me, who was always there for me, then so be it. I'd do it again. That's what *loyal* people do." And I was going to continue to be loyal to her no matter what.

"There's loyalty and then there's stupidity. Loyalty is not leaving someone you love to take a beating alone. Another minute or two and you would've been dead."

I couldn't do it. Couldn't believe it. Not her. She would've stepped in.

"You're wrong." I'd gone from staring at him, ready to do battle, to looking out the window above the desk at the swirling universes. I could accept what he said about anyone else, but I wasn't going to believe it.

I slumped against the wall, looking out at the view again, hearing the sounds of the waves creeping in when no one spoke. I could see more cliffs in the distance, the glittering ocean crashing into the dark rocks, making them look like black diamonds. The view reminded me of its owner—harsh and yet devastatingly beautiful and intriguing. Both capable of utter destruction.

That was what his words were doing to me right now. Ripping apart the only thing I had left.

"Maybe she would've," he said a moment later, after the silence had become all the more deafening in comparison to our raised voices.

I looked back at him, catching that look on his face. "I don't need you to placate me, or your pity. I'm fine."

He gave a single nod, as if he wouldn't belabor the point. "Is there anything else you haven't told me? Any other allegiances I'm unaware of?"

Other than Gram, who was once again lost to me, I had no one. My state of being was so low that I didn't have the fight left in me to pretend, or pick a fight. Who was I kidding, anyway? Like he'd said, I had nowhere to go. I couldn't even get lost in Nowhere.

"No. There's no one else."

He waved a hand toward the door.

I turned and left, not waiting for him to say anything else or lay down any more rules. I hobbled along, wishing I could make my legs go faster, wishing I hadn't left that bedroom after all.

ELEVEN

I'd spent the last two days walking around my room, trying to get the kinks out of a body that had spent more time in bed than standing the last couple weeks. Once I could move in a somewhat normal fashion, I expanded into the hall. I did laps back and forth, always keeping an ear out for Kaden.

Trying to avoid Kaden wasn't as difficult as I'd imagined. He seemed to be avoiding me as well. He had to be, because I didn't see him once while I paced back and forth in the halls. Maybe he was in the city, visiting Antoinette. As long as she wasn't here, I wouldn't look a gift horse in the mouth.

If he had gone out, it would be even better, because today, I was venturing downstairs again. The first thing I was doing was finding a way out. I might have nowhere to go, and he might've kept me from leaving, but that didn't mean I wasn't finding the escape hatch.

The trip downstairs was an epic workout on its own.

The place was vast. They might've gotten a little greedy when they were carving up the mountain. There was a room for everything, and some of them looked abandoned. The place, everything in it, had a feeling of ancientness.

Servants would walk past with a nod, but no one stopped or asked what I was doing. It wasn't clear if that was because they didn't care or had been instructed not to. Either way, it was working out well for me.

I kept creeping along, examining every room on the first floor that I could gain entrance to, slowly making my way toward the only door out I'd seen so far. The closer I got, the more I expected something to happen, someone to run up to me or start yelling on high alert.

No one came, even as I stood in front of it. No one seemed to care. Maybe Kaden didn't think I'd try to leave, which was worse. He thought I was so pathetic that I wouldn't even attempt it. I'd sit there and do as I was told. A couple of weeks ago, I might've. That was how low I'd fallen. Today? Not so much, and tomorrow might bring even more surprises.

I grabbed the handle on the massive door, swinging it open. I stepped out onto the small stoop and leaned over, seeing the craggy rock way down beneath. How did people get in and out? Squinting, I tried to see if there were any piles of bones below, but it was too far down.

I backed away before anyone got the crazy idea of putting a boot to my ass. I made my way back upstairs before Kaden appeared, ready to gloat.

Soleil showed up with a plate of food fifteen minutes

later, as if she'd seen me and known I'd worked up an appetite.

"Thanks," I said, taking the bowl of stew and going over to the table and chair I'd pushed closer to the window, the place I took every meal.

"What is that song you keep humming?" Soleil asked. "Is that from Topside?"

I frowned. Had I been humming? "I don't know where I heard it. It just got stuck in my head."

I settled down to eat, but Soleil didn't leave.

"What's wrong? I thought you liked stew?" she asked, watching me.

"No, it's great." All the food here was. It was sitting in my room alone for every meal that I didn't like. Kaden was avoiding me anyway. Why not at least take my meals in a different spot? Sit by that large fireplace I'd seen? Read a book downstairs? Get out of here before I threw myself out a window onto the rocks?

"It's just, I was wondering..."

"What?" she asked.

"Is there anywhere else I might eat?"

"Of course. Where would you like to eat?"

"Well, I saw a dining room, not that big one but the smaller one. Could I eat there?" The small room was still huge by any standards, but it wasn't the size of a ballroom. I'd only seen the kitchen from a distance, and even then, I'd caught enough stares to feel awkward going in. That place might as well have a flag flying in front of it declaring it off-limits, and there was no way I'd risk alienating anyone else. I had enough people who hated me.

"Of course. I'll bring all your meals there from now on." She smiled and then patted me on the shoulder, as if she were proud of me.

She turned to leave, and I began to hum again, happy at the prospect of branching out.

IT WAS my third breakfast in the dining room, and it seemed as if the staff here were trying to encourage me to continue. Instead of the normal eggs and toast, there was an entire spread laid out on the buffet. When I'd told Soleil it was too much, she insisted it was no problem. What I'd really hoped for was some company to eat it with. I was tired of talking to the walls.

I was taking another bite of eggs, after dipping them into the weird cream sauce that I was now addicted to, when Kaden walked in. I choked on the bite.

He stopped and looked at me with a raised brow. Clearly he was still averse to speaking to me, even if it was a simple *Are you okay?*

I nodded, motioning that I was fine. It took me another minute to stop coughing. I hadn't seen him in days. What was he doing, strolling in here like nothing was amiss and fixing himself breakfast? *My* breakfast. It was all mine. I'd wanted company, but not *him*.

He was filling his plate as if this were a normal occurrence, before moving on and helping himself to coffee.

He took a sip of it and made a sound of distaste. Good. I was glad he didn't like the coffee.

"Why is this so bad?" He was looking at me as if I were to blame.

"Really? I think it's delicious." I sipped mine as if to prove it.

I might've made my inclinations for lighter coffee known, but I'd improved conditions by getting rid of the typical mud Kaden preferred. Most people didn't like coffee that made the hair on your chest grow.

For all his groaning, he continued to drink it.

Maybe he'd take his eggs and coffee and go. That would be fine by me. I might be desperate for company, but I wasn't so desperate to need his. I wasn't sure where he even *had* breakfast anymore. If he did, it was somewhere I never saw him. He could go off and hate me somewhere else, and I'd continue my silent resentment of him in peace and quiet.

No such luck as he settled down at the table.

That was when I saw the paper in his hand. A month ago I would've asked him for the crossword. A couple weeks ago I wouldn't have had to ask at all. Now I didn't want the crossword. Well, I *wanted* the crossword, but not from *his* paper, and I doubted he'd give it to me even if I did.

I took a sip of my coffee, focused on my food, refusing to speak to the only company I had. It wasn't like I wanted to talk to him anyway, but I finally had company for breakfast, and it was almost worse than being alone. At least alone, I was just lonely. Now? I was lonely *and* awkward. This was a net negative for sure.

My plan was to ignore him until I departed this

place. When would that be? I wasn't quite sure, but it would happen, and I would be busy not speaking until such a point arrived. He'd made it very clear how he felt about my actions, and although he'd saved me, his disdain couldn't help but evoke a similar feeling in myself. In my book, if you could hate me for no reason? I could hate you right back, especially if I *had* reasons. At least I hadn't kicked him out of my outpost or tried to boot him from an entire city. I was the one who was allowed to be angry.

I was continuing to be polite and hate him in an indirect manner, but then he turned and looked at me.

"Are you still stiff, or do you think you can move around all right?" he asked, returning his gaze to his paper before I responded.

Had he already changed his mind? My heart rate shot up from its normal seventy range to something closer to an Indy 500 racer about to take the lead.

"I'm good. I feel good." Let him tell me to leave. I *wanted* to leave. I'd survive fine on my own, in spite of what he thought.

He shot me a glance that said I was the worst liar ever born.

"I'm good," I repeated, continuing the lie. I was. Kind of. I mean, maybe I wasn't getting out of bed as fast as I used to, but so what? I might be an old beater at the moment, but once I got all the parts warmed, oiled up a little, my engine would roar like a V8. This old junker would hold her own. I wouldn't fall back on some lame excuse about being hurt. I didn't need him or his big black cave. That's all this place was, a big, overgrown cave, and who needed it? Not me.

"Then we start tomorrow morning." He flipped the page of his newspaper.

"Start what?" It would be great to know what we were starting, but again, he seemed to abhor speaking to me.

"Making you more resilient," he said.

So that was the plan? Get me up to par so he could get rid of me? Had the crew given him some sort of lecture or something?

"My resilience isn't your issue," I said, stabbing a piece of egg.

"It is."

"It isn't."

He put the paper down and looked at me. "I feel it is, and your saying otherwise won't change that."

He stared at me as if that were the final word.

"I feel that it isn't, and nothing you say will change my mind." *Ha! How do you like that one, Mister Bossman?*

He narrowed his eyes. "Are you saying you're rejecting my help to make you stronger? Because that would be idiotic, considering your situation."

I didn't *want* to give him that point, but it was a hard one to dispute. "No, that is not what I'm saying. What I mean is that I will take your offer but that my resiliency is *my* issue."

He raised his brows before going back to reading. "Fine. It's your issue that I will help you with."

"Yes, fine," I said.

He didn't hand me the crossword.

I didn't ask for it. I drank more coffee, making a delighted humming noise, so he realized how much better my way was.

TWELVE

Kaden had asked if I was sore yesterday, so it stood to reason whatever we'd be doing today was physical. A pair of leggings, a sports bra, and I was ready to work out. He didn't want me—hated me, in fact—so my assets shouldn't be a problem. If Antoinette showed up and disliked it, then her boyfriend shouldn't have supplied these clothes. It wasn't as if I'd picked them.

I walked into the hall, listening for sounds of the monster. I'd been waiting for Antoinette to show for days —unless they'd broken up again. I wouldn't know, because I didn't care enough to ask. I wouldn't ask Cookie either, or the guys. I'd ask no one, because I. Didn't. Care.

My breakfast was waiting, and the dining room was clear. My first sip of coffee was perfect, so Kaden hadn't gotten to the staff yet. My morning was starting off with a win.

Kaden walked in a few minutes later, running his

eyes over the length of me. He didn't say anything as he went to pour himself a cup, but he didn't have to. I'd seen the pattern of his perusal and the different landing stops he'd made with his eyes before he looked away.

I leaned my hip on the buffet, arching my back a little, not because I wanted him, or wanted him to want me. It was good business. Keeping him off balance would only be a benefit. Why shouldn't I use what I had? There might be a little spite and gloating, but not *that* much.

He drank his coffee as he fought to keep his eyes on my face.

"You need to..."

I leaned forward slightly. "I need to do what?" I asked, trying not to smile because I'd thrown him off. He wasn't a man that was easily toppled, and it was hard not to do a little mental muscle flex.

He had his pick of women. Even now, in jeans and a sweater, he was looking...

He looked nothing. There would be no appreciating the way he looked, even if it was innocent, because nothing about him was pure or simple. He was someone to keep at arm's length.

Wait, why was he in jeans?

He cleared his throat and then forced himself to look everywhere but at me. "You need to grab a sweater. We're going to the cellar."

Huh? Cellar? I'd had one job in a few days, discover all the nooks and crannies of this place, and I'd failed. How had I missed the cellar?

"We're working out in the cellar?" Was there a gym

down there? This place looked a little too ancient to have a finished basement, with workout equipment. Stranger things had happened, though. I couldn't believe there was a home gym and no one mentioned it.

"Finish your breakfast, grab a sweater, and meet me by the door behind the stairs," he said, walking out of the room.

I grabbed two croissants and then ran upstairs. I was back in less than a minute, excited to see what kind of setup he had. Kaden was waiting at the back of the stairs, in front of paneling, a torch in hand. Was that the door? No wonder I hadn't seen it. This place had its own set of tricks.

He pushed it open, and lo and behold, there were stairs. He headed below, disappearing with his torch into the dark. I wasn't sure I wanted to work out in a place that required a torch. Or that was pitch black.

If this was someone else, I wasn't sure I'd be willing to follow them. But Kaden could've left me for dead a lot easier than bothering to heal me. My belief didn't waver even as we kept going lower, and lower, and then even lower. By the time we stopped, I was surprised the place wasn't filled with seawater—not that I could see much in the dark.

"Wait here," he said, lighting torches along the wall as his steps echoed.

The huge, cavernous space slowly came into view, one torch at a time, and it was definitely not a home gym. The walls and floors were all that same black, honed stone I'd seen everywhere else. The space was fairly empty except for monuments and statues lining the perimeter. What really caught my eye were the symbols etched into the walls, from floor to ceiling. Different symbols and sketches. The ceiling was a mural of Nowhere's sky. The place was pretty, in a mausoleum kind of way, but not exactly somewhere I'd want to hang out.

He circled back, putting his torch in a holder nearby, before walking over to me. "There's something I need to explain to you before we go any further."

Kaden? Looking to explain things? I hadn't been nervous following him down here, but this was concerning.

"We have to talk here? We couldn't have discussed it over morning coffee?" I asked, looking around the place some more. If he was trying to put me on edge, it was working.

"We're down here because it's safer." He looked around the room, at the markings, as if they were a replay of memories from his past.

"Don't you trust your staff?" I'd never gotten the impression, not even a little, that they weren't to be trusted. Yet here we were, hiding in a cellar? If there was an issue, he might've disclosed it earlier.

"I trust them implicitly." He faced me again, his expression deadly serious. "What we need to discuss carries a certain weight. The words alone might travel on the wind."

Yeah, and he just kept upping the creepiness factor of

this conversation. This was why you didn't follow people into dark cellars.

"The forces that are gathering against you, they won't quit, and your odds of survival aren't high."

He was talking about my odds like a statistician and not like he'd declared me a dead woman. Talk about a harsh delivery. I should've known this wouldn't go well, considering talking wasn't his forte. Well, he could say whatever he wanted, but it didn't make him correct.

"You don't know if they'll come for me again. They might forget about me." Yes, they were angry about Chaos. Maybe they'd get over it? He didn't know every mind in Nowhere.

He let out a low sigh. "Trust me, they *will* come for you again, and if you don't agree to what I suggest, you won't survive. You won't have the skills needed. I'm your only hope."

He was standing there, looking so certain that it was hard to brush off his words. Getting beaten to near death might have also contributed. Either way, I didn't have the luxury of not hearing him out.

"Well? Tell me. What is it that you suggest I need?" I took a few steps toward the stairs, leaning against the rail. I attempted to appear as if I were getting comfortable, and not that I was afraid I'd need the support for what I was about to hear. I shrugged, hoping it added to the effect.

He looked me over for a second. If he knew I was scared, he didn't comment.

"In order to teach you what you need, for you to be

able to do some of what I can do, I have to give you a piece of myself. I have to mark you," he said, and then went silent again, as if he was walking me slowly through whatever this day was going to hold.

"Like, a tattoo or something?" Maybe something like all the markings on the wall? Or how he'd drawn on me when I was hurt?

"It's a bit more involved than that. A part of what I can do comes from *what* I am. I have to give you a piece of that and make it a part of you."

"And what exactly are you that you'll be giving to me?" I'd always suspected he wasn't your run-of-the-mill tinker, but I'd never had a moment like this to pursue it, a point where it wouldn't look like prying or digging. He couldn't suggest what he was talking about and not tell me. It was a necessity.

"I'm a Kradix," he said casually.

"What's a Kradix?" I'd wanted to ask him what he was for so long now, and I had to admit, the answer? Little anticlimactic.

"The name wouldn't mean anything to you. It's not something that would've made it to your books on Earth, but it's something quite a bit stronger than your average tinker. It's the name of people who are native to Nowhere. There aren't many of us." He walked over to a column and leaned his shoulder on it, watching my every twitch and blink.

"What can you do?" I asked, careful to keep my emotions locked away as he studied me. I didn't want to seem eager, and have him asking too much in return.

"My powers are immense, but most of them aren't important, since they won't transfer. What *will* transfer is strength, durability, and a stronger hand at persuasion. It'll give you a fighting chance going forward," he said, matching the calmness I was trying to portray.

I was pretty sure *he* wasn't faking his calm persona, though.

"Will I stay me? Or the version of me I am now?" What he suggested sounded good, but everything came with a price.

"Many Kradix have tried to transform people into one of us. In all the times they've tried, it's never succeeded. I'm not arrogant enough to think this time will be any different."

I pushed off the railing, needing an outlet for the fizz of excitement starting to bubble up. The horde had run from Kaden when he showed up. If I could have even a little piece of that, I could walk the streets of Nowhere without fear. I could get on with some sort of normal life.

Do it and have a fighting chance against the next threat that cornered me, or be afraid all the time? Afraid and hiding, or brazen but with risk? Fortune favored the bold. I'd always thought that saying was foolish because the bold ended up in ditches just as often as everyone else, maybe more. Everyone knew about the Wright brothers, but no one talked about all the people who died or got injured before them. Then again, I'd already gotten injured and almost died. Was there really any choice to be made? It was boldness or death.

I did another short pace. "So I'll be stronger and have

a little more 'juice,' so to speak, when I want to persuade someone."

"And you'll be harder to kill," he added, as if that had more weight than everything else combined.

"Will it affect you at all?" I shouldn't care. It was his decision. It wasn't as if I were asking him to do this, but I'd never been a taker. Maybe I'd spent too many years worrying about everyone else, and that habit didn't die easily.

"Slightly weaker, especially initially, but I'll regenerate almost all of it back."

There was only one word that stuck with me. "Almost?"

"I'll lose a fraction of a percent." He shrugged.

Fraction of a percent? That was something I could live with. I wanted this. I was nearly vibrating with want.

"So what's the cost to me?" I asked, hoping I didn't sound as eager as I was.

"Nothing."

It was a gift that would help me survive and yet it was free? It seemed too good to be true. Nothing was free. Sometimes it was a little and sometimes not. Costs tended to be proportional to the "gift." This one sounded quite hefty, and it wasn't adding up. I looked at him, thinking this was a gag, but he wasn't smiling. No, he was serious.

"Why would you do this? You're still mad at me. You barely talk to me, but you're going to give me this?"

He didn't answer for a second, his features stoic. I waited, demanding an answer with my unflinching stare.

"I feel a responsibility for what happened to you." It seemed like someone was stealing the words from his body, and with a struggle.

I stiffened. There was only one way he'd feel responsible, and if it was what I feared, I'd walk out of this place right now. If he wanted to stop me from leaving, he'd have to kill me. It was a betrayal too deep to even tolerate his presence.

"I thought you didn't tell them about Chaos."

"I told you I wouldn't, and I haven't." He shook his head, as if even the suggestion was an insult. It was the exact reaction I'd expect from him.

"You're going to have to explain how it was your fault?" I asked, seeing no connection. If he hadn't told anyone, how could he be to blame for the beating I took?

His jaw twitched. "You weren't ready for Nowhere. I told you to go Topside, but I didn't follow up on it. I allowed you to stay against my better judgment."

That was why he blamed himself? I had a mountain of anger toward him, but one tiny piece was chipped off. He might've kicked me out of the outpost, and tried to evict me from Nowhere, but maybe he wasn't as evil as I'd wanted to believe. He'd turned his back on me but hadn't completely stopped caring. He'd feared for my staying in Nowhere, and that was why he wanted me Topside. In my book, he'd still wronged me in so many ways, but I might've been closer to a slow simmer at the moment and not the rolling boil I'd been.

"I didn't go Topside because I chose not to. That doesn't mean you're to blame." Even if I'd like to use him as a scapegoat, it was too far a stretch even in my deepest rage.

"I could've made you go," he said, as if that was how his world worked.

"Except whether or not I went Topside was my call. Not yours. I decided not to, and I wasn't going." Sometimes his attitude on things was as ancient as this place. Even when he was being civil, I wanted to punch him.

"That's what you think because you're young and naïve. I shouldn't have allowed it." His voice was growing harsher, but it was directed at himself.

"I am not naïve. I'm an adult who makes her own choices." I *was* going to kill him if I stayed here. He was trying to give me something that would help me stay alive, and I was going to kill him before he could.

"Look how that's turned out. You still have no idea what you've gotten involved in." He was running his hand through his hair, seeming as on edge as he was making me.

Deep breaths. I needed to take many, many deep breaths. It was as if since I got here, since the beating had taken place, his mission in life was to anger me. He was exceptionally good at it, too. I'd lived with a drunk my entire life, a person who'd never lacked for hurtful things to say, and yet I'd never felt quite so out of control as he made me.

No. I couldn't let him get under my skin this way. He could only upset me if I allowed it, and I wouldn't. I refused to let someone else rule my emotions.

"We're going to have to agree to disagree." I didn't

give him an opportunity to launch into anything else on the subject, knowing that it would lead to my trying to punch him or storming out. It didn't matter what he thought. He was wrong and I was right, even if he didn't know it.

"Now back to what you're suggesting—you said it might be the only way I can survive and have any independence. There must be another way," I said.

He'd be giving me something that would cost him because he felt guilty. This was not the way I wanted to get stronger. In fact, nothing about his motives were appealing. I might be unhappy with him, but to do this?

He was shaking his head before I finished talking. "It could take decades, if ever."

"I can train and do—"

"Take it or never leave this place." He shrugged, as if he didn't care how this was achieved, but it was going to be done.

"So you're going to force this on me?" It was as if he were allergic to being nice. Every single time I started to soften, he undid his goodwill somehow. "You can't force this on me if I don't want it."

"No. You have a choice. Eventually you'll be able to leave, but not until the other side is dead. I can't say for sure how long that will take."

"Why do you care? It's my problem, not yours." I was stumped, watching him as he threw out his dictates. It was as if he'd lost his mind. He was being overly protective, as if he wanted to put me in bubble wrap, at the same time as he was being an utter ass.

"Because I don't want to *have* to save you again. I don't have the time to clean up your messes," he said.

I was a hair away from blasting him, telling him what an absolute lunatic he was, when he turned and gave me his profile. In that split second, his guard had dropped and he seemed gutted. He looked at me as if he were seeing me on that night, and his anger nearly filled the cavernous room. Maybe it was misplaced guilt, but what had happened was eating him up.

Maybe I couldn't trust him completely, but I was coming to believe he didn't want to see me hurt—not physically, anyway. Emotionally? Yeah. He'd been the one to leave me wounded on the ground when he kicked me out of the outpost and rejected me. But maybe his intentions were pure here, in this moment.

Living with that kind of guilt, whether it was deserved or not, was life-ruining. If it wasn't for him, I'd be dead. If he needed this to get past whatever it was he was going through, I had to do it just to settle my debt to him.

But that was it. I wouldn't let him in. I could let him do whatever he needed to my body, but I'd keep my heart soundly in my chest.

"Let's do it. What do you need from me? How does this work?" I took a step toward him, showing my willingness.

The tendons in his neck smoothed out, as if he'd just heard he was the one that was going to be saved.

"We do it here, now, and all you have to do is take my hands," he said.

"Does it have to happen down here for some reason?" Between the dark walls and the weird writing, I almost expected to hear a howling wind or something. Sitting in front of a warm fire, busting out a couple of marshmallows, might take the creepiness factor down and calm my nerves about what I was going to be doing.

"There might be an energy signal. If there is, this place is engineered to absorb the power."

I nodded, and then took a second to walk around the cavernous room again, stalling for time now that I'd agreed. He was going to take a piece of him, put it in me, and it was so forceful that it could send out a signal into Nowhere? And whatever was in this room would block it? This sounded like something that was sitting on the edge of insanity.

"You're going to do this how, exactly? Just by holding hands?" I ran my fingers along a carving of a crazy-looking creature, half dragon and half some other sort of beast.

The idea he was going to be able to give me a piece of himself like this was also crazy. The things I'd believe now were leaps and bounds more than a few months ago, when I thought my future was as an accountant. Most people had a normalcy bias, never believing the world as they knew it would ever significantly change. My bias had been blown to smithereens, and what little pieces were left were still being smashed into dust. I'd learned the hard way that you never quite knew what could happen.

"You'll feel power entering, and I'm not saying it's

going to be overly enjoyable, but it'll be done fast." He held out his hands, his gaze locked on mine.

I took them, feeling some strange closeness in this simple act, even though it was a means to an end. I'd never realized how intimate holding hands could be.

"Fast, right?" It better be. I'd avoided risk my entire life, and this was going to take some getting used to.

"Yes." He closed his eyes, and I could feel his flesh growing warmer, almost as if I were holding a warm mug. Then he grew hotter, just shy of uncomfortable.

Was I really doing this? I had no idea what was even going to happen.

Don't think. If I did, I'd pull away.

"You need to try to relax, be open," he said.

"Okay." Could he feel the emotional wall I'd erected around myself? It had been built block by block, starting the day he turned his back on me in the alley. It wouldn't be that easy to tear it down at a moment's notice.

I closed my eyes, thinking open thoughts. *Open, open, open.*

"Are you trying? You feel impenetrable." He shifted his grip on my hands.

"I'm trying." *Open, open, open.* I was nearly singing it in my head.

"You need to try harder." He spoke as if he needed this more than I did.

"I'm *trying*. You're not helping by making me agitat-ed." I opened my eyes to find him staring at me. "I'm trying my hardest, so whatever you get is what you'll have to work with. Just do whatever you have to and let's be done with this. If you can just force it, then do it." Because I was pretty certain I was as open as I could be at this point. He'd turned his back on me, humiliated me in his outpost. What did he expect?

"You're sure? It's going to hurt more that way."

"I don't care. Just do it." I firmed up my grasp on his hands.

He didn't ask again as the room exploded with power that was palpable, feeling like it was frying the air around us, and then a blast of pain hit so hard that my vision blurred and I fell to the ground. That was the last thing I remembered.

THIRTEEN

I'd only gotten small glances of the bedroom I woke in. It wasn't exactly the clean-lined decor of Kaden's town-home, with a bed that looked like it had been carved from a redwood that had lived an eon, but it fit the fortress it was in and also the man sleeping like the dead beside me.

The shooting pain that had taken me out was gone, but I felt like one big bruise. There wasn't any hint of damage on my skin, but I felt as if my insides had been put through a blender, pureed, and then poured back in. It wasn't just physically, either, but as if my soul had been ripped apart. Then it had been roughly stitched together but was still oozing from the damage.

I sat up, wanting nothing but to retreat somewhere alone and lick my wounds. And get food. The hunger was nearly overwhelming.

I moved to get out of the bed.

Kaden's hand wrapped around my wrist.

"You can't leave yet." His eyes were barely open and

his voice was raw, as if he'd spent the night screaming. "We have to make sure the marking took before you can get too far from me."

"Is that what I'm feeling? That raw sensation?"

"Yes. It'll go away." He was already closing his eyes again, and letting go of my wrist.

If I'd had a rough night, he looked like he'd been pulled from the brink of death. His normal healthy glow had a grayish tinge, and his breathing seemed shallow.

I dropped back down on the bed, afraid to leave him even if I could.

"How long will this last?" I wanted to reach out and feel his forehead but fisted my hand, keeping it to myself.

"Sometime before tomorrow," he said, not bothering to open his eyes.

"Then we'll both be normal?" I'd never seen him like this. I wasn't sure he could lift his head off the pillow, and the sight rattled me more than the raw feeling inside.

It sounded as if he'd hummed an agreement.

"What if I want to shower?" Would that kill him? Would he die if I left?

"You'll have to use my bathroom."

He looked as if he were barely clinging to consciousness. I reached for him again but stayed my hand before it touched his skin. We weren't close like that. We weren't even friends. Most days he barely tolerated me, and yet this compulsion to touch him was nearly unbearable.

"Are you sure you're okay?" I asked, staring at him now that his eyes were closed, wringing my hands in the blanket.

"I'm drained, but I'm fine. I'll bounce back quickly." His voice was raspy, as if his breathing were labored.

"You sure?" How weird would it seem if I put my ear to his chest and listened to his lungs?

"If you're worried, I called in reinforcements."

Wait, called in reinforcements? I hadn't been worried for me, at least until he said that. He looked about to drift off, and I should've let him. Whatever he'd done, it hurt him more than it hurt me, but he'd been the one to drop that bomb. How was I supposed to let that go?

"Why do we need reinforcements?" I whispered, as if softening my voice were nicer somehow.

"In case the cellar didn't manage to block everything and they decided to hit while I'm weak." He rolled onto his side away from me, sending a clear signal he was done talking.

They were probably my grandmother and her group. And hit? Yeah, he obviously thought they wanted to kill him. Did they? That was not a conversation worth delving into right now.

I settled back down onto bed and turned on my side toward him, watching his chest rise and fall, just in case he stopped breathing. If he did, I'd have to try to resuscitate him. It was the only decent thing to do. I would've done it for anyone. I mean, if he died now, it would be because of what he did for me, and I didn't want blood on my hands.

I lay like that, watching his chest rise and fall for a good fifteen minutes before I forced myself to look away. I glanced around the room, taking in the smaller details.

I was checking out the area rug when he rolled back toward me. He wrapped his arm around my waist, pulling me into him. His leg bent, draping over mine.

I stiffened, as much as I could, anyway. I'd gone from looking around one second, totally platonic, to being cuddled. It wasn't sexual, exactly, although his leg was bent at an angle where it seemed he wanted to dip it in between mine. He had no idea who he was cuddling, or he definitely wouldn't be doing it. We weren't on cuddle terms. I should probably pull away.

I didn't. Obviously he wasn't feeling well because of what he'd done for me and was looking for comfort. No decent person would withhold that from him. I was on the winning end of things, so if he needed to cuddle to feel better, then so be it.

Unless...

Did he think I was Antoinette? No. Not possible. Even in a state close to death, he must feel the difference. She was lean and long and model-esque, and I was...definitely not those things.

Antoinette had pointed out our differences more than enough for them to be clear. No need to beat a dead horse. If she could see us now, she'd be beating me until *I* was a dead horse.

I lay there trying to rest, even though I wasn't that tired. I tried to examine the rug again, and then the dresser, the walls, the paintings on the walls, but all I couldn't think of now was Antoinette. I didn't want to be cuddled on false pretenses. It was one thing to offer comfort, but as her?

"Kaden?" I whispered, not trying to fully wake him but bring him to the edge of awareness. "Kaden," I whispered again.

He hummed in acknowledgment, still not opening his eyes.

"It's Billie," I said softly.

He hummed again, and his arm tightened around my waist.

It would have to be enough. He was either too out of it to register what he was doing, and still thought I was Antoinette, or maybe he didn't quite hate me as much as he seemed. I'd go with the latter.

He might not completely despise me. He still might not like me, but I didn't like him either, so that was fair.

I wasn't sure why I was smiling.

THERE WAS a rap on the door a couple hours later. Kaden was so dead that he didn't stir. I laid a hand on his forehead, checking him for a fever for the umpteenth time. If he could cuddle me, his leg swung over mine, not putting my hand on his forehead seemed a little idiotic.

He wasn't hot. His breathing seemed even, but the longer he lay here like this, the more I wanted to pound on his chest to make sure his heart was beating.

There was another rap on the door, this one more persistent.

Cookie's familiar voice rang out. "You letting me in or what? What the hell are you two doing in there?"

I untangled myself from Kaden, who still wasn't stirring even with Cookie's racket.

I opened the door, realizing it had been locked.

Cookie pushed it open the rest of the way and looked me over. "Well, you're dressed, so I guess it isn't that interesting." She looked at the bed. "He said he'd be out of it, but he looks like he's dead."

My heartbeat ratcheted up a few beats. "He said he's fine. That this is normal."

Cookie's frown was growing, as Kaden still wasn't stirring. "Normal for what? I've never seen him like this, and I've known him for a very long time. He could survive a nuclear blast standing at ground zero."

She pushed past me and laid a hand on his chest, then his neck, looking gentler than I'd ever seen. This was the Cookie not many got to see, the loyal, ride-or-die chick that would fight to the death by your side.

"What happened?" she asked.

"He did something so I could protect myself better. Gave me something," I said, talking softly so as to not wake him. I wasn't sure I *could* wake him at this point. He looked like he was in a coma, and the longer he lay there like this, the more I was ready to straddle his hips and pound on his chest.

"Like what? His soul? He looks like a zombie," she asked.

"Not his soul, but part of him and what he is." I glanced back to Kaden's still form.

Cookie was staring at me, lips parted and eyes wide. I

wasn't sure I'd ever seen her speechless before, but she appeared to be having trouble with her words.

It took another couple of seconds before she got it out. "You're saying he marked you? Is that what you mean?"

"Yes. That's what he called it. You think he's okay? He said this was normal, but..." I reached out and felt his forehead again.

She looked in his direction. "Now it makes sense. He'll be fine." She nodded and looked me up and down. "That was a serious gift he gave you," she said, a smirk starting to form. "I couldn't imagine why he'd need any kind of backup, and he was being pretty tight-lipped about it. But it makes sense now. He's regenerating." She laid a hand on his chest again and then nodded. "Yeah, he's fine. I can't believe he marked you."

She was examining me like she was moving chess pieces into place and I was her rook or something. I might've cared more if my hunger wasn't growing more intense by the second.

"Can you do me a favor? Can you get me some food? I'm not supposed to leave his side until it settles in, and I'm so hungry right now I feel like I haven't eaten a meal in eons."

She laughed. "Got it. You go sit near him and I'll get on the food issue."

Soleil showed up ten minutes later with two trays heaped with meats, cheeses, fruit, and bread.

"Thank you so much," I said. "I'm starving."

She smiled and put the platters down on the table off to the side.

I was already digging in when she came back with a platter heaped with chicken parmigiana. It might've been a coincidence that it was my favorite, but somehow I didn't think so. I'd never seen it in Nowhere. Another servant followed her with a platter of burgers, wings, and fries. There was hunger and then death by eating. Were they trying to kill me?

"You're going to feel like you have a hole in your stomach," Soleil said before she left, as if she knew something I didn't.

I took a couple fries and then moved on to the chicken. I was sitting in bed, halfway through my second burger, when Kaden stirred. He sat up, looking as if he'd gotten some life back into him.

"How are you feeling?" he asked, as if I'd been the one who was incapacitated most of the day.

"Getting normal."

"The effects will take a little while to kick in," he said, then fixated on my burger.

I was fixated on the way his stomach muscles bunched. When had he lost his shirt?

While I was distracted, he took a bite from the burger I was still holding, his lips grazing my fingers. There was something so sexual about the act that if someone walked in at that moment, they would've assumed we'd slept together. My heart was racing like we had.

"Here, take it." I would've dropped the burger in his

lap if he didn't have fast reflexes. "There's a whole platter of burgers over there, too."

I jumped out of the bed like I'd just gotten caught doing something wrong. I hadn't, but it sure felt like it. Or was that my guilty conscience playing tricks on me because I'd liked how it felt when he lay beside me? Maybe I'd tried to lie still so he wouldn't wake?

"You're looking better," I said, trying to keep my tone neutral.

"You can go if you want," he said, watching me as I inched toward the door.

"Yeah, I'm going to head back to my room and change and stuff." I took another step toward the door and then glanced over at the food. Why should he get to keep it all? "I'm just going to take some of this with me, though, if you don't care."

He nodded, watching me.

I grabbed the platter of chicken parmigiana and high-tailed it out of there. I was halfway down the hall when Connor yelled, "Where are you going with that platter?"

I turned, smiling. Dice was standing next to him.

"There's more food downstairs, and apparently there's been some interesting developments happening here we'd like to hear about," Dice said, grinning back at me.

"Make sure she brings the food," Cookie yelled from somewhere out of sight.

I headed toward them, a little bounce in my step. I had my crew back, at least for now.

FOURTEEN

I was eating breakfast when I spotted the little mouse in the corner. I was in a castle, in a mountain. A few mice weren't exactly shocking.

"You want to eat breakfast with me?" I tossed a little piece of croissant in its direction.

He took it, nibbling the edge before running away. Even the mouse didn't want to eat with me.

Kaden walked in a second later and fixed himself a plate. He sat down, took a sip of coffee, and groaned. "Why am I still drinking coffee that tastes like dirty water? I told them to fix this."

I sipped my perfectly brewed cup without comment.

"I don't understand how anyone could possibly like their coffee this way," he said, and then settled in with his paper at the table.

If he remembered spooning me barely a day ago, he wasn't acting like it. Or he was in denial. Either way was fine by me. I wasn't looking for a discussion either.

He opened his paper to read.

I focused on eating my food, my stomach feeling like it would never be full again. Filling my stomach was more important than what he was doing.

If he didn't want to give me the crossword, so be it. I understood. I did. I really, *really* did. He'd marked me, which seemed to have stunned everyone when I sat down with Cookie and the guys. He'd given me a piece of his magic. That was a much bigger deal than any stupid crossword.

I wouldn't ask for the dumb thing, either. He knew I wanted it. I *always* wanted it. If he kept his crosswords piled up, unused in a corner somewhere, that was his business. We weren't friends, after all. He clearly still hated me because of the connection to Gram. I hated him because he'd so utterly and completely turned his back on me, refusing to hear me out. He'd done me a solid, but no way would I soften to someone who wouldn't hand over a piece of paper.

Where were Cookie and the guys, anyway? Some chitchat would at least break up this weird breakfast tension. The guy spooned me the day before and now couldn't get a civil word out. I wasn't leaving this room either, not until I finished eating, even if I was struggling to swallow. This behavior reinforced why I was justified in hating him as much as he hated me.

The paper ruffled as he flipped the page. I kept my attention focused on my plate, refusing to glimpse in that direction. It ruffled some more, and then a corner of it appeared beside my plate, impossible not to see.

I swallowed. Was he really giving it to me? Yes. It was a single sheet. It wasn't as if he'd put the whole paper down and it accidentally encroached on my side of the table.

I glanced up at him, but he'd already gone back to reading.

"It's only a crossword," he said, as if he could feel the stirrings of my confusion and needed to contain my reaction.

Was he really afraid I'd make too much of it?

"I know. I'm fully aware it's just a scrap of paper. Trust me when I tell you, I won't be groveling at your feet over something you were going to throw out in an hour."

If I hadn't been staring at his profile, I might've missed the slight uptick of the corner of his mouth. As it was, it seemed like an illusion that he'd show any kind of humor in my presence.

I looked down, biting my lower lip so he couldn't see my smile. I didn't even know why I was smiling. Like he'd said, it was a crossword.

Then I realized I still needed a pen, and that took care of the smile. I'd take the puzzle and find one later, or ask Soleil. No way was I asking him for anything. The fact that he'd given me the paper was a huge step in itself. We were at least on the road to being civil.

"Are you taking this, or am I supposed to sit here holding it forever?"

I looked up. Kaden held a pen out to me as he continued to read his paper.

"What's wrong? Can you not even solve one of those clues?" he asked.

I took it and then looked down at the paper, without reading it.

My eyes were burning. What the hell was wrong with me? Like he'd said, it was a crossword. And now a pen.

I swallowed hard, trying to get a grip on myself. I couldn't be growing feelings for this man. There were way too many issues for that. First off, he *hated* me. He might've handed me the crossword, but he'd made it clear it didn't mean anything. It was, after all, only a crossword puzzle.

Second, he had a girlfriend. I might not have seen her around, but that didn't mean her claws weren't dug in. Not to mention the girlfriend he did have, he didn't make a priority, and she hadn't wronged him anywhere near the amount he accused me of doing. In spite of those very sound reasons why I shouldn't want him, I was sitting here feeling like I was a pile of mush because he'd handed me a crossword.

I could feel his eyes shift to me, as if he knew something was wrong. I kept my gaze down, like I was guilty of something. If I looked at him, he'd read my feelings all over my face, and they weren't true. I was confused and in a bad mental space. That was the only reason I was being so soft. It would pass.

No sane human being would go there with this man. He was unreliable. He might've saved me, but not before he'd turned his back on me like I was nothing, garbage to be discarded. No. I'd had too many of those people in my life already. I wouldn't knowingly get involved with another.

He was still staring, and I forced myself to meet his gaze.

"What? Is there a problem?" I asked, trying to steel my features the way he did, not let a drop of the silly emotions leak out.

"You looked out of sorts for a minute. You're not, *are* you?" His voice was soft, concerned—*worried*. For all my hard exterior, he sensed my softening anyway.

He might as well have said we were nothing and never would be. That was how clear the message was, hand-delivered, so I wouldn't miss it.

"I'm not out of sorts. At. All." Years of rejection in every form lent strength to the denial. Even if I had started to soften a second ago, it meant nothing. I wouldn't be laid low twice by this man.

Our gazes met, and then got stuck.

He squinted, his lips parting slightly, as if he wasn't sure he liked my answer. Like he didn't know what to do in response to what he'd asked. What he'd clearly wanted to hear.

I didn't break my stare, refusing to be the one who turned away in embarrassment, confirming what he might've thought. No. I was fine. I would be fine, and that was all he was getting from me.

The heavy sound of the front door opening and closing echoed down the hall and into the room.

"Where is he?" Antoinette's voice rang out like nails on a chalkboard, breaking our stare.

Suddenly I realized why no one else had been here for breakfast. They'd known she was coming. It would've been nice if they warned me. I'd been nearly beaten to death less than a month ago, and not one of them could help a girl out and tell her the devil was on its way?

There was a murmured response in the hall. I had barely enough time to shovel down the last couple of bites.

"I'm fine. I'll see myself in," Antoinette said, those simple sentences ringing with arrogance, as if she didn't need *their* help. That they were beneath her.

Before I could fully prepare myself, she was there.

"Oh, look who's here. So lovely to see you up again and looking so..." She looked me over, as if struggling to find a compliment. "So stout and hardy."

Hardy? She might as well have called me a lumberjack, the way she said it. Yes, stout and hardy. That was me.

Kaden stood, kissing her cheek, his hand going to her waist. There was an attentiveness there, an effort I hadn't sensed before. They'd gone from breaking up to *this*?

She turned back to me with a grin a mile wide.

"Nice to see you, too." I nearly vomited on the words. "Well, I've just finished up, and I've got several things to take care of. I'll be off so you two lovebirds can have your privacy." That last line almost choked me, but I'd be damned if I let either of them know I cared.

She preened like the silly bird I'd called her.

"Billie, dinner is at eight," Kaden said.

I nearly tripped as I was leaving. Dinner? Was she going to be there? I was going to have to eat with both of them? I was suddenly feeling a stomach bug coming on and felt ready to lock myself in my room for the rest of the day.

I left them knowing I'd been on the verge of idiocy, and over a crossword, no less. I'd started to soften. I'd been ready to sob over a piece of paper and a pen, like a pathetic soul willing to take any scrap of kindness I could get. It would be the last time. Not again. Never again. Not if I wanted to survive this place.

FIFTEEN

"I don't know why we all have to go eat with his batshit-crazy girlfriend," Cookie said as she sat on my bed, waiting for me to finish getting dressed. "It's bad enough he's dating her again. Must we all have to be exposed?"

I rifled through another drawer as she continued to complain. She'd been at it for a good fifteen minutes already, and damned if I wasn't taking longer than normal, trying to find something that made my butt look a little smaller.

"What is taking you so long? Throw on whatever. I want to get this over with." Cookie flopped backward on my bed, her legs swinging and kicking the bedframe.

Cookie wasn't all talk. She was backing up her sentiments by wearing sweatpants, a ratty t-shirt, and steel-toed boots. What people thought about her wasn't on her radar. She wasn't equipped with the part that made most people care about others' opinions. She'd somehow yanked it out of her psyche and hammered it into pieces.

She was right, too. Who was I trying to impress, anyway? Definitely not Kaden. He'd delivered his message loud and clear, and I wasn't going to strut into the dining room like I had something to prove. I grabbed a sweater, threw it on over the jeans I was already wearing, and called it a day. It wasn't like anything I wore would make my butt and hips shrink. No. Showing up like this said I didn't care what anyone thought.

"I'm ready," I said, as if we were about to walk into battle together.

She got off the bed and joined me by the door. "Let's do this thing," she said, as solemn as I was.

Everyone was waiting for us by the fireplace in the massive formal dining room. I preferred the smaller dining area myself. Antoinette was decked out in full cocktail attire, her arm looped through Kaden's, eating up this grand atmosphere like a cat with a bowl of cream.

One glance at Dice and Connor showed they were as miserable as Cookie and me, both holding nearly empty rocks glasses. Looked like that was how they were planning on getting through the evening. I wasn't much of a drinker, but that could change by the end of tonight.

"We should probably head over there and say hi." Instead of doing that, Cookie let out a long sigh and remained by the door.

"Come on. Let's just get this over with." I headed forward and then had to glance back at her. She shook her head but finally began to walk.

We all exchanged nods and forced smiles, and then the silence spread out.

"Shall we all sit and eat?" Antoinette said after a stalled moment. She'd gotten here this morning and was already picking up the mantle of lady of the house? How long was she going to be staying? She might turn this whole house into alcoholics.

It didn't matter if it was her suggestion. The sooner we ate, the sooner we were done. I turned toward the table and was nearly trampled by the stampede past me. The reason became clear as I saw the only empty place setting left was beside Antoinette. At least Cookie was to my right.

There was some mundane conversation about the weather, started by Dice. Connor didn't speak much on a good day. Cookie wasn't attempting to speak at all.

If I wasn't so hungry I might've begged an illness, but I might as well get a few bites first. Plus, these rolls were amazing. How many more could I take? Had everyone else gotten some?

If I could be forced to eat with her, I didn't care how many I had. I was taking more. I was about to reach for the last when Kaden beat me to it. I stared at him, narrowing my eyes.

"They'll bring more," he said.

I nodded, biting my cheek. I really wanted to ask *when*. It could be another twenty minutes before more came, and it might come down to bread or escape.

I looked at the bowl of potatoes, or what I thought were some sort of potatoes. There wasn't that much left, mostly because of me and Kaden. The guys were more interested in drinking their dinner. Cookie didn't like them. Antoinette surely wouldn't stoop to eating more than the tiny spoonful she had. After the stunt Kaden pulled with the roll, he didn't deserve more potatoes.

I was about to reach for the bowl when Kaden got to it first.

I gasped.

"There will be more," Kaden said, catching me eyeing up his plate and reading my mind.

"*E-ven-tu-al-ly*," I said, enunciating each syllable.

He picked up his plate and leaned over the table, dumping half of them onto my plate. "Are you happy now?"

I eyed up the piles, checking for equal distribution. It was hard to tell, since his pile looked a little wider, but mine might be higher.

"I can live with it." No need to be petty and split hairs.

I didn't realize how comfortable we might've appeared with each other until I noticed Antoinette's dagger gaze was out.

"My, aren't you hungry. It looks like you're eating even more so than usual. Trying to keep your *health* up, I guess," she said, then dabbed her mouth like she'd actually eaten anything.

She was staring at me alone, as if Kaden hadn't kept up with me bite for bite, not to mention his grab on the last roll.

"Yes, I do like to eat a healthy diet," I said, then smiled.

"On to more interesting news." She laid a hand on

Kaden's arm closest to her and said, "Should we tell them? That's what this dinner is for, after all."

"Go ahead," he said, seeming a little stiff.

"I'll be moving in here. Part-time initially, but hopefully full-time soon enough. Well, when we aren't in the city together." She was smiling wide, her fingers nearly digging into Kaden's arm. She seemed to be watching me more intently as she waited for reactions.

Forcing every emotion I had down into a bottomless pit, I said, "That's very nice."

If she could make it work, good for them. It wasn't any of my business. None, and I refused to care, at all. Things would simply go back to the way they used to be, where I avoided her at all costs. This place was large enough to steer clear of her. If that was who Kaden wanted, so be it. It was his life. There was no denying her beauty, that was for sure.

"That's great," Dice said, then threw back the last of his drink.

"Congrats." Connor raised his glass before following his brother in arms, taking a healthy sip.

At least that pulled her analyzing stare from me.

"That's wonderful to hear, you know, considering," Cookie said, sounding as sugary sweet as could be. The statement might've seemed innocent enough if I didn't know better. This was a tone never heard coming from Cookie before, and something about it sent off alarm bells.

She was sharpening her little poker into a fine point and was about to stab someone with it. Her mark was sitting across the table, looking as confused as I felt, as she tried to figure out where Cookie was going.

Dice grabbed the liquor bottle, topping off his glass and then Connor's. Kaden narrowed his eyes in Cookie's direction. Antoinette was squinting as she attempted to figure out what was coming.

We didn't have to wait long, as Cookie barely skipped a beat before continuing. "I can't imagine how much there is to cover after what Kaden did for Billie. It's going to take weeks, I'd imagine, with all she'll need to learn. Obviously I don't have any experience with what was done, but it would only stand to reason."

The guys were refilling their drinks again as they watched. I could feel Kaden's anger roiling off him. This had to be about the marking, but why would that be an issue? I wouldn't ask right now. There was a heaviness that was building in the room. I wasn't going to be the first to break it and direct that energy my way.

Cookie obviously knew it was a problem, though, or she wouldn't have picked this subject. She didn't miss her mark. She could be holding a twig five hundred yards away and she'd manage to poke you in the eye.

Cookie continued eating as if nothing were amiss. Antoinette was staring at Kaden, her mouth flattened. She didn't have the fullest lips, and now they were nearly invisible. Kaden was staring back with a resigned expression, knowing Cookie had set off the nuke. Now we waited to see how bad the explosion would be.

"What did you do?" Antoinette asked, her stare not moving from Kaden. The awkward strain of her voice was like she wanted to scream but was trying to repress it. I wasn't sure anyone was falling for the calm charade.

"We should talk about it later," Kaden said, putting his napkin down. Something had finally killed his appetite.

"Tell me you didn't..." Antoinette looked over at me. She sucked in a loud breath, as if she'd taken a gut shot. She turned back to Kaden. "You did, didn't you? Were you even going to tell me?" She jumped up from her seat, and her chair tipped over and crashed to the floor. She threw her napkin on the table, and although it landed in the center, I was pretty sure it was aimed at me. I was glad it wasn't something hard, although that might be coming next. I'd have to keep an eye on her wine glass.

"I had every intention of telling you." Kaden let out a long sigh, glancing at Cookie.

Cookie shrugged, playing stupid. It was a piss-poor performance.

The guys were staring, riveted.

"You wouldn't even *discuss* doing that for me when I mentioned it, but you did it for her." She stabbed her finger in my direction. "You said you'd never do it for anyone, but you didn't mean that, obviously."

"She *needed* it. You don't have all of Nowhere trying to kill you." Kaden's tone was matter-of-fact, as if everyone knew I was a dead woman walking.

There was no denying the mob that had come for me, but *all of Nowhere*? He had to be overstating things a bit, no?

Cookie leaned toward me. "Technically I think it's closer to ninety-five percent. You've got some holdouts on your side."

My mouth gaped open. Was it really that bad?

She grimaced, reading my expression. "Well, maybe ninety? It's not like I've taken a head count."

I needed to work on my poker face, especially if I was going to be a pariah from here on out. Wouldn't do me any good to be walking around Nowhere broadcasting to everyone that I was an outcast and depressed by it.

"I can't believe you did that, and for *her*," Antoinette yelled.

It might've been better than the fake calm that no one had bought. She spun and walked a few steps, only to turn back and close the gap again, inching closer to me.

"I told you why. You'll have to accept it because it's done," Kaden said, as if that would end this fight.

He couldn't possibly believe that would work, could he? Was it possible I knew his girlfriend better than he did?

"Of all people, *her*?" She was pointing again.

Her. She kept putting this accent on *her* when she referred to me. What was that about? Like I was some sort of sludge that formed in the swamp where daylight never reached? I'd never punched a person in my life, but I was alarmingly close at this moment. I had to leave, and now.

Antoinette loved to drag me into her fights with Kaden. I already had a presence in this one, but I was trying to remain in the lower cast. There was no need to be a star in their drama. They already had two leads, after all.

The guys, unusually quiet, had made their way nearer to the door, ready to make a quick getaway.

I glanced at Cookie and tilted my head in that direction, suggesting we make our exit. She ignored me. I reached for her arm, trying to get her attention. She shrugged out of my grasp with an irritated look and shook her head, hissing in my direction.

I'd have to leave her to her own defenses—not that she really needed backup. The term "tough cookie" might've originated with her. At least I'd have someone who could fill me in afterward.

I got up and headed toward the door.

Antoinette was back to glaring at me.

Kaden was leaning back in his seat and running both hands through his hair. "Antoinette, I did what needed to be done."

"And why is that? She shouldn't even be here. She should be dead." She turned her full wrath on me, moving to block my exit.

Antoinette was messing with the wrong girl. I'd been dreaming of what I should've done when the horde beat me, how I should've fought harder. If she thought standing in my way was going to do anything but give me a target to unleash my anger on, she was more delusional than I might've imagined. I was a powder keg of regrets and repressed rage, looking for a match.

"Get out of my way," I said, not recognizing my own voice.

Kaden was on his feet, stepping in between us. "Antionette, this was my choice. You're venting your anger on the wrong person."

Antionette kept her stare on me. "Why aren't you dead already?" She leaned closer. "You're an abomination, and all the people in Nowhere know it, *finally*."

The room went still. It felt like all the air had been sucked out in a flash, as if everyone were sensing the same thing.

The way she said that, the pieces finally clicked. It had been her. She'd told everyone in Nowhere about Chaos. Kaden claimed to not have repeated that information to anyone, but we all knew how pillow talk worked. Unfortunately for me, his taste in women ran toward the psychotic, vengeful type.

"It was you? You told everyone?" I asked.

Kaden was staring at her, as if he couldn't believe she'd done such a thing. Did he not see her at all? Was he that blinded by her beauty?

"Of course I told them, you idiot," she sneered. "Why would I protect *you*?"

She didn't merely dislike me—she'd tried to have me killed. I'd had a rough go of it in life, but this? No one had ever hated me enough to try to end my life.

I could hear Cookie growling beside me.

"I need the room," Kaden said.

If he'd wanted me gone, he should've gotten rid of me before. Now he'd have to carry me out of here. I made a move toward Antoinette, and she backed up. Kaden grabbed me around the waist, holding me back.

I pushed at Kaden's chest while she smiled at me.

"This is my situation to handle now," I said. "She's not only your crazy girlfriend anymore but the woman who almost got me killed."

"She did it because of me. I'll handle it." He wasn't relaxing his grip.

We were all so fixated on our little bubble of three that no one noticed Cookie walking toward Antoinette until the last second. I spotted her right before she pulled her arm back and decked Antoinette, dropping her to the floor like a sack of potatoes.

Kaden's hands dropped as we all stared at Antoinette's limp form.

"You had to do that? I said I was going to handle it," Kaden said.

"Yeah. I really did." Cookie shrugged and nodded.

I stared at Antoinette's still form for another second. It wasn't like I could walk over and kick her while she was out of it. Well, I could, but under the circumstances, it was a bad look. No matter what she'd done, what kind of person she was, she was unconscious. I needed to at least wait until she came to. Not to mention, there was nothing that I could do that would make me feel better. The damage was done. The only thing I wanted now was to never see her again.

"Okay, well, I guess you can handle it from here," Cookie said. She looped her arm through mine and tugged me out of the room with her.

They guys had already vacated, knowing the show was over.

We were heading upstairs. "She'll probably make sure Kaden kicks me out after tonight, no matter what she did. But it doesn't matter. I can't stay in this place with her."

"He'll boot her," Cookie said. "I've called a few things wrong with him lately, but trust me, he's going to get rid of her. What she did is a betrayal that cuts too deep for him."

"I'm not so sure."

I hoped whatever his marking did to me kicked in soon, because I'd need it back in Nowhere. I'd jump out of the window and scale down the side of this fortress if I had to, but I wasn't staying here with her. Maybe I'd have to hide out Topside for a bit, until I sorted some things. Still better than staying here with her.

"Do me a favor, just give it until tomorrow. If she's still here, I'll help you leave, okay?"

A night. I could manage a night. "Okay, I'll stay until tomorrow. But then if she's still here, I'm gone, even if I'm jumping out a window." I looked Cookie dead in the eye, trying to impress upon her how serious I was.

"Got it, and I don't blame you." She looked back toward downstairs and then smiled. "Hey, if Kaden hadn't blocked you, you were going to beat her into a pulp, weren't you?"

I threw my hands up. "I was going to give it try."

She slapped me on the back. "I like this side of you."

SIXTEEN

I felt more exhausted in the morning than I had when I'd gone to bed. Sleep wasn't something that was compatible with rage, and the more I thought of Antoinette trying to have me killed, the more elusive sleep had become.

I didn't know what Kaden's idea of handling the situation was, but I couldn't remain here if she stayed. This was his house, fortress, whatever it was, and if he could tolerate her presence, then that was his choice. I'd risk death instead of having to see her regularly. Even if it were possible to stomach her, it might be more dangerous here than going back to the city. She'd probably try to poison me next.

I was packing a bag, just in case, when my door swung open.

Antoinette was standing there looking—*wrecked*. It wasn't because of her swollen eye, although that didn't help matters. There were no words for the agony etched into the lines of her face, the way her shoulders looked too heavy for her body, the droop of her chin. She wasn't someone stopping by on their victory tour. If rejection had a smell you could bottle, she could stock a thousand shelves. Cookie was right—he'd told her to leave.

Whatever Kaden had done or said, he'd been thorough. She looked as if she'd received a death sentence, and as much as I wanted to kill her myself, there was still a little piece of me that pitied her.

She strolled in, looking about the place, especially at me, like it was toxic. I wanted to walk out. Except this was my room. I couldn't walk out. It was too ridiculous.

She finally finished her lap and stopped in front of me. She made an obvious perusal of me from my feet to my face.

"You won, but it won't end well for you," she said.

"I'm not trying to win." All I'd done since I stepped over that bridge, what seemed like an eternity ago, was try to survive. Survival didn't come with first-place ribbons. It was a pass-fail situation.

"He won't love you. He'll never love you. If he couldn't love me, you certainly won't be the one." Her face contorted with such disgust and rage, it stole some of her beauty.

"I'm not expecting anything from him." I answered her before I could stop myself, feeling humiliated by the entire topic. Everything she said was true. I was stupid enough to imagine he'd ever love me. I wasn't an idiot. Not even my parents had loved me. Why would anyone else?

"I'm leaving, so he's all yours to chase until he kicks you to the curb. I'd give it a few weeks at most."

"I'm not trying to catch him, Antoinette." Did part of me want him? Maybe, but I wasn't as foolish or delusional as her. I knew what would happen if I let myself go in that direction. In a month, maybe a year, I'd be looking like she was now. Or worse, like my mother, who had turned to booze at the cost of everyone around her. After my last boyfriend, it was clear my judgment was not to be trusted when it came to men. All of that didn't matter anyway, because Kaden didn't want me.

"You've got him lulled with this victim act. You play the damsel-in-distress bullshit, but I see what you are, and he will—"

"Antoinette, you were asked to leave," Kaden said, filling the doorway.

She stiffened, looking at me with a hate so strong it sent chills down my spine. This wasn't someone who would fade off into the night. She'd tried to have me killed once, and she'd do it again, and again, until one of us was dead. This woman would have it out for me until the day she died, or I did.

She walked out of the room, but this wasn't over. I had acquired another target on my back, along with the many others. They were starting to stack up so high that long-term survival was beginning to look less and less likely. The only thing I was sure of was she wouldn't be the one who would take me out. I'd kill her first, even if I was my last act, with a dagger stuck in my back.

She stopped in front of Kaden. "Don't worry. I didn't

touch your precious Billie." She laid a hand on his chest, as if she couldn't stop herself from touching him.

He glanced down at her hand like he couldn't figure out why it was there. She dropped it. Somehow that seemed like a worse set-down than if he'd flung her hand off him.

"You'll regret treating me this way, but I won't be waiting for you when you do." She was trying to cling to the last shreds of her dignity, as if there were any left.

"I'll see you out," he said. There wasn't an emotion left in his face. He was colder, more aloof than I'd ever seen him—or anyone, for that matter. I'd seen glaciers with more warmth. Even when he'd been furious with me, I at least got some show of emotion from him. I'd prefer that over the man who was standing there now.

She turned and walked away, and he followed. She might stab someone to death on the way out if he didn't. She might've murdered me if he hadn't been here. Or tried.

I dropped onto the bed, glad I wasn't going to need to pack but so numb I couldn't think of anything else. That final look she'd given me would haunt my dreams if I let it. I wouldn't, though. I had too many other things to fear than letting some jealous girlfriend with crazy ideas take up space in my brain. It was already crammed full of murdering hordes and plotting grandmothers.

Kaden walked through my open door a few minutes later, stopping beside my bed. I sat up quickly, hoping I didn't look as spent as I felt, at least not over her.

"She won't be a problem," he said. He rested a shoulder on the bedpost, watching me.

I wished I could believe that was true, but she'd be a problem for a different day.

I sat up straighter, and then got to my feet. Standing was a better idea for the next hurdle I had to cross. "Why did you tell her?" He'd said he wouldn't tell anyone about Chaos, and I'd believed him.

He lifted his chin, as if flinching. "I didn't. You gave it away the day we saw you leaving Alaric's."

"What are you talking about? I never would've said a word in front of her." I hadn't thought she'd try to *kill* me, but trust her? Never.

"That day you told us you wouldn't be leaving Nowhere. She asked if that was a good idea. She had been referring to staying in general, because I'd told her you would be leaving. She didn't know the details, but everyone was aware that we'd had a falling-out. When you replied, you didn't care what people figured out, and in doing so, you told her there was a secret to be sniffed out.

"All she had to do was put together the Chaos incidents and the dates I'd left for emergencies. The picture became pretty clear. She told me as much last night. She might not always be pleasant, but she's cunning."

I dropped back onto the bed, rethinking that day. I'd been shakier than a pissed-off rattler when I saw them as I walked out of Alaric's. I'd set out the breadcrumbs for her, and she hated me enough to snatch up every little one, right to where my worst vulnerability lay.

It was hard to believe how careless I'd been, and yet it was still better than thinking he'd broken his word. I wasn't sure I'd be able to take another betrayal this soon.

"That's why you got rid of her?" I asked, wanting to confirm that she was really gone. I might have to hear it another ten times before I felt comfortable.

"Yes. I told her not to come back. She knew I wouldn't want that information spread, and yet she did it. That's not something I tolerate in an alliance."

An alliance? Weird name for a relationship with a girlfriend, but with someone as cold as Antoinette, perhaps fitting. At least the *alliance* was over and the fortress was once again a safe place.

"I'm sorry. I know you were trying to make it work with her. I didn't mean to get in your way." Even if he did have the worst taste in women imaginable. If I was honest about it, I'd done him a favor.

He shook his head. "You weren't the problem," he said, but didn't elaborate any further. "How are you feeling?"

"Other than being hungry every minute of the day? Normal."

"Good. Then we start training tomorrow."

SEVENTEEN

When I'd thought we were going to get physical, Kaden threw some magic mumbo jumbo at me. Today, when I thought we were going to do all that magic mumbo jumbo, he decided to torture me with combat training. We'd been at it for ten minutes in the large dining room, where mats had been laid down.

"Keep your hands up. You leave yourself wide open." Kaden tapped the bottom of my fists, bumping them up a foot. "Stance."

I turned slightly. It was probably a good thing I hadn't punched Antoinette. Apparently the way I made a fist, I would've broken my thumbs instead of her face.

"*Hands,*" he said, again. It was maybe the tenth time he'd reminded me, and his tone sounded like it.

I raised them. For some reason I couldn't seem to focus on my fists and angling sideways at the same time.

"I'm not sure what the point of this is. If you think I'm going to be able to fight my way out of the next attacking horde, you're in for a big disappointment." We hadn't been doing this long, and it was already clear I wasn't a natural.

"Better control of your body means better control of the power." He was shaking his head at me again. He'd been doing that a lot in the last few minutes. "Angle your body. S*mall* target."

I did what he said, knowing I'd probably get distracted again in a few minutes.

He lifted one of the pads he was holding, motioning for me to hit it. I did, and even I could see my swing was pathetic. If Kaden and Cookie hadn't stepped in, Antoinette might've kicked my ass. When I was boiling with rage, I seemed to have formed some delusions about my abilities to handle myself in a fight. My calmer head was now clearing up that delusion with an acid wash. I sucked at physical combat to a degree most would think impossible.

"When does that magic you gave me start taking effect?" Because I'd woken up yet another day feeling the same, and viewing my current circumstances, that was really bad. How was I going to stand on my own two feet, be self-sufficient?

"It depends. Could be tonight, or it could be in a month. The time varies greatly. You'll know, though."

"Can we work on bringing that out, since I'm not very good at this?" He might think he could turn me into a fighting machine, but it wasn't happening. Not this month, next month, or next year.

"We're not starting on anything else until I'm sure it's

completely set. I don't want to dislodge it." He tapped the bottom of my fists upward again.

They didn't stay there and dropped to my sides.

"Wait, what you did can be dislodged?" I hadn't asked to be marked, but at night, when all the anxieties I'd ignored during the day haunted me, the prospect of being a little less vulnerable had become my security blanket. Now he was telling me I could lose that, and I was already feeling the chill.

"From what I know, it's a possibility."

My mouth gaped open, and my stance had completely gone to hell. This was getting worse by the second. There were two problems as I saw it: that I could lose the magic he'd given me and that he didn't seem sure of anything.

"A possibility? I've noticed you seem a little shaky on some of the details. How much do you actually know about what you did?"

"I've heard a lot." He motioned at me, telling me to get back in position, as if dropping that bomb was a minor detail.

"How many times have you done this to people?" I ignored his gesturing to get back to fighting. I had more important issues at the moment than pretending I had a shot. "How many?"

He stopped, looking upward, as if he had to do some serious mental math. Perhaps this wasn't that bad. It wasn't as if I expected him to have done this willy-nilly, after all. Just maybe a few times, so that he hadn't just experimented on me with no clue.

"That would be one," he said, nodding.

"One? You mean one before me, right? And I'm two?" Please let there have been another guinea pig before me that he'd worked some of the kinks out on.

"One, including you." He grinned and then pointed at my hands. "Get your guard back up."

It was the first time he'd smiled at me since we'd started talking again, since he kicked me out of his outpost. The timing didn't go unnoticed, nor my stupid reaction to it. He didn't bother to charm most of the time, but it wasn't because he didn't have the skills. His smile could melt the North Pole.

Instead of yelling at him, or lecturing about how he should've told me that, I said, "A heads-up that this was your first go-around would've been nice." I tried to sound stern, and not to let the warm gaze work on me. Considering we hadn't been on speaking terms for months, it was hard to throw down completely.

"Let's try something different." He dropped the pads and waved at me. "Try to hit me. I know you want to," he said, smiling again.

"Hit *you*?" He was right—I wouldn't mind getting a shot in. Killer smile or not, you didn't do what he did for the first time and not give a warning. Plus, he'd fired me. He hadn't given me the crossword at breakfast that first time, either. It was enough to get me swinging for real. I launched myself at him.

He groaned, but not because I'd hit him. I missed by a mile. He wasn't supposed to move out of the way. He made it seem like he was going to stay put and give me a free shot.

"Did you even try?" He scratched his shadowed jaw.

"I was going to be an accountant. Not a boxer. I'm not used to hitting people. It's not my thing." I threw my hands up in the air.

"That's painfully clear."

"I'm not a thug. How long until we can do the other stuff?" At least tinkering I'd taken to easily. It was something to be optimistic about.

"We work on the other stuff after I'm sure it's set." He dropped out of guard, stepped forward, and grabbed my hands. "Don't. Let. Them. Drop."

"I'm not trying to drop them." He acted as if I were *trying* to be this bad.

"You're not trying to keep them up, either." He stepped behind me, gripping my hips, shifting my body sideways. "Smaller target, remember? You stand like you want to get punched."

"I know," I said, having a hard time arguing when my head was getting muddled with other thoughts. The last time a man had grabbed my hips that way, we'd been in bed, and he hadn't dripped sexuality the way Kaden did.

Kaden moved back in front of me. I hopped up and down, as if I were trying to warm up. That was why my cheeks might look pink, and nothing to do with his touch.

Other thoughts. Any other thoughts.

"Was there ever a government in Nowhere?" I asked, knowing that was a mood killer.

"There was for a short time. It only lasted a couple of weeks," he said.

"What happened to it?"

"They tried to pass some laws and formed a police force of sorts. It didn't go well. They were killed shortly after, and no one has suggested it since."

"If I died, or anyone in Nowhere was murdered, for that matter, would anything happen?" Yeah, this really was a mood killer. More than I'd counted on, and not just for me. There was no trace of a smile on his face.

"Like what, for instance?" he asked, feigning a punch in my direction and then shaking his head at my clumsy attempt at ducking.

"I don't know—would there be some sort of punishment? Anything?" I could've died from that beating, lying there in the street. The idea that the people who'd done that could walk away with no repercussions at all was a hard pill to swallow.

"Depends on who knew the deceased and how well they were liked." He threw another mock punch. "You need to at least put forth an effort."

I put my hands back up, trying to pretend I was invested. "So a militia-type response, is what you're saying?"

"Yes. You could call it that."

There wouldn't have been a militia forming for me. Cookie might've attempted to avenge my death, but there were too many on the other side and only one of her. Kaden would've told her it was a lost cause and to not waste her time. She might've gotten Dice and Connor to help, but her loyalty to Kaden would've eventually won out, and she would've heeded his advice.

I didn't blame her. She'd known him for decades, and who was I but some chick she had to constantly help? The people who'd beaten me would've walked away from my death free and clear.

Kaden stopped his mock attack and was looking at me a little too astutely. I reached for my water, trying to buy some time.

"Maybe we should call it quits for the day. I've got to go eat. This hunger thing is killing me," I said.

"Sure," he replied, not putting up a fight, which was completely unlike him.

I headed out of the room.

"Billie," he called before I got to the door.

"What?" I asked.

He paused for a few seconds before he said, "You would've been avenged."

"I'm sure Cookie would've tried," I said, pausing.

"*I* would've avenged you." His voice was deadly serious.

I turned, not sure what to say, too stunned to speak. All I could manage was a nod, and even that was a lot, because if I didn't leave that room, in that second, I might've started to cry. He cared enough to mark me, to keep me alive, to avenge my death, and suddenly my world was spinning again.

"You were part of my crew. It's only what's right," he said.

I nodded, his nonchalance tempering my upcoming

meltdown. "I'm fully aware it's just part of your duty. After all, it's just a little revenge, right? I won't be groveling at your feet for doing what you think was your responsibility." The conversation took on a sense of déjà vu from the crossword. The paper had been a lot easier to brush off, but if he wanted to act like it meant nothing, I wouldn't fight him.

"I have to go eat."

He nodded and walked over to a punching bag, throwing a few shots. I backed toward the door and got out of there before things got weirder.

EIGHTEEN

I'd eaten two breakfasts, three lunches, and I was the first one there for dinner. There was no telling who would show up or when, so I'd given up on waiting for people days ago. Plus, not eating felt akin to torture, and my stomach would wail like it was taking a beating.

I glanced over and noticed the little mouse standing on its hind legs, as if it was waiting for me. I tossed it a piece of croissant, and it ran off.

Dice and Connor filed in a few minutes later as I was already halfway through a steak. Cookie had been cryptic when she left to run an errand today, saying she wasn't sure if she'd be back for dinner.

Soleil walked in with a huge bouquet of flowers and set them down next to me.

"For me?" I asked, looking at the exotic blooms in a pale blue color.

"Yes. Nicest bouquet I've seen in a decade," she said, and then left without saying who they were from.

I dug around and found a card.

"Who are they from?" Dice asked. Connor's head popped up as well.

I opened the card.

WE KNEW you wouldn't let us down.

FRANK, Hank, and Tank.

"WELL?" Dice asked.

"Nothing. The bridge guys."

"They 'get well' flowers or something? Little late, but a nice gesture," Dice said.

"I don't think they've ever sent flowers to anyone else," Connor added.

"Uh huh. Very nice," I said, pocketing the card so no one could snoop.

Kaden walked in a few minutes later and narrowed his eyes at the bouquet but didn't say anything. I kept eating, not sure what to say to him. His declaration about avenging me was still swimming around in my head. I was actively trying to not look his way until I drowned that little tidbit.

Dice and Connor were shooting each other looks, as if something was going on I wasn't aware of. What this dinner desperately needed was Cookie's brashness to break up the silence.

As if I'd summoned her, she strolled in a few minutes later. Her pace was a little slower than normal, her boots hitting the floor with less of a stomp. She bypassed the buffet of dishes and slumped into a seat at the table.

"That bad?" Dice put his fork and knife down, as if his appetite had died.

Connor was moving some bites around his plate but had stopped eating as well. Kaden leaned back in his chair, looking at her pointedly. Wherever she'd been off to, everyone here knew something.

She shook her head. For the first time since I'd met Cookie, she looked like she was on the verge of tears. *Verge*. Nothing actually made it past her iron grip of control, but it looked like a fight that was hard won.

Kaden nodded but said nothing. He stood, leaving a full plate of food on the table. "I've got a few things to handle. Cookie, find me later." He left the dining room.

"Seriously? Are you really saying..." Whatever it was Dice wanted to ask, he didn't seem capable of getting it out.

"Yeah. Larken is gone." Cookie made a fist and thumped it against her thigh.

"I can't even believe it," Connor said, slumping so low he could rest his head on the back of the chair as he stared at the ceiling.

Cookie got up and left, not saying a word.

"I'm sorry about Larken," I said, not sure what else to add, since I didn't know what he was—a friend, family, associate?

I wasn't sure Connor heard me, as he remained still in his chair, staring at the ceiling.

Dice nodded. "Thanks. Larken was one of Kaden's people, almost like a mentor. We all got pretty tight with him. He'd gone silent for a while. Word was hitting the street that…" He looked at me, then took some time choosing his words. "Word was he might've come under some opposition." He glanced away quickly, as if afraid if he looked at me too long, he'd cast blame in my direction.

"From the people my grandmother runs with," I said, the knowledge hovering like a noxious fume.

He looked at the table as he nodded. Connor got up and walked out of the room without a word to either of us.

I didn't ask anything else, and Dice didn't offer.

For the first time since Kaden had marked me, my appetite had dulled. "I'll see you in a little while. I've got some things to do."

"Billie, you know we trust you, right? We know you wouldn't do anything bad," Dice said.

"Thanks. I'll see you in a bit. I'm going to go stretch my legs."

I WAS SITTING in my bedroom, where I'd been hiding all night like a loser. For someone who hadn't done anything, I sure felt a mountain of guilt by association. Every time I went to leave my room, I pictured one of them seeing me and looking at me as if I were the enemy.

It wasn't as if I could stay in this room forever. I was now hiding in the spot that I was holing up in? Not to mention my stomach was screaming at me, demanding food. I wanted a steak, or a plate of pasta, or a—*grilled cheese*. I hadn't had one of those in a long while. Bet they had good cheese here, too. It might be a weird color and called something else, but it would be close. This kitchen was stocked like crazy.

I snuck down to the kitchen, hoping no one was around, and not solely because of earlier tonight. The amount I was eating was becoming borderline embarrassing. I needed to find out how long this phase lasted.

The doors to the den were open, and light spilled out into the hall. It was probably one of the servants straightening up or something. I never saw them in that room during the day. Didn't matter. I only needed to make it around the corner.

The sound of muffled voices reached me. I couldn't make out what was being said, but it was definitely Kaden and another man, or two? It wasn't anyone I recognized. Who would be here now?

I froze. Was Kaden going to kill me now? He'd turned on me before because of my grandmother's deeds.

Eavesdrop, or trust he wouldn't screw me again? Survival vs. grilled cheese? It should've been a much easier choice, but I stood still for a few seconds before I tiptoed closer toward the voices. This was merely a delay, and survival had to take precedence over my sandwich, at least until I ruled out a threat. I glued myself to the wall as I moved slowly closer until the voices became clear.

"I haven't seen you all in a while, and this is why you came? Not Larken, but this?" Kaden asked.

"What happened with Larken is done. This is more important. We know you marked someone," an older male voice said.

"We want to meet her," another man said.

How did they know he'd marked me and that I was a she? So much for the creepy cellar blocking the signal. I guessed there were enough rumors that he'd brought me here. If Kaden had planned on doing it to Cookie, Dice, or Connor, he probably wouldn't have waited decades.

"She's unavailable," Kaden said.

"Really? We can sense her nearby, listening. Hiding her won't change anything," the older man said.

I stopped breathing, afraid they could hear that. How could they know I was here? Was that even possible? Yeah, probably, since all sorts of things I'd never thought possible happened on a daily basis.

So what should I do? Did I go in there? Kaden had said I wasn't available. He didn't think I should. What if he didn't want me to talk to them because *he* was hiding something? Maybe I should go in?

"I said unavailable. She's none of your concern." Kaden's voice was low and lethal. Well, whatever his plans, it didn't sound like he was handing me over to them. If he didn't want them to see me, odds were he hadn't called them here to kill me.

That was all I really needed to know. I should head on over to the kitchen now and whip up that grilled cheese.

"You went against our rules doing what you did. You're supposed to come to us before you do something like this."

More people angry about the marking. We could probably form a club of people pissed about it at this point, and yet I seemed to be the only person who didn't know why. How did that make any sense?

"Larken is dead, and all you care about are your rules and procedures?" Kaden asked.

"We're as upset as you are, but—"

"I doubt that," Kaden said.

"Eons of tradition were put into place for a reason," one of the older men said.

"You relinquished your authority to demand anything when you gave up," Kaden said.

Gave up? What did they give up? Someone was talking, but it was too soft to hear. I inched slightly closer.

"We *will* speak with her," the older man said, sounding like the pushier of the two.

"You don't have the right to come in here and demand anything." There was a moment of silence before Kaden added, "I'll let you speak to her, but it's my decision, not yours."

Oh shit. Kaden expected me to talk to them? I should've chosen the grilled cheese. I could make a dash for it, and pretend I wasn't eavesdropping, but they all knew I was here. Then they'd think I was a coward.

Run or stay? The clock was ticking.

"Billie, come in here," Kaden said.

The sound of my name made me go rigid. My joints

cemented together, not wanting to unfold enough to allow me to walk. I could still pretend. They hadn't seen me. Maybe I had a head cold and my hearing was bad? I looked toward the stairs, wondering if they'd follow me.

If I ran from this, I might never stop, because the problems heading toward me weren't going anywhere. If I couldn't find the guts to go into that room with Kaden backing me up, I wouldn't have the nerve to face anything.

I shook out my arms, forcing myself to get moving. My stomach growled so loudly it might as well have been a trumpet announcing my arrival.

"She's clearly hungry. That's a good sign," the pushy man said.

I walked into the room as if I hadn't been caught eavesdropping. As if there hadn't been a delay in my walking in. As if I hadn't been heralded by my grumpy stomach.

The two older men stared hard as I approached, making no bones about their appraisal. The lines on their faces grew more severe as I approached.

My expression might not have been any better. I thought we were immortal? We didn't age? If that was true, what happened to the two of them? It was one thing to wrap my head around living forever, but going through eternity with my bones creaking? As frail as these guys appeared? They looked like they'd crawled out of a grave. They made my grandmother's old body look like a spring chicken's.

Not to mention the wizard robes. Kaden wore jeans

and sweaters, but never this kind of draping, theatrical getup, and in blazing silver, no less. They looked like they were getting ready for a role in *The Lord of the Rings*.

The oldest of the old stepped forward. I didn't need to hear his voice to know this was the pushy one.

"It's taking. Does she feel anything?" he asked, tilting his head toward Kaden, as if I were some inanimate object standing in front of him, incapable of comprehending or responding.

"Farrow, she can hear. She also speaks," Kaden said, leaning on the back of the sofa.

"I asked you because I don't expect her to recognize the signs." Farrow let out a very loud sigh, but then turned his nearly silver-eyed gaze to me. "Do you feel any different?"

My urge was to look at Kaden for some reassurance that it was okay to speak to these men. That would undo everything he was establishing, that I didn't need him to answer for me.

A few months ago, I wouldn't have hesitated to speak, but it was getting so that I didn't trust my judgment anymore. I'd found out how small my world had been, that my grandmother wasn't human and crazier than I'd imagined. Worst was that I'd thought I could survive in Nowhere on my own, on pure will alone. I'd been wrong so many times in the last month that it might now be prudent to do the opposite of every instinct I had.

"I'm hungrier than I've ever been in my life, but other than that, I feel the same," I said.

Farrow nodded and then glanced at his companion, who nodded as well.

"Anything else? Maybe some strange warming in the chest?" he asked.

I woke up this morning with a burning, but it had passed. It came back after breakfast, then lunch, but passed again. I'd never been prone to heartburn before, but with the constant overeating...

"No, I'm normal." I wasn't sure why I lied. Maybe it was to test them? I was flying blind.

Farrow narrowed his eyes, and so did the other one. I broke my control and glanced over at Kaden. He was pinching the bridge of his nose.

The two older men circled me, as if they could see through my clothes as they stared. Glances passed back and forth between them.

"What is it?" I asked.

Farrow turned and looked at me. "You want answers? Then answer ours. We know you're holding out. I can hear the lie in your voice."

"Fine. I'll speak frankly if you promise to as well," I said, this time sounding a little more confident and ignoring the urge to look at Kaden.

"Agreed," Farrow said.

"I've been getting something that I believe is heartburn. It didn't seem worth mentioning." I shrugged. It wasn't normal to tell complete strangers about every case of indigestion I had.

They looked at each other and nodded again.

"It's taking," Farrow said.

"I can sense it growing in her, too," the other man said.

They looked at each other and in unison headed toward the door.

"That's it?" I asked.

"We're done," Farrow said to me, and then looked at Kaden. "We understand why you had to do what you did." They continued out.

I waited until the main door opened and closed.

"They're your people?" I asked, feeling the need to confirm. Everything about those two felt shadier than a big old elm tree at noon.

"My race. Not my people. There's a difference," he answered.

"I thought I wouldn't age?"

"Only if you choose to," he said, looking toward the window, as if sensing their departure.

"What is it they didn't want to say?" I asked. I hadn't liked the way they'd looked at me, and left right afterward with nothing else to say.

He kept watching out the window, as if he were as eager for them to be gone as I was. "I'm not sure, but we'll find out when they're ready."

I didn't like the sound of that.

NINETEEN

There was no mention of the mysterious Larken the next day at breakfast. Cookie, Dice, and Connor were acting as if nothing had happened, as if they'd shut down those emotions and tucked them away.

Things felt strangely back to normal as Cookie looked at Dice's plate and made a pig noise.

"Me? Have you seen what she's been putting down?" Dice waved his hand toward me.

I was currently shoveling in another couple bites of eggs, a croissant ready in my other hand to wash it down with.

"She doesn't count. She's growing new body parts," Cookie replied.

"She eats like she's growing a twin," Dice said.

I might've cared a couple of days ago, but that was quickly wearing off. Instead of interjecting myself in the debate, I grabbed another croissant.

Kaden walked into the room and looked at me. "Grab

a sweater and meet me in the cellar. We're practicing down there today."

He left. Dice, Connor, and Cookie all stared at me, and not because I was still eating.

"What?" I asked.

Cookie pointed in the direction Kaden had departed. "He thinks it's taken enough to start working with you magically."

The creepy old guys last night had said it was taking, but I didn't share that. There was something about those two men that made me hesitate to mention them, like they'd somehow know I'd gossiped about them. I had better things to do, anyway, like getting my magic on.

I grabbed the last croissant, getting ready to leave, and the three of them stood.

"Oh no, you aren't coming." I wasn't taking another step until they sat their butts down.

"What do you mean we aren't?" Cookie asked.

"I don't know what I'm doing yet. You have to give me a few days." I pointed to her chair.

"So you don't look stupid?" Dice asked, then laughed.

"Like we've never seen her look idiotic before," Connor added, laughing as well.

Cookie joined in. "You have to admit, you've had some low points. Remember the day you showed up at the outpost like a drowned rat? You finally realized that everyone was telling you the truth and you couldn't stay Topside? I highly doubt you'll look worse than that." She shook her head as if it were impossible.

"What about after she came in from seeing Chaos and we thought she wasn't going to leave her room for a year?" Connor asked.

"Thinking she had to scrub the floors was probably the best. I still have pics from that," Dice said, as if this were turning into a competition of who could recall my worst moment.

"You've got pics of that?" I asked, stunned.

"Yeah, the cleaning crew took them. The chick you thought was child labor? You pissed her off pretty bad." Dice dug out his phone, scrolling. "She even got audio of you gagging."

"You guys are definitely not invited to watch now. Not even if I'm good," I said as I walked out of the room.

I wasn't sure they heard me. They were too busy listening to my retching in a bathroom.

They were lucky I usually liked them. I might've killed them otherwise.

Kaden was waiting for me downstairs. The place was lit with torches.

"So how's this work? What are we doing?"

"I need you to hit me."

"I thought we were working on magic stuff?" Not this crap again. I sucked at punching. This was supposed to be fun, or at least productive. I'd come down here, to this dark, muggy room, to throw punches?

"It's the easiest way for you to start utilizing what I gave you and incorporate it. You weren't born with it, so you need to sync it to your body. One way to do that is being physical. So swing at me."

He held his bare palms up, waiting.

"Don't you want a pad for your hand?"

"No. I need to feel the energy you're putting out this time." He waved his hand for me to swing. I hit his palm, and he immediately said, "Do it again."

I continued, trying to keep focused on hitting his hands, and not that his arms were flexed and tan.

"I want you to keep going until you stop thinking about what you're doing. Until it's automatic. Don't put so much energy into it that you tire out. It's the movement I'm concerned with more than the impact."

I smiled. "I thought you said I didn't hit hard?"

"You don't. I'm sure it still tires you out, and I need you to keep going for a while." He wasn't smiling. That wasn't even a joke, which made it more insulting.

I hit a little harder, but he didn't seem to notice. He wasn't feeling it, and I was getting wiped out, which was almost as bad as listening to my retching sounds come through Dice's phone upstairs.

I backed off, trying to conserve some energy before I was crying for a break and proving his point. I kept punching, going through the motions until my body was moving on its own, and my muscles were tiring.

"Good, keep going—but as you do, that burning sensation you felt in your chest? Try to focus on it. Imagine it burning now."

I continued to punch while talking myself into having heartburn. Except I didn't have heartburn, and my chest didn't want to burn.

"Don't be concerned if it takes a little while," he said, his focus intent on every move I made.

Burn, burn, burn.

I was feeling a little hot and sweaty, but nothing was burning. I couldn't stir up even the smallest amount of acid, and I was beginning to think maybe that's what it was. Maybe the old, creepy men didn't know as much as they thought, and I *did* have heartburn.

"Maybe it's not taking? Maybe you didn't mark anything?" I kept punching, hoping it was going to burn. I *needed* it to burn. I needed this to work.

"I did and it is," he said, dropping his hands.

"Yeah, I'm not so sure." I crossed my arms in front of my chest.

He moved closer, and I jumped back.

"What are you doing?" I asked, as if he were the weird one and I hadn't overreacted to his nearness. Why did I have to be so attuned to him? So aware that I broke out into a sweat when he got close? I was acting like the weirdo Antoinette accused me of being.

"I'm going to help you feel it." He was talking to me as if he couldn't understand my issue.

"How?" I added a little accusation to my tone, trying to deflect my crazy back on him. There was no way we were leaving here with me owning it, or what was at the heart of it.

It was his fault. Ever since he told me he'd have avenged me, he'd shifted something, chipped away at my walls. It was business. He'd felt obligated to do so. I had to keep that in the forefront of my mind. I couldn't afford to be soft, not with him.

"It's part of me. I'll be able to help you find it if you let me," he said, taking a step forward.

He was watching me like I was a scared rabbit about to sprint away.

"Maybe I don't want you rustling around in my insides, looking for shit?" I shot off the first excuse that came to mind, even if it sounded stupid. I took another step backward in spite of my decision not to act like a weirdo.

He ran his hand over his shadowed jaw. He had a really good jaw. It was the perfect width and angle for his face.

"You want to be independent? You want to be able to walk down the streets without being a hair away from death?" His eyebrows were raised, as if he'd presented me with a question we hadn't covered.

"Obviously." He was wearing his black sweatpants today. They were my favorite. Maybe it was that they seemed to hang lower on his hips.

"Then let me help you," he said.

He was rubbing the back of his neck in a way that accented his forearm, and his shoulders too. Couldn't forget them.

"Billie?" he asked.

"What?" I asked, belatedly registering that he was still speaking to me.

"I need to show you," he said. "But there's something else I need to tell you. I probably should've mentioned this earlier, but I wasn't sure if what I did would cause an issue."

"What issue?"

He walked over, grabbed his water, and took a long swig. Kaden was the type to say whatever he wanted, but he was taking his time.

"The marking. It can cause a certain...*sensitivity*," he said.

"Like a skin thing? A sun thing?" Although I guessed a sun thing wouldn't be an issue in Nowhere.

"More like a libido thing. As it kicks in, you might feel an attraction toward me. I wanted you to be fore-warned in case it happens."

He was staring at me, as if he expected me to tell him if I was already feeling something.

He'd known why I was acting weird. I was glad the lighting down here was horrible. It meant he might not see the raging fire across my cheeks.

"Really? Nothing has changed." That was partially true. As much as I'd like to blame it on the marking, I wasn't stupid enough to believe it myself. I'd always appreciated his body. That was it, though. I wouldn't go anywhere near the man.

"So then I can show you?" He was staring at me as if he wasn't completely buying my denial. "Unless you're suddenly afraid of me?"

"Of course not," I scoffed.

It wasn't as if he hadn't seen me naked. I'd been laid out nude while he painted my body with intricate patterns. What was a little closeness?

He stepped near me, and I resisted the urge to back away.

"Are you sure you're okay with this?" He lifted a brow, silently taunting me.

"I think I can handle a few minutes of touching. Show me." I inched up my chin, trying to force my body to relax.

"Do you feel more comfortable facing me or away? I need you to be as relaxed as possible while I'm holding you."

If I faced him, he'd be able to watch my face. I'd watch his, and they'd be uncomfortably close.

I turned, giving him my back. He came up behind me, wrapping his arms around me, and it was immediately clear that there was no good option, front or back, eyes closed or open. I could feel him molding to every curve, and they all fit together too well.

He took a deep breath, and I could feel every muscle surrounding me.

"Your heart is racing," he said.

"Just shut up and do whatever it is you need to— unless you don't think *you* can." I closed my eyes again, trying not to focus on him, even as he was surrounding me.

"There," he said, his voice so close to my ear his breath tingled. "Do you feel it?"

"Yes." I shivered in spite of myself. "It's chilly down here," I said, even as every inch of me was burning. I pulled out of his arms, trying to focus on the spot he'd seemed to bring to life in my chest. "Why couldn't I feel this before?" I laid a hand on my chest, sensing something different within me for the first time. How had I missed this?

"I buried it as deep as possible, hoping it would take better."

He was watching me with a strange look I couldn't put an emotion to.

"It's... It almost feels like it's got a pulse of its own, as if I have two hearts beating within me." I looked into his eyes, wondering if I'd see him staring back at me like I was crazy.

"It does," he said. He took my hand, laying it over his chest. "Can you feel my heart? It's beating to the same rhythm as what I gave you."

We stood like that for a minute, and I felt the matched beating.

"That piece of me makes it very hard to kill you, even if you never convert any further to my kind," he said. "As long as I'm alive, that piece will beat within you. I'm not saying there aren't ways to kill you still, but it won't be easy." He spoke as if this was what he was most proud of accomplishing.

I had to admit, it would make me sleep a little easier tonight.

"Focus on feeling that, connecting with it, and we'll try again in a few days," he said.

"So it is taking, just slowly." I was going to be okay. I wouldn't be hiding forever. I'd be able to get a life back.

"The slower, the better. It means it's working more than I could've expected," he said, and then his gaze became transfixed on where my hair was lying over my shoulder. He picked up a lock and fanned it between his fingers. "Your hair is changing. Have you looked at it recently?"

Actually, I hadn't. It wasn't that there was no mirror in my room, but lately I showered, dragged a brush through it, tossed it in a ponytail, and called it a day. Vanity had taken a back seat to survival, plotting, and the general business of staying alive. If my wardrobe hadn't been provided and laundered for me, things might've taken a worse turn.

I looked down at his hand. There, within the dark red tresses, were a few pale blonde locks.

"The crew told me that tinkers morph instead of aging. I thought I'd have longer, though."

"It's happening fast." He was fixated on my hair, not really talking to me, when he said, "Sun and night."

"Sun and night? What are you talking about?" I asked.

"Nothing." He dropped my hair, taking a few steps away and seeming to distance himself mentally as well. "We're done for today. I need to go handle some other matters. We'll pick up again in a few days."

He was already halfway up the stairs when I said, "Okay."

TWENTY

I was sitting in the window seat in my bedroom, staring out at the swirling universe, and missing the sunshine. Cookie and the guys weren't anywhere to be found, so there were no distractions to pull me away from my worries, and I was very good at worrying. Recently I'd graduated from exceptional to expert. It was the only area in which I seemed to be gaining ground.

Hand-to-hand combat was a lost cause. What if I never got good enough at the magic he'd instilled in me to walk the streets confidently? It would be so easy to be a coward, stay here indefinitely, but when would it end? Would I stay in this place forever, existing as...what? What I was now?

I might as well be one of the statues in the cellar for all my purpose, and being around him all the time wasn't a good idea. My guard was dropping. I was getting soft, in spite of myself. Kaden smiled at me and my anger wilted. He neared me and I went into a panic.

I needed a better plan than hanging out here and relying on his charity. There needed to be an exit, and Kaden had to understand that as well. He'd probably lock me away indefinitely so he could relieve himself of whatever guilty feelings were breaking through his uncomfortably cold soul. Or worse, turn on me at the first imagined slight.

Well, I wasn't going to stay here waiting to get the boot. I marched my way downstairs with more confidence than I'd had in weeks. I was laying down the law. I would plot my own path, wherever that might lie.

I checked all Kaden's usual haunts but only stumbled across Soleil in his office.

"Have you seen Kaden? I can't find him anywhere."

"I believe he's in the pool room," she said, dusting some books.

"There's a pool table around here?" This place was so sprawling that it was easy for things to be missed.

"No. A swimming pool."

"Pool? There's a pool here? Like, inside of this place?" Whoever had carved out this fortress really had been an overachiever.

"Yes. All the way down the back hall, last door on the right," she said, grinning and nodding.

I spun around, trying to remember which hall was the back hall. Left and then right? Left and straight? What about that weird hallway that went—

"The hall behind the kitchen," Soleil said, before laughing softly.

"Thanks."

I found the hall, grabbing a muffin from the kitchen on my way. I must've gotten detoured by food before I'd made it this far last time.

The door she'd specified was small, closet-sized, but as soon as I opened it, I could smell the water. I walked down a steep set of circular stairs that seemed to be never-ending, even steeper than those that descended to the other cellar. A strange blue glow reflected off the walls, lighting the way.

Kaden was swimming laps—naked. He made his way to the far side and turned like an Olympic swimmer in a pool that looked as if it were carved out of the stone floor. His body moved through the water like he was born to it.

He finished his lap back toward me and stopped at the side of the carved pool, resting his arms on the edge.

"I wanted to talk, but if this is a bad time..."

"I was just finishing up," he said, and then jumped out of the pool.

I tried not to stare. I really did. At least I managed not to gawk, until he turned around and grabbed a towel off the nearby stone bench. He ran it over his head before he bothered to wrap it around his waist, not that he had anything to hide.

His skin was perfect, the color of dark honey and not a blemish anywhere, just smooth satin over a perfect form, highlighted by the rivulets of water dripping down and accenting the lines of his body. No wonder I found him attractive. I was a woman who liked men, and he was about as close to perfection as a male specimen could get.

I looked away quickly as he turned, but not fast

enough. He'd definitely caught my checking him out. I'd done worse.

"What did you want to discuss?" He was finger-combing his hair away from his face, his stomach muscles flexing with the movement.

How was I supposed to have a conversation this way? The only fair thing would be for me to rip off my shirt. How would he like that? See how well he could concentrate. I wasn't sure why men's breasts got all sorts of freedom. Like they had no effect on women?

He was staring at me, brows raised. "Billie?"

Concentrate, you ninny.

"I know you want me to stay until I'm more self-sufficient, better at self-defense and all that. Still, I think we need to set up goals and a clear exit strategy."

He narrowed his eyes, rubbing a jaw that seemed to be growing more stubborn by the second, as if I'd hit him with something out of the blue. He couldn't have imagined I'd stay here indefinitely.

Except he looked like he might've.

He took a step toward me, close enough I had to bend my head back.

"I'm not sure you understand the situation." He was speaking with that tone, the one that made me want to kick him.

Right now, no number of smiles would make me wilt.

"I'm aware of the situation, but you can't expect that I'll be here indefinitely. I'm sure that's not what either of us wants." Why was he being so stubborn? Oh, that's right—he was Kaden. What else would he be?

His jaw twitched. For someone getting an easy out, he was really going to dig into this white-knight act. Maybe the novelty of it amused him, but white wasn't his color. It showed too many bloodstains.

"You realize they're going to come for you as soon as you leave here?" He stared at me as if I'd stuffed my head full of rocks. As if I didn't have a brain cell left after the beating I'd taken.

"I'm not an idiot. I know if I leave here now, it'll be a problem. But I *will* be leaving, and we need to come to realistic terms. Survival is never a hundred percent." If he thought it was, he was the one with a head full of rocks.

He scoffed. "Oh, well, that explains it all. How good of a chance were you looking for? You might have a five percent chance. Is that good? Or what about ten percent? Will that satisfy you?"

"You're being unreasonable." I crossed my arms, not an ounce of humor showing on my face.

"This is life or death, and right now I'm the only person between you and dying. You certainly can't rely on your grandmother."

"Don't bring her into this. You don't know her like I do."

"I know her better," he said, not hesitating a second.

"She doesn't hate you. Did you know that?" I asked, stretching out every inch of my smaller frame.

"Of course she doesn't hate me. I'm not trying to rob her," he said.

Rob him of what? My grandmother had never taken

anything that wasn't hers, ever. Now he was saying she was a thief?

Why was I terrified to ask? Was his dislike starting to warp my belief in her? Either way, he was derailing this conversation *again*.

"To be honest, this was a courtesy discussion," I said. "I'll leave as soon as *I* think I'm ready." He clearly thought every decision was his for some reason, and it was time he reassessed the situation. The truth was, the only reason I'd stayed was because I'd been scared. I hadn't even admitted it to myself until something came along that scared me worse. Him. Having *feelings* for him was more terrifying than the horde.

"You're not ready. End of discussion." His jaw was clenched as he walked across the room, dismissing me.

"Why can't you have a civil discussion? Look, I did things you didn't like, and you did things I absolutely *hated*, but I can talk to you like a sane person."

He turned. "Really? Because you're screaming right now."

"If I am, it's because you drove me to it." Yep, he was right. I was screaming. I'd never been a screamer in my life, but then, I'd never had to deal with someone like him.

"If you can't control your emotions, you're not ready." He walked over to the bench where he had his clothes piled and dropped his towel to get dressed, as if I weren't standing there.

I was boiling hot, and it wasn't from looking at his physique. I wanted to walk over and beat him. One of these times I was going to do it, too. When I was nice and calm one day, I'd walk over and beat him, just so he couldn't blame it on my being out of control.

"And you're so controlled?" I yelled at his back.

"Still screaming," he said.

His tone might be soft, but it was far from calm. It might've sounded angrier than mine. This wasn't going anywhere good.

I took the stairs two at a time and marched right over to the front door, swinging it open to the death stoop.

"How the hell does anyone get in and out of this place?" I yelled.

At least a few of the servants heard me, but no one offered a reply.

Why hadn't I asked Cookie? Where the hell was she? I was walking out of this fortress just to prove a point, even if I didn't go far. I was in charge of my own life.

TWENTY-ONE

Cookie and the guys didn't come back here tonight. Figured they'd stay at their places in the city just when I needed to harass them for answers.

I'd searched this place with a newfound determination, making a hand-drawn map. Servants came and went, and I didn't care who saw me. I carried on, searching every nook and cranny. At the end, I determined there was no other entrance.

The only positive that came out of it was finding this place: a balcony off the fourth-floor observatory. The access had been hidden behind yet another small door, which hid a staircase that climbed to the top of a tower. It had the most magnificent views of the ocean, with lounge chairs to recline on and watch the swirls of all the galaxies above and the glittering reflection in the water below. It was so breathtaking it made it easier to forget my trivial role in life and embrace the beauty around me.

It was so quiet and peaceful that I almost forgot how angry I was. *Almost.*

Footsteps rang through the room behind me. I didn't want to recognize them, but I did. I'd like to blame it on that piece of himself Kaden had given me, but it had been like this for a while. His scent, his sounds—all seemed to trigger some sort of alertness in myself. Maybe some wiser part of me knew he was a threat? Except no matter how furious I'd ever seen him, I'd never felt threatened.

Whatever. Life didn't always make sense. If I decided he was a threat, then that was what he'd be, no matter what logic said.

He walked out onto the balcony and over to the railing, leaning his forearms on it with his back to me.

"This is one of my favorite places," he said.

That was the worst news I'd had all day. So much for dreaming of lounging out here and avoiding him.

"I'll leave you to it." I'd finally gotten my pulse to a place where I might be able to sleep tonight. Every moment I remained near him would cost me a few more beats.

He turned around. "I came up here to talk to you."

"Now you want to have a conversation?" It was clear he was holding out an olive branch, but after earlier, I was ready to snap it in half and throw it into the woodchipper. It was no less than he deserved for the attitude I got when *I'd* wanted to have a conversation.

"Your grandmother left you for dead," he said, hitting me out of the blue with a new topic to fight over.

I got up, heading toward the door.

"I'm not trying to pick a fight. I want to explain why I was less than receptive earlier. Will you please sit and listen to me?" His tone was much softer, and a lot less arrogant than normal, chipping away slightly at my wall.

He'd also said "please." I wasn't sure I'd ever heard him use that word before. I was waiting for him to break out in hives from uttering it. I might need to fetch an EpiPen or some antihistamine for him.

He had his hands raised in surrender. "Hear me out?"

"Fine. But I want it on the record that it's only because you said please." It wouldn't hurt to wait a few minutes to see if those hives were going to pop up.

He waved a hand at the lounge chair, as if he didn't believe I'd listen if I was standing. I sat back down, stretching out my legs and looking up at the swirling sky. If he pissed me off, I'd just focus my attention above and ignore him.

He moved back to lean on the balcony railing. "Can you discuss your grandmother unemotionally?"

"Can *you*?" I countered. If he could, he hadn't shown any history of it.

"I can strip the emotion out of any situation needed," he said matter-of-factly.

That right there was why I could never fall for this man, ever. If I did fall in love again, it was going to be with someone who couldn't stop their feelings for me, even if they wanted to. Someone who led with their heart, not cold logic and a cynicism so ingrained it was probably part of their DNA.

"I'm not quite as adept as you are, but I'll give it a go," I said. "Why don't we start with what you think my grandmother took?" The first time he'd mentioned her trying to rob him, I wanted to run from the room, afraid of what I'd hear. But it was at the heart of the issue that I'd been dragged into the middle of. I couldn't run. There was nowhere *to* run.

"Her and a man named Herrick, the person she works for, want Nowhere, and they want it at any cost."

"Why do they want Nowhere? I mean, not that it's not nice, but why here?" I asked.

"You see what's above you?"

I glanced up, already having admired this view so many times before. When I was at Cookie's, I used to stare out the window when I couldn't sleep, wondering what was happening in all those other worlds.

"Everything?" It sure looked like it.

"Exactly. Nowhere is at the heart of everything. And I mean *everything*. What you're seeing isn't just some universe. It's every universe in existence."

He was looking upward as well, as if this view never got old.

"Nowhere is called Nowhere because it's not in one place. It's nowhere and everywhere, all at once," he said. "The only way to get here is through an outpost or portal, and you can get everywhere else the same way. This place is the key to getting anywhere. With control of this place, you have the upper hand in any battle or conflict. Imagine Earth. Then think what it would be like if the forces of three other planets, or one advanced planet, were able to populate all their arms almost instantaneously while the people on Earth don't even have interstellar travel? You have control of *this* place, and you could colonize every other planet and universe simply by moving arms and people through here."

I would've fallen on my ass if there wasn't a lounge chair underneath me. I stared above, and the view took on a whole other level now that I realized what was possible. The places you could go.

I couldn't stop staring now. I could go to one of those glowing nebulas tomorrow, and another one the next day? Suddenly the variety of people and creatures in Nowhere made perfect sense.

A year ago, planning a trip to Asia was a big deal. The places I'd planned on going were endless. Now that bucket list felt more like a crumpled-up tin can compared to what lay all around me.

"Your grandmother and Herrick want to control Nowhere, and all it has to offer. In order to control this place, they need to get rid of me and my kind. We're the only ones standing in their way."

My grandmother was with people who wanted to control the multiverse? I was still speechless as I looked at him.

"Takes on a whole new meaning, doesn't it?" he asked.

"Just because she's associated with this Herrick person, we don't know if she really wants—"

"That's why I didn't tell you." He kept looking upward. "Even now, you can't believe it."

"Maybe the people she knows want to do that, but..." Gram? No. It couldn't be true. She was just getting thrown in with their plans. My grandmother might be quirky and crazy, but this wasn't her. "Can you keep this Herrick person from doing it? Are there more of your kind that are willing to help?" The conversation from the other night with Farrow and the other man was making a lot more sense.

"There are more of my kind, but I don't know if there's enough left willing to fight. Most of the people in Nowhere aren't from here, and my kind are a dying breed." He walked over and settled into the lounge beside me. "I'm not trying to rehash things to frustrate you, but we need to discuss the night of the beating. Your grandmother knew you were in trouble. I believe the people she's associated with might be the reason she didn't step in. I think they might've been the catalyst that drove the horde after you."

The only saving grace to that comment was he said it calmly and seemed to be looking to just establish past history. Plus, I was going to prove I could discuss things as coldly as he could.

"Just because she didn't step forward, if she *was* there, doesn't mean it was her people. She probably thought it was beyond what she was capable of. There were a lot of attackers." Would I have stepped in without thinking? Yes. But she'd gotten me help, which was better than both of us dying.

He turned toward me, his brows raised. "Your grandmother could've taken out that gaggle of idiots nearly as fast as I could've. She wasn't looking for backup."

Then she'd simply left me there to continue to take blows. The slim possibility that he was correct made my soul lurch off its axis. Kaden hated her, though, so everything he said was tainted by that. Until there was proof, it was all speculation.

I pulled my knees up, toying with the rip in my jeans.

"I'm not saying that to hurt you." His voice was softer than it had been.

"I know." For all I might accuse him of, Kaden wasn't intentionally cruel.

Even if I didn't like what he was saying, I let the idea bounce around for a few moments.

"Why would her people want me dead?" I asked. "I don't see how that makes sense. Why would they care about me at all? I have nothing to do with any of this."

"I don't know if that was the goal, but I can sense Herrick's fingerprints all over this." He took a long breath, his hands fisting at his mention of Herrick.

"But why bother with me?" I asked.

He shook his head. He either had no idea, or wasn't ready to share. I might not be ready for more sharing anyway. My head was spinning with all the information.

I leaned back, letting the ideas swirl around my head. I'd never met any of these people. "The only way they'd care about me..."

No. That couldn't be it. I was a nobody.

"You could hurt them somehow?" he asked, as if he could read my thoughts. "We have to go with the assumption that Herrick and the people she's with have an interest in you specifically."

And anything that might be detrimental to them was a positive to Kaden. Was that why he marked me? Or part of it? I'd seen guilt in his eyes, but that didn't mean there wasn't more to it.

"I don't think that was a mindless horde but a directed attack," he said. He gave me a minute, watching every twitch of my fingers, flick of my eyes.

"An attack led by your girlfriend?" I added. He was so quick to accuse my grandmother, but where was the blame for her? She'd played a large part.

"She was a tool. That's all."

An *innocent* tool? I shook my head, letting it go. She was gone. I'd have to let sleeping dogs lie for now, or at least until she reared her ugly head and began barking again. Right now, she was nothing but a nuisance, if Kaden was correct.

What would happen if this Herrick person was behind the attack? If he were, and he took over Nowhere with an eye on expansion, I was dead. I'd be hiding under rocks for the rest of my existence, and that immortal life seemed much longer all of a sudden.

I would've loved to hear Gram's side of it, let her defend herself. I'd ask about Herrick and what they were doing, but she wasn't anywhere to be found. Constantly beyond reach.

"I'll stay. At least for now or until I know more." Until I could leave this place and know I could defend myself.

He didn't say anything. Just nodded as he lay on the lounge beside me.

TWENTY-TWO

I was back up on the balcony the next morning, drinking coffee and staring at the sky.

Cookie walked over and stood beside my lounge, eating a croissant. "Kaden called everyone into the den. Said he has something to tell us."

"Any idea what it's about?" I asked before sipping my perfectly brewed coffee. They were still making it the way I liked. I'd take a win wherever I could.

"No idea," she said. "He won't tell us until we're all there, so you gotta get up, because I want to know."

I got up, heading to the stairs. "You got any more of those?" I'd already eaten five this morning, but my hunger was returning. It was becoming the only predictable thing in my life.

"A new platter was just put out."

That made me move a little quicker.

"I've been looking for you," I said as we made our way downstairs. "Where'd you disappear to?"

"Had some jobs scheduled that had to get done, even though we're all trying to lie low right now. Why? What's up?"

I missed doing jobs, being productive. I couldn't even get out of this fortress.

"How do you get in and out of this place without dying? Is there another door? The front door is a deathtrap."

She laughed. "There's stairs. Kaden probably has you blocked."

Well, that wasn't acceptable. He might want me to stay, but hiding the stairs? That was petty.

A hair was yanked out of the back of my head.

"Ow! Why did you do that?" I rubbed my scalp, turning to look at her. I was used to her pushing and pulling, but this hair business was not going to fly.

She was squinting so hard, her lip rose. She held up my hair to examine it. "It's changing colors, but I think it's turning platinum blonde. Didn't see that coming. My bet was on redder, and definitely not this quick."

"Oh, yeah. I know." I took the strand from her. "Why is it all blonde? And not just blonde at the root, where it's changing?"

"That's how human hair changes. You're not human anymore, remember?" She was squinting in the direction of my head. "Look, there's another."

I jerked away from her, afraid she'd try to yank more out.

"You've got blonde hair coming in all over the place under there," she said.

I pulled a chunk of hair forward, over my shoulder. Nearly a quarter of it was blonde.

"It's happening fast." I'd checked my hair after Kaden mentioned it, and there'd been a few hidden strands. It seemed as if it were changing almost overnight.

"You guys coming?" Connor's voice boomed from below.

Cookie was already moving again, my hair color shifted to the back burner. I ran past her so I could grab a couple of croissants from the dining room before settling in.

Kaden was leaning on the table as we all dropped down onto the chairs and couches.

"I wanted to give everyone a warning. I'm calling a gathering. It's time to see what our numbers are," he said as soon as everyone was settled.

Cookie groaned. The guys were pretty quiet, so it couldn't be that bad.

"What's a gathering?" I asked.

"It's a party, but not a purely social one. This is more strategic in nature, with the faint veil of socialization," Kaden said. "See who's willing to come and be counted. Showing up at all says something, since I'm sure they're watching and going to note all who come."

"Not sure I'd give them much credit. Half of them are just busybodies." Cookie was slumping into the couch, looking as if she were about to throw a hissy fit. "And those are the interesting ones."

"It's not that bad," Connor said, looking at her like she was being a diva.

"That's because you barely talk to anyone," Cookie said.

Dice shifted in his seat, repositioning his gun in his holster. "I don't think it's that bad either, to be honest."

"Because you walk around like a freak ready to shoot the place up. No one *wants* to talk to you." Cookie shook her head, as if she couldn't fathom his stupidity.

"Either way, it has to happen," Kaden said. "If things are going to come to a head, we need to know where everyone stands."

"How long will it be?" Cookie asked, running her hands through her hair so hard it was stretching her forehead.

"A week," Kaden said. "But no one will stay that long. They never do."

"I'm assuming all the regular jerks?" Cookie looked at me and shook her head again, like I had no idea what was coming. "They never want to get their hands dirty. They want to skate by on other people's work."

"They're going to have to understand that the time of being able to skate is coming to an end," Kaden said.

"So it's really coming to a head, then, huh? This is the beginning?" Connor asked.

"They'll make a move soon, unless we do it first. Either way, the clock is ticking. They think we're weak enough to take out. Now I need to figure out if they're right," Kaden said.

What happened if Kaden was right, and this was the beginning of a war for Nowhere? What did that mean?

I looked around the now-silent room. Cookie's

dramatics had shifted into something more sober as she sat there, not talking. If this crew was concerned, the people that would toss someone into a river without blinking, what did that mean?

Dice stood. "I gotta go buy some more guns."

"I'll come with," Connor said.

Cookie didn't say that she was leaving. She just shook her head for the last time and went.

The room emptied, except for me. I kicked my feet up on the table, watching Kaden.

"You need something?" he asked, raising a brow and tilting his head.

"Yes. Why are you including me in talks when you don't trust me? No judgment. I don't trust you either." I shrugged. We were beyond pretending at this point. The man had taken my stairs, after all.

He smiled a little too confidently. "I have faith things will work out."

"Things? You mean that I'll decide my grandmother is an evil person?" It was never going to happen. She might be mixed up with the wrong people, but I'd never turn on her, no matter what he said.

"Your words, not mine," he replied, unfazed.

His continued confidence was bleeding mine out, not that I'd tell him.

I got to my feet, ready to do battle for the next topic. "I want stairs. I decided to stay because I think it's a good idea. Not because you stole my means of escape."

He smiled and then actually laughed. "Fine, you get stairs. But be aware that there might be spies watching. I don't know how close they'll get, but I wouldn't wander far."

"I'll wander as far as I deem safe," I said.

He continued to stare at me, as if he doubted my words.

"I'm not an idiot. I'm not going far, but it's my choice," I said, staring him down, daring him to say something.

He waved a hand toward the door, which I took to mean my stairs had already arrived.

I didn't waste any time heading right to the front door. No longer was there a stoop of death but a treacherous set of stairs. It had to be five flights down, narrow and steep. Whoever had carved this deathtrap didn't feel the need for a handrail? It was as if they'd exhausted themselves on the inside of this place and then decided to cut corners when they got out here.

I made my way down a few steps, to test them out, clinging to the stone wall. As far as I could see, there was nothing but mountains and forests. Where was I going to go? What had been the point of hiding them? I didn't have a death wish—not most days, anyway.

Still, it was nice to be somewhere out, even if *out* were steps. It was so nice that I went back inside, grabbed a jacket, and returned to sit some more. The view here was no less stunning than the balcony, with a rocky coast coming right up to a forest that appeared ancient, with trees that would dwarf even redwoods. Every so often, large white birds would swoop across the sky, almost glittering and opalescent.

A silver butterfly flapped its wings, flying up the stairs and coming to land on my bent knee. I leaned forward, looking closely at it and realized it wasn't actually a butterfly at all but a piece of silver paper folded in that shape. Its wings spread wide, and it lay open, going still in that position. My name was written across it in my grandmother's writing.

I plucked it off my knee, unfolding the paper that was so thin it seemed like gossamer.

MEET me at the large boulder at the base of the highest mountain after everyone else goes to sleep tomorrow night.

IT WAS SIGNED with a crooked smiley face, the kind she'd always scribbled next to *Gram* whenever she'd written me a note in the past. She'd found a way to reach out to me, even here. There wasn't a question of meeting her. Even if she wasn't my grandmother, I'd go because I wanted answers. The memory of seeing her that day in the distance, backed by what Kaden had told me, left too many open questions. Even if I hated her, which I didn't, I'd still go.

The only question was: did I tell Kaden? Or any of them? Could I risk it? I had to go, no matter what.

I still had the note in my hand when Kaden walked outside, his eyes on it. I might not have recognized what that paper was right away, but he clearly did. The choice was taken out of my hands. The only other person who might've sent me a note was Alaric, and that was probably a stretch. He still hadn't replied to the message I'd sent through Cookie, so his stance was pretty clear. He was steering clear of me as well.

"How did you know?" I held up the folded sheet. The timing of his arrival was too close to be a coincidence.

"I can feel every trace of magic that crosses the boundary of this place. I wasn't sure what caused it, so I rushed here." He nodded toward the message. "Gram?"

"Yes. She wants to meet me." He'd figure as much anyway. He'd realize there wasn't any more information on the thin sheet. No sane person would lay out their plans and deliver them to their enemy. Even Gram wouldn't be that crazy.

"She might've heard about the invitation to the gathering."

He was staring at me as if waiting to hear what I was going to do. If I was planning on meeting with his enemy. The last time I'd tried to hide such a meeting, it hadn't ended well.

That was the problem with our situation now. I couldn't live my life making decisions based on fear. Even if she shocked me and was bad as he painted her, how could I align with someone that I didn't feel like I had an equal relationship with?

I was going, so he might as well know now. If he kicked me out, so be it. At least I had stairs to leave.

"I'm going to meet with her," I said, waiting to see if

he'd explode. "I told you once that I'd never act in a way to hurt you. I won't. But I don't want to choose sides."

He nodded. "Go to your meeting. I won't ask you about it. You'll tell me or you won't, and I'll trust that you won't betray me. I know it's not easy to walk away from someone who's family. I hope you don't have to make a choice, but I fear you will, and not because of me."

He turned to leave.

"That's it? With no repercussions? You won't turn around afterward and decide to throw me out again? Or demand to know every detail?"

He turned back and calmly said, "I'm giving you my word: that won't happen."

"No matter what I do? No matter what comes from the meeting?"

"Yes. I realize that I tried to bully you into seeing what I believe instead of letting you live it yourself, and in the end, that's the way it has to be. So go, meet with her—do what you need to do."

He waited, as if expecting I'd have more questions. I was too stunned to say a word.

He nodded and walked away.

TWENTY-THREE

Kaden was there for breakfast, sliding the crossword over to me as if nothing had happened. Then we went through rounds in the basement, my swings worse than ever and not even a tingle of magic rising.

He didn't seem concerned, even though I was.

I had dinner in my room, barely able to eat anything. The day passed in a blur, and the only thing I could focus on was the meeting with Gram.

Cookie hadn't been around, relieving me of the decision to withhold my plans from her. She was about as unpredictable as they came, but once she did make up her mind, she'd be dogged in getting her way. If she didn't want me to go, it would be like having a bulldog's biting hold on my leg and dragging me away.

As the house grew quiet, I paused. I should be anxious to go, to hear why Gram hadn't helped me, but I wasn't.

What if she lied, and I knew she was lying? Or was

that Kaden getting in my head? He had such a hatred of her and her people, believing the worst of her. There was always another side. She deserved to have her say.

I grabbed my jacket, still wary but set on my decision. I trekked down the steep stairs and then headed toward the closest, highest mountain. It towered over the others but was close enough to walk to twenty minutes. It didn't seem like a far enough distance, considering the hate Kaden held for her, but I hadn't picked the locale.

I couldn't help but look over my shoulder every few minutes, expecting to see someone following. Was Kaden really going to let me meet her? The last time I spoke to her, he'd fired me and then thrown me out of the outpost.

Yet here I was, walking to meet her with his full knowledge? It had to be a setup, even if it hadn't seemed like one. How could it not be?

I scanned the forest and caught sight of a glimmer in the distance. Not only was she meeting me this close, but she'd started a fire, as if she had nothing to worry about.

I walked into the clearing and, for the first time in my life, hesitated to hug her. I kept envisioning her standing there while I was taking a beating that nearly killed me.

Just. Standing. There. Not making a move toward me. I had to have imagined it, right? She couldn't have done that. Not her. I'd expect it from my father, my mother, but not Gram.

If she noticed my hesitation, it didn't show. She came right over and hugged me, as if nothing were amiss. I only hesitated another split second before I wrapped my arms around her.

"I was so worried about you." She was rubbing my back the way she had when I was a kid, and all the hurt of the last few weeks felt like it wanted to bubble up and choke me, make me melt into a puddle. How many years had I leaned on her? Cried to her? But that seemed like it might've been a different person now, and not just because she looked different.

I pulled back, trying to get a handle on my emotions but knowing I couldn't go another minute before clearing the air.

"Did you see me that night? Did you see it happening?" I asked, wiping at my face because, in spite of my trying, a few tears broke free.

"Why would you even think such a thing?" She wrapped her arms around me again, as if trying to reassure me.

"When I was lying there, I thought I saw you." How many hits had I taken to the head? It had been the blows. It had to be. She wouldn't have walked away from me like that.

"I wasn't there. I got word something was happening. I immediately reached out to someone who could contact Kaden. I knew he'd be able to get to you faster. I've been sick to death ever since." She pulled back, watching my face, as if to make sure I believed her.

I nodded. I had no reason not to. If she said she wasn't there, she couldn't have been. She wouldn't have left me like that. She was the only person who'd really loved me.

"I need to know what's going on. What's happening

with these people you're involved with?" I moved my hands closer to the fire, rubbing them, trying to stay calm until I was sure I shouldn't be.

No matter how much I told myself that Gram was a good person, that I really did know her, it was getting harder and harder to believe. I was letting Kaden get in my head, and he'd been the one who tossed me out. Gram had always been there for me, *except* maybe the night when I needed her the most. Did that erase a lifetime?

No. It was an illusion. It had *to have been.*

"Why? Has he told you something? We see things very differently. He's a stubborn man." She stood next to me in a body that was more femme fatale than grandmother, and I wasn't sure if I'd ever adjust.

"He says you and your people want to control Nowhere."

"We do, but did he tell you why?"

Even with this new voice, I could hear the change in her tone. When I was a child, it would've been after I'd cut her marigolds. But that was a childish game, and now we were both grown and the stakes were much larger.

"Because it's the hub of everything?" I asked. Calling that a "large stake" was probably a gross underestimation.

"He makes it sound like we want to have control. The problem is he wants things to continue as is. We're trying to protect it. If someone doesn't step in, others *will* come and take this place. There's rumblings all over the multiverse," she said, as if she were lecturing a small child.

But I wasn't a child anymore. I'd been through hell

and back in the last few months, and from the sounds of it, she was doing exactly what Kaden accused her of.

"So you *are* trying to take control of Nowhere?" I asked.

"Only to save it from a worse fate," she said, toning down the lecture and shifting into more of a conspirator's tone.

I was doing it again, letting Kaden twist my thoughts and opinions.

"What protected it all these years before?" I asked, trying to keep an open mind. There was never a wrong or right side. She'd taught me that.

"Him and his people, but they're a dying breed. There aren't enough of them left. He's clinging to what used to be instead of dealing with reality." She threw her hands up as she paced around the fire.

"Maybe you can all sit down and talk this out? If you both want the same thing—"

"We've tried that many times. He doesn't listen, and he's making things very difficult for all involved. You can't imagine how frustrating it is to try and try, but he won't hear us out." She circled back, stopping in front of me. "At some point I might need your help persuading him. No one wants a war. Maybe you can get through to him somehow?"

"He's his own person and, as you said, not very flexible." No. I wasn't getting dragged further into this mess. I shouldn't have come. Nothing good was coming out of this meeting. I'd wanted to come here to listen to her reassure me she'd never have left me there taking a beating.

I'd wanted to walk away with clarity, but instead I felt like I was trying to look through fogged glass.

"Women have a way," she said, sounding confident in what I could do.

I snapped my head toward her like a whip. "What are you saying?"

"Billie, you're a grown woman. Not a virginal child. Don't look so affronted. This is the way of the world. You use what you have."

"The way is to sleep with someone to get them to do your bidding? Even if he wanted to sleep with me—which he doesn't, trust me—that would not bring him to heel. He's not that type." Did she know him at all? They both seemed to have these crazy delusions of each other.

"Billie, you underestimate your appeal." She took my hands in hers, holding them and looking as if she were going to say something more. Lecture me on the way things worked. Instead, she stared at my hair.

"What? Do I have more blonde hair coming in or something?" I asked.

"Just a few," she said, smiling as she stared, transfixed on it. "Very unusual, but becoming."

My grandmother had touched my head, brushed my hair, so many times. Yet as she picked up a lock of my hair, I nearly jerked back. She was running her fingers over it almost reverently.

"Gram, stop. You're making me self-conscious of the weird coloring." I shifted my head, encouraging her to let go.

She seemed to be struggling to pull her eyes away

from my hair, but she finally forced her gaze to my face though struggled to keep it there, her eyes darting back to my hair repeatedly.

"I'll let you get back. I don't want to alarm Kaden with your being gone, but I'll be in touch again."

She went to hug me, and I returned it, swallowing back the urge to get away.

She pulled back first, as if she could feel the tension in my body, my desire to retreat, but then gripped my shoulders. "Billie, you know I love you, right? No matter what, that will never change."

A glimmer of my old gram showed in her eyes. I wanted to ask her again if she'd been there when I was beaten. I wanted to hear her say again she hadn't. Maybe if she told me enough, I'd believe it fully and shed this horrible dread once and for all.

"You need to get back, but I'll see you soon." She smiled and waved me off, as if eager to get on her way.

TWENTY-FOUR

No one was waiting for me at the door to the fortress. I walked back in as if nothing had happened.

Down the long main hallway, I saw the light from Kaden's office glowing. Was he waiting for me? If so, I'd rather have it out now than tomorrow over eggs and with witnesses.

I walked in, and he was standing behind the desk, looking over papers. If he'd followed me, he was putting on a convincing show that he'd been in here for quite a while.

He looked up. "Did you have a good meeting? I'm sure it was nice to see her again," he said.

He sounded like someone trying to go through the pleasantries of normal conversation, without a hint of an edge. With anyone else it would've felt natural, but this was Kaden. He didn't do pleasantries. He either had something to say or he didn't bother talking.

"I did." I held my tongue, refusing to chase that with

a list of everything said, or come up with fluff to throw him off. If he reneged on what he'd promised, if he turned around and threw me out, so be it. If this situation was going to work, he was going to have to trust me. I'd have to trust him as well.

I stood, waiting for him to turn on me, practically daring him to with my shoulders squared and a stance ready for battle.

"Was there something else you wanted?" he asked, as if he didn't know why I was waiting.

"No." He really wasn't going to question me? He wasn't telling me to get out or calling me a traitor? He was letting it go. He was attempting to trust me. Or so it seemed. I turned as if about to leave, but stalled for a few seconds. "Well, goodnight," I said, giving him one last opportunity to show his true colors.

"Goodnight," he said, sounding pleasant enough.

I nodded, walking out slow enough that I'd hear him if he tried to call me. I stalled by the foot of the stairs for another few minutes. I made my way upstairs, still waiting to hear him. I was in bed for a good twenty minutes before I began to truly believe he was going to try to trust me.

I padded upstairs barefoot with a blanket wrapped around my shoulders a half an hour later, craving the view of the swirling stars and the sounds of the ocean crashing.

Kaden had beaten me to the spot. He was reclined on the lounge, his arms behind his head, with only a pair of sweatpants on, oblivious to the cold.

His presence should've made me want to leave, or so logic would seem to say, and yet I motioned to the other lounge when he looked my way. He nodded, signaling he didn't mind the company, before returning his gaze upward.

I got comfortable, looking up at the stars swirling in the universes above, and realized some strange shift had occurred in our dynamic. I didn't know why. Couldn't say how. But it had.

When I met with Gram, I'd wanted to run away from her for reasons I couldn't make any sense of. My nerves had felt like they'd had a razor taken to them since then, and now, sitting here, the frayed ends were finally smoothing out.

But this place calmed me. It was why I'd come up here. It wasn't *him*, because it couldn't be him. I wouldn't let it be.

I was lying there, trying to convince myself that I was pulled in by the tranquility of the moment, when my body started to rebel. That strange heartburn feeling was happening inside my chest again, except with a little something extra this time. A heart palpitation combined with the shock of electricity, and that strange sense of warmth.

"Everything all right?" he asked, looking at the hand I'd laid on my chest.

"Just some burning and tingling. But that's normal, right? It's just settling in a bit?" I waited for his answer a little too intently.

"It is." His gaze flashed to my hair that seemed to be growing blonder by the day.

I nodded, wondering what he was thinking. It seemed as if there was something more to say, but then he went back to looking above, sipping a drink.

He still wasn't asking me anything about my meeting, and for some reason that made me want to speak about it, or parts of it. The part that haunted me most.

The part I couldn't get past.

"She confirmed she wasn't there the night of the beating," I said.

He didn't argue or try to convince me otherwise. Didn't say a word at all, and somehow that bothered me more, not that it should.

"It doesn't make sense that she'd be there and not help me." I glared his way, as if he'd given me an argument. Daring him to fight.

He stayed silent, still looking upward and relaxed.

"You don't believe it, so you should just say it," I said, pushing him to fight.

"Whether I believe she was there or not doesn't matter." He continued to sip his drink.

"Seriously? That's all you've got?" I turned so I was sitting facing him. I wasn't buying this act. Nope. "You don't want to fight about it anymore because it doesn't make any sense. Why would she call you but not help me if she was there? You have no idea what you're talking about. That's why you're not talking."

I should've stayed in my room. This was about as

relaxing as getting tossed around in a barrel for a few hours, and he wasn't even fighting back.

I spun back around, reclining again. Fighting with yourself got old quickly.

"Just so you know, I think Gram and her people are open to discussions," I said. "All they're doing is trying to protect this place."

"Not surprising that she'd put it like that," he said, and then fell silent again, not asking for more details.

"Maybe they feel like they're being persecuted when they want to do the right thing?" I asked, wondering why I couldn't shut up.

"Yes, noble souls, the whole lot of them. Surprising that they sneak around like they do, considering that they're so aboveboard in their intentions." He stood, walking to the door.

"Can't be bothered to argue that one either?" I asked. "What? Do you want to kick me out now?" I got up and walked over to him, daring him to show me the door.

"Is that what this was about? Testing me?" he asked, holding his ground. "Because no, I don't plan on kicking you out for the crime of being blind. I am going to leave you, though, so that I don't throw you off the balcony."

"Amusing," I said.

"I'm glad you think it's a joke." He walked out.

He was right. It didn't matter what he thought, only what I believed, and I was starting to not like where those beliefs were headed. I dropped back onto the lounge, hating that my unease had nothing to do with Kaden and everything to do with my meeting earlier.

Why couldn't I believe her when she said she hadn't been there? Why?

Cookie showed up ten minutes later and dropped into the lounge he'd abandoned.

"I guess no one can sleep tonight," I said.

"Nope. Got word people are going to be arriving soon. They'll probably stop in the town first and be here by tomorrow night." She was crossing her arms and shaking her head.

"How many are coming? Any idea?" I asked.

"No, but probably not as many as should, and then some who shouldn't. There's always some people that want to be nosey. A lot of people find it easier to leave than stand and fight."

"What if they aren't looking for a fight? The other side, that is?" I asked.

Cookie groaned. "Shit. You did talk to good old Gram again, huh?" She snorted and rolled her eyes.

"He told you?"

"More like warned us not to intervene if we saw you out there with her." Her tone made it clear she disagreed with that.

"He did?" He'd not only not interfered but helped me? That man would never cease to surprise me. He was like Jekyll and Hyde.

"Yes, he did. You try to sell Kaden this peace-talk crap?"

"We don't know that it's crap, and yes, I did."

"How'd that go?" She was laughing, and I hadn't even told her yet.

"He left. Said it was that or throw me off the balcony."

"You're lucky he left. That water is cold as hell when you get tossed. Sucks the air right out of your lungs." She shivered.

"You've been tossed over this balcony?"

"Just a few times." She shrugged, as if getting tossed from this distance into a violent ocean wasn't a big deal. "It was a thing one winter. I can't complain, because I started it by knocking Dice over. It became a running joke to sneak up on each other. It was all fun and games until Soleil complained about us tracking salt water through the halls. Kaden said we either had to stop or clean up after ourselves. Obviously we stopped."

"No one was worried about dying on cliffs?"

She jumped up and sat on the rail, looking over the edge and pointing. "The balcony overhangs. It's a clean drop. No big deal."

These people were insane. I was surrounded by crazy people.

TWENTY-FIVE

Cookie was looking over the pants and shirt laid out on the bed. She groaned, rubbing both hands over her face.

"What? It's a good outfit." It was black slacks and a white blouse with beading. It was sort of business on the bottom but with a little evening flair on top. How could I go wrong?

Cookie held up the offending wardrobe pieces as if this couldn't possibly be true. "For tonight?"

"Yes. For tonight." I plucked my clothing out of her hands and laid it flat again, before she wrinkled it. The place would be crawling with guests in a matter of hours, and I didn't want to have to worry about ironing anything.

"Good thing I was prepared for this." She walked to the door then went and stood in the hall, looking as if something or someone would be arriving soon.

"What are you doing?" Cookie standing on patrol for

something made me almost as worried as a horde showing up to beat me again. "Cookie?"

There was a rattling sound, and her face lit up. "Ah, here we go."

A minute later, Soleil rolled in a clothing rack, filled with dresses in every color of the rainbow.

Cookie grabbed the other end of the rack, helping her steer in. "This is what I'm talking about. Soleil, you are a lifesaver."

"What are those?" I asked. "I've got an outfit." No one needed saving right now.

Cookie looked at Soleil and then tilted her head toward my clothes on the bed. Soleil widened her eyes, and then they both laughed.

"It's a good outfit," I said.

"This is the opening night of the gathering. There are certain expectations," Soleil said. "People are going to show up looking a certain way, and they cannot see you in that."

Soleil and Cookie began laying out dresses on the bed, over the chairs, on the dressers. Everything I saw was shimmering or sheer, with crystals or metallic. I'd never worn anything close to what they'd chosen in my life.

They began walking around the room talking amongst themselves, glancing at me every so often.

"I think we need to steer clear of the reds," Soleil said. "Not her color."

They'd walk a few more steps, stand in front of a dress, and then continue on.

"What do you think of either that or that?" Cookie asked Soleil, pointing to different options.

"I think we should go with the white," Soleil said. Neither of them seemed to feel the need for my opinion.

"Not the silver? I was leaning toward the silver," Cookie said.

"No, definitely the white." Soleil reached forward, touching the nearly transparent fabric of the skirt.

"You want me to wear that?" The skirt was nearly sheer, and the rest of the dress looked like nothing more than a bodysuit.

"This is a typical outfit for the kind of event we're having," Cookie said. "And it's more cover than what you had on display at the tinker party."

The two of them laughed again.

"Fine. I'll wear the white one." I would have agreed to worse to not relive that particular memory.

"And you need to leave your hair down. No ugly ponytails," Cookie added.

Soleil nodded in agreement. "It's one thing to walk around here like that, when no one cares how you look, but it's not good."

"Fine." I needed to get these two separated and out of here. It was as if they fed off each other's pushiness.

"I've got to go get ready myself," Cookie said, but then didn't move. She glanced at Soleil, who nodded. It was as if Soleil was promising to make sure I was presentable. It seemed to do the trick, because Cookie left.

Soleil reached into her pocket and pulled out a

jewelry box. She opened it, revealing a huge teardrop diamond pendant. It was hanging from the thinnest platinum chain, so flimsy it was hard to see how that stone didn't break it.

"For tonight," she said, putting the box on the dresser as if it were an afterthought.

"I can't wear that." The thing was priceless, or at least a price I couldn't pay, so it might as well be. I'd be sick all night with that thing dangling from my neck.

"You have to wear something. If you don't, they'll all wonder why you have nothing. Then they'll start imagining a rift between you and Kaden. You can't have that." She wagged her finger at me.

"Do you have anything sturdier?"

She shot me a look that said I was absurd.

"I'm not going to be on the hook for that thing getting lost."

She waved a hand at me, saying it all, before she pushed the rack of clothes out of the room. So much for having another dress or jewelry option.

She wheeled past Kaden on her way out. He walked into the room, was already dressed in black evening clothes, hair perfect and looking every bit the man who would own a fortress.

"I need to prepare you for tonight."

If I heard anything else, I was going to be tempted to hide in my room. "Okay," I said, even though I didn't want to hear whatever he had to tell me.

"Watch every word you say. There's undoubtedly rumors going around. You have to expect anything you tell them to either be used against us or circulated. They're going to seek out any details they can that could give them an edge."

"I thought these people were possibly allies? At least not enemies." I hadn't been looking forward to the party before. Now it seemed like I'd be walking into an inquisition.

"They are possible allies, but they could easily flip to enemies. The one thing they're all coming to see is you, now that the rumors are running rampant."

"So what's safe to say?" I asked.

He rested a shoulder on the bedpost. "Hello, nice to meet you, and goodbye."

"In other words, don't talk."

This was going to be a long night. Depending on how long they stayed, a long week. Luckily I'd found out that there were cottages nearby that most of them would stay in. The upper floors of the fortress would still be a safe zone, as long as we didn't get any wanderers.

Was this why his relationship with Antoinette had lasted so long? This crowd probably wouldn't bother her. Me? I hadn't even met them and I was dreading it. No, I wasn't cut out for this, *at all*.

He was looking at my dress for tonight as if he were inspecting a ledger book. The numbers must've added up, because he nodded.

He turned to me. "If anyone asks about your hair, try to evade answering."

"Why? My hair is an issue, too?" What was the point

of meeting these people if I was going to be afraid to utter one word or walk into the room?

"It's better than broadcasting how fast you're changing," he said, as if nothing were amiss.

"My hair might be changing, but that's it. Nothing else has changed at all."

"The rest will follow." Something flickered in his eyes but was gone in a flash.

"Is there something more I should know?"

He took a moment, as if he were debating saying anything. "The longer it takes to develop, the stronger it tends to be. I believe the mark took better than we could've expected."

"But I'll never be fully one of you, right?" I took a seat on the bed. I'd already been overwhelmed before he walked in.

He crossed his arms, still leaning his shoulder on the post. "Even if you transition by ninety-nine percent, you'll never close that last bit, so there won't be an issue. You would need a catalyst to change completely."

"What if I could transition completely? Maybe that would be better." What if I could be as strong as Kaden? What would it feel like to not be scared anymore?

He straightened, his stare growing more intense. "It wouldn't be."

"Why not?" He seemed to be doing pretty well. Why would it be bad for me?

He walked to the other side of the room, looking out the window. "Because it wouldn't, so you need to let that go."

"In other words, you gave this thing to me but you don't want it to work that well. You want it to be just enough to help, but keep me at arm's length from turning into a true Kradix?" I knew how this went. He didn't think I was good enough to be one of his kind. What if he had to truly bring me into the fold? Treat me as an equal?

"Can we focus on tonight for now? There are other issues," he said.

Looked like I wasn't the only one on edge tonight.

"Sure. What else?" I got off the bed, finding things to busy myself with while he got the rest of it out of his system. If he noticed something off about my tone, or picked up on the fact that I was done speaking, he didn't remark upon it.

"Other men of my kind might be interested in you because of the marking. There aren't many females of my kind, and they'll sense you're transitioning. Be prepared for interest in that area."

My lips parted, but it took another few seconds for me to get out my big, whopping response. "Oh."

"It's wise to not encourage any interest."

Wait a second. Now I couldn't even flirt? Not that I'd been proficient at it anyway, but still. This night was getting worse and worse.

"What if I'm attracted to one of them?" I asked.

"Do you think this is the time to get a boyfriend?" he said with such arrogance that I couldn't help but push back.

"You can't time love," I replied in a sappy voice, just to dig in.

"I'm asking you to use caution. You don't have the best track record."

I'd thought I was done speaking to him before. Now? He was lucky I hadn't kicked him out of my room. "You want to talk about poor judgment in dating? I'm not the only one with a psychopath in my past, lest we forget Antoinette. She tried to have me killed."

"She made her own missteps." He shrugged.

"You're defending her?" I wanted to take those shrugging shoulders and push them out the window he was conveniently standing by.

"How is saying she had missteps defending her?"

He didn't want me to talk, totally transition, or do much of anything. Yet his ex-girlfriend almost got me killed, and that was a "misstep"?

"You know, let's just focus on tonight, as you said. I have to get ready."

He had the nerve to look irritated at me as he left. Yes, I was overreacting. It was all me.

TWENTY-SIX

Cookie was right—this was nothing like a tinker party. That had been pretend play. This was a whole different level.

The room turned and took me in all at once, and there were many more of them than I'd been prepared for. Surveying the crowd, I decided caving to Cookie and Soleil on the dress had been a smart move. This scene couldn't have been more different than the tinker gathering. Where that had been a mixture of casual and dressed, this was full-on "bring your best or don't show up at all." It wasn't just the level of dress, either—the women were all showing skin, as if flesh were the dressiest part of the night. The only things that rivaled the skin on display were the flashing jewels.

I walked forward as if I owned the room. My head was high and my spine was so rigid and straight that it was about to break under the strain. I'd survived hell, only to turn around and walk into the lion's den. Only this time, I refused to be the prey. I might not be the toughest one here, but I'd be damned if I showed it. I'd never curl into a ball and beg again. Next time someone tried to take me out, I'd fight like a demon with the wrath of the devil himself seeking vengeance.

Kaden was speaking to two men across the room. He gave me a slight nod, as if to say I had this. I lifted my chin, agreeing, grateful that he didn't cross the room to meet me. The people here needed to know I could hold my own. I didn't need a savior, nor did I want one.

Cookie was with another group in the corner. She rolled her eyes when she caught my gaze.

I smiled wide, showing her how well I was faking it. She responded with a pained grin of her own.

Dice and Connor were in a different spot, both talking to a single female, who looked to be smiling at both of them. They didn't even realize I'd arrived.

Right when I had to make a crucial decision on where to turn, who to approach, Kaden took his first step toward me. He held out his arm as we stood amidst the crowd, the center of attention. His gaze slowly ran the length of me before rising back to my face.

He hadn't said a word, and I still blushed like a tween.

"Shall I make introductions?" he asked.

"Let's get this over with."

He turned us to the right, and it was nice to have this particular choice taken out of my hands.

"Are all of these people the same as you?" I asked.

"Kradix? Some, but not all. The only thing all of

these people have in common is they have something they can contribute." Everyone was watching us, as if who we greeted and in what order was a huge tell.

He steered me toward a couple in the corner. "Larian and Viola, may I introduce you to Billie. They're from the Herecta district," Kaden added, as if I'd recognize that place."

They both nodded politely, but hardly gushed with friendliness.

We'd barely spoken before he was steering me in a new direction, to a new group. He rattled off more names, and there was another brief exchange, and then we headed on again. Kaden had to translate some of the greetings, as I couldn't understand a thing they said. After several more rounds, I realized this night would be most terrifying because of its tedium.

"So this is it?" I asked, in between one greeting and the next.

"Don't expect much. They don't know you. They aren't going to speak freely in front of you. Most of them won't speak freely with me, who they've known considerably longer."

"Are you going to make any progress?" I was beginning to find it doubtful.

"That remains to be seen. Just the amount who showed up plays in our favor."

I couldn't tell if he was truly happy about that because he had his game face on.

"Farrow came?" I asked, surprised to see the creepy

old guy off in the corner, looking my way. I'd gotten the impression he'd given up on fighting for anything.

I smiled in his direction, trying to not burn any bridges. I got a barely discernible nod in return. It was more than I expected.

"He's probably here to check on your progress," he said.

I grabbed a glass of wine off a passing tray as we headed toward another group.

We were intercepted by a younger man. He wasn't classically attractive, but there was a certain charm to his smile that was hard to ignore.

"Duncan. Glad you could make it. This is Billie," Kaden said.

"Yes, well, I'm happy that I came as well," Duncan replied, and then sent a pointed look in my direction, smiling slightly wider.

"Nice to meet you," I said.

Kaden followed his gaze, his game face cracking just slightly. Did he not like Duncan?

Dice neared, standing a handful of feet away. He caught Kaden's eye and nodded over to the side.

"I'll be back momentarily," Kaden said, and then looked at me.

I got the message loud and clear. "I'll be fine," I said, shooting him a look that replied, *I won't say anything stupid. I know my place well.*

Duncan grabbed another glass of wine off a tray and handed it to me. I hadn't realized I'd downed the last one.

"So how do you like the countryside?" he asked.

"It's quite beautiful," I said, keeping my answers short but pleasant. How could that possibly get me in trouble?

"You don't mind the remoteness of it?" A sandy lock of hair fell forward, lending to his charm somehow.

"Not when I look outside and see the beauty of the place. No, not at all." I could spend weeks up on the balcony and doubt I'd ever grow tired of it.

"You know, I heard Kaden had a beautiful house-guest, but considering some of his past company, I wasn't quite sure what to expect." He smirked in a knowing way. "I'm sure you knew Antoinette?"

Keep it pleasant and light. Don't reveal too much.

"Yes. She was..." No. There was no way I could utter something nice about that woman. It didn't matter what the stakes were or who he might repeat it to. It wasn't as if she didn't have a reputation.

"Yes, she was definitely that." He laughed.

A bell rang, and then the doors to the grand dining room opened.

"Would you allow me to escort you to dinner?" He held out his arm to me like some gentleman of old.

"Thank you."

I'd never been escorted anywhere. Even when I dated Johnny, we might've *gone* places, but that was it. There was definitely a difference.

There didn't appear to be set seating, and Duncan walked us over toward the center of the table. Kaden cut him off.

"Duncan, I wanted to speak to you during dinner. Come sit by the head of the table, will you?"

Without abruptly yanking my arm out of Duncan's, there was no choice but to be tugged along.

Duncan pulled out a chair next to his.

"Actually, I wanted to include Billie in this conversation as well. It might be easier if she takes this chair," Kaden said, pulling out the chair on the other side of his.

Duncan's fingers tightened on mine for a moment, his arm tensing before he said, "Of course. That makes sense."

"You could always fill me in later," I said, not sitting right away. After our talk earlier this evening, I'd planned on sitting with pretty much anyone but him.

"Wouldn't want you to miss any of the details," Kaden said.

It was either cause a scene or take the seat. I took it. There were enough eyes on me already.

Dinner started, and all those discussions, details, and plans Kaden had alluded to seemed to vanish. The only time he seemed to have something pressing to talk to Duncan about was when Duncan turned his attention on me.

The dinner was about as intriguing and enlightening as the cocktail hour had been. By the time people were making their goodbyes, I was struggling to hide my yawns.

The guests were slowly filing out, and Kaden was otherwise occupied by the people, when Duncan managed to catch me alone.

"It was very nice meeting you. I hope we can talk again?"

"That would be nice," I said, knowing this was the exact thing Kaden had told me not to do. Right now, I didn't care. If I could get a few minutes of pleasant company in this fiasco of a gathering? I'd take it.

"Forgive me if I'm being forward, but I won't be stepping on any toes, will I?" he asked, glancing toward Kaden, who was surrounded by departing guests at the door.

Kaden was looking right at me when I told Duncan, "No. Not at all."

TWENTY-SEVEN

I made my way to the upper balcony and dropped down onto a lounge, letting the swirling stars and universe lure me in with their beauty. I needed any distraction from today, and this place had a way of smoothing out the frayed nerves.

My peace lasted for a handful of minutes before Kaden strolled out onto the balcony. He walked over to the rail, looking out at the same view.

So much for peace. I would've been better off staying in my room, tossing and turning. I should get up and leave, but it would gall me if he drove me out, although this was his house, fortress, chunk of stone—whatever he wanted to call it. Common sense said leave, but stubbornness won out and kept my butt on the cushion.

"You know, I didn't think it was possible." He took a sip from his glass.

He was still drinking? He seemed *off*.

"Are you drunk?" I asked, knowing I was currently

sitting in a glass house, or at least one with an awful lot of windows. How many glasses of wine had I had? Couldn't forget the port I'd had to top it off and the second I'd brought to my room.

He lifted his glass, taking another sip and ignoring my question. "I didn't think it could happen. And then one day it did, I don't know what the hell to do about it, and you're certainly not helping the situation."

"What situation?" I asked. What was he talking about? It was probably drunken rambling, but it wasn't like he was falling over, or even stumbling.

"It's bad enough it happened. I won't be compounding the issue by consulting with you for advice."

"I think you should go to bed." And I definitely should, or at least leave. My relationship with Kaden was shakier than a raft in the ocean. If I didn't leave, someone would be drowning tonight, and I didn't doubt it would be me.

He turned to face me. His eyes took a long, slow path up my legs, over my hips and breasts, before resting on my mouth, and then finally my eyes. "You plan on going with me?"

No. He couldn't have meant it like *that*. He was drunk. We hated each other, or he at least hated me and I disliked him. At this point my beef was mostly because... where did he get off still being mad when he'd hardly been a saint? It might sound ridiculous, but people hated much for less.

"Now I *really* think you should go to bed." I got up,

taking my own advice before he remembered he hated me and things took a turn.

He pushed off the railing gracefully in spite of his obvious intoxication and walked slowly toward me. Self-preservation told me to leave, but the lure of what he might do was too strong to deny.

He was going to kiss me. If I stood there and waited, he would.

Instead of being sane, I stood there. I could tell myself I didn't want him, but when he was here, right within my grasp, I couldn't seem to deny the craving that overruled all saner thoughts. I wanted to taste him. That was all. Just to see what it was like.

It was curiosity with a touch of loneliness. I was young and healthy and hadn't had sex in...how long? He was an exceptionally virile man. No reason to make too much of it.

Kaden stopped so close that his shirt brushed against mine. He reached around my back, pulling me until I was flush against him. My hands landed flat on his chest from the suddenness of the motion.

"Not even a halfhearted attempt to push me away? No feigned denial?" he asked, his eyes shifting to my lips, hot with need.

I'd die before I admitted I wanted him. If he walked away, so be it.

"My little, naïve Billie. I never thought I'd be the one played, but here I am, feeling like I've lost control." He tilted his head ever so slightly closer and breathed deeply, as if he wanted to devour me.

He lifted his other hand, running it through my hair and caressing the base of my skull and then tugging my head back.

"Admit you want me."

My lips parted against my will, but I didn't say a word. I couldn't. Having this moment, this taste of him, was one thing. Saying those words? Building this into something else? Pretending it *could* be something? No. I'd take my taste, but I wouldn't play his games.

His stare was intense, and then he smiled, as if I'd admitted it without saying a word. Maybe it was the way my spine bent, pliant to his demands, or the way I licked my lips as I waited for what seemed like the inevitable. I didn't care. He was leaning closer, the smell of whiskey merging with wine as we both did something we might never have allowed ourselves to do sober.

He finally dipped his head and grazed the side of my neck. The feeling of his lips trailing over my sensitive skin was like the devil delivering me a slice of heaven. He continued his path to my ear, as my breathing became erratic. I wanted to grab his head in between my palms and kiss him.

His tongue traced the curve of my lobe before he said, "Tell me."

Damn him. He wouldn't even let me have this. I shoved at him and stepped away. He didn't try to stop me.

"Is that what this is? Are you trying to control me? Is that your game?"

I wanted to punch him. He didn't look too pleased with me, either.

"Maybe I am. Maybe it galls me that what *you* want and need seems to have such sway over me. I. Don't. Like. It." He turned his back on me, walking to the railing as if he couldn't wait for me to leave.

All I could seem to focus on was that he said he cared about what I wanted. Was that true?

"You do." It was sort of a strange revelation, especially since it didn't seem like he'd wanted to make it— even appeared to regret that revelation already.

I took a step toward him, torn between pushing him and running away. I should run. I knew I should.

"If that's true, if you do care about what I want, why did you do what you did? Why wouldn't you talk to me after you saw me with my grandmother? You turned your back on me like I was nothing." I hadn't brought this up in weeks. Hadn't talked about how he'd tried to evict me from Nowhere. Not once had I ever told him how low it had made me feel.

"Go. You did us both a favor." He barely glanced over his shoulder at me.

Rage burned in my veins. *This* was the man I hated. Right here, in front of me, dismissing me with dripping arrogance.

"Just when I think you aren't a total ass, you always turn around and prove me wrong. How anyone can maintain any humanity at all around you is a miracle."

He wouldn't even look at me as I yelled, and I *was* yelling.

"You know what? I hate you. I'll stay and do what I have to. I'll be civil and act the part in front of company, but don't think for a second I want to be anywhere near you."

He gripped the railing so tightly, it looked as if the metal might bend. His muscles tensed. I was getting to him, and it felt good. No, not just good. It felt absolutely brilliant.

"What? You don't like hearing how much I hate you? Maybe you shouldn't have thrown me out of your outpost like a vagrant."

"Don't say that again." He spun, rage in his eyes.

Looked like I'd poked the bear. I should be worried. Instead, excitement was fizzing through my veins. I'd been spinning out of control for weeks, and I was tired of being in this place alone. Tired of being the only one who cared. I wanted to unravel him, just to prove I wasn't standing alone and bereft. I didn't know why, and I wasn't going to think any deeper. I didn't *want* to.

"What? That I *hate* you?" I asked, poking him some more. "Well, I do, and I'll say it every single day if I want. What are you going to do about it?"

He was walking back toward me, his energy nearly exploding outward. His eyes were a little crazed.

He wasn't completely sober. Maybe if *I* hadn't drunk so much, I would've worried about that. As it was, neither of us were in our right minds.

We were standing toe to toe again. He was staring at me, as if dissecting every thought in my head, reading every little minutia from the way my breathing hitched to the way my lips parted.

"If you think you're going to get me to say I want you, dream on," I said.

"I don't need you to."

He grabbed me, pulling me against him. This was nothing like the slow seductiveness of a few minutes ago —it was an unleashing of pure want and need. It was a surge of desire so strong it was undeniable. He wrapped an arm around my waist, hoisting me higher, fitting me to him, as his other hand found my hair again. My toes barely grazed the floor as he pulled me close.

His mouth crashed over mine, demanding a response. If I could've kept my senses, I might've held back to spite him. There was something infuriating about melting into his arms after all that had gone on between us. Yet that was exactly what I did. I opened for him like he was a long-lost love I'd been yearning decades for. I couldn't get enough of his scent, his taste, the feel of him.

My thirst for him seemed to multiply his own until we were inseparable. My hands were gripping his shoulders and his mouth didn't leave mine; he only deepened the kiss. One hand angled my head, and his other had a handful of my backside as a growl reverberated through his chest.

I felt the lounge at the back of my legs, knowing exactly where this was heading, and I wanted it as much as he seemed to.

Then suddenly I slid down his body and had no idea why—until Cookie spoke.

"Sorry," she said. "Not trying to break up your little after-party, but you've got some rowdy guests downstairs. No one wants to deal with them, so we need you to handle it." She threw up her hands as if she were sorry to interrupt.

For some reason, I doubted that. Cookie wasn't the type to shy away from a little rowdiness.

Kaden glanced at me for a split second and then departed.

"You know, you're very lucky you have me." Cookie dropped onto one of the lounge chairs. "What would've happened if I didn't interrupt?" She was giving me one of her motherly looks, as if she'd saved my soul or something.

I walked over and took the lounge next to her. Maybe she *had* saved me. I wasn't sure what else would've stopped us. If she hadn't come, I might've been lying on this lounge with Kaden in between my legs. Or bent over the railing. Or...

I needed to stop thinking like this. What was wrong with me? I'd thought a kiss would make me feel better. Instead I was hotter for him than ever.

"It's stupid to get involved with him. I know. It had to be the wine." I was going to have to limit alcohol consumption around him.

"No!" She scowled and shook her head. "That's not what I'm saying. You two would be great together, but you can't hand over all the goods right away with him. You don't know him the way I do. I know he seems normal, but he's emotionally stunted. We've got to lead him along with breadcrumbs. You give him the whole cake and he's going to binge until he's sick. You gotta slow-play him."

I should've known she'd have some other plan up her sleeve. She always did. But her plan was emotional suicide.

"I'm not looking for a future with Kaden, not fast or slow. I don't want someone I have to trick into wanting me. Tonight was a mistake."

"Not a trick, and he already wants you. He's got his reasons for being the way he is, but want has nothing to do with it."

"And I've got mine, which is why we're better off separate."

TWENTY-EIGHT

The place was quiet, the breakfast crowd already departed, as I snuck my way downstairs in search of food.

Soleil must've been expecting me, as the buffet was still heaped full.

I grabbed a plate and loaded it up, happy to have the place to myself. It didn't last long. I turned to find Farrow staring at me.

He didn't say hello but continued to stare at me. It was as if I were an anomaly he couldn't quite figure out but was certain he didn't like.

I nodded in his direction, refusing to speak first. He'd probably be insulted that a lowly person like me wasn't genuflecting at the feet of his almightiness. That was one of the good things about having bigger issues—almighty whoever didn't make me shake in my boots.

I walked around him and sat down, digging into my eggs. I would've continued to ignore him until I was done with my breakfast, but he followed me.

He didn't sit. He hovered. Probably too stuffy to eat with the likes of me. I wished he was too good to be in the same room, but that didn't seem like it was a problem.

"Do you realize the gift you were given?" he asked. The lines on his face deepened in a most unbecoming manner.

I'd wondered if I was imagining his dislike before. Now I was certain his feelings toward me were what killed his appetite.

"Excuse me?" I asked. I knew exactly what he was talking about, but Kaden was the only one who had a right to know how I felt about it. This guy? The one who looked at me like I was worse than the dirt on the soles of his shoes? Yeah, he didn't deserve anything.

"You don't understand the depth of what's happening, do you?" He was leaning closer, almost as if he thought I was hard of hearing.

The way he was looking at me now, my remembering how strange the creepy old guys had acted the first time I met them, was sending little trickles of apprehension down my spine.

"Why don't you explain it to me, just to be sure." I put my fork down, finding myself more interested in what this man had to say than breakfast.

He leaned his hands on the table. "You think it's only use is protecting you, but you're wrong."

"Farrow, did you come to speak with me?" Kaden asked from the doorway. He was standing there, practically guarding us, and he knew exactly what he was doing.

Damn, that man could be a thorn in my side.

Farrow looked at Kaden and then me. "Perhaps another time," he said, pretty much confirming I was screwed.

Kaden didn't want me to know what had been about to be said, and now I wouldn't. Farrow left, but not before shooting me a look I didn't understand. Did he want me to find him later? Did he think I was psychic now too? I wasn't, because I had no idea what that meant.

Kaden walked into the room, and my awkwardness increased. I'd prepared myself to see him in a crowded room, with lots of people around. I'd come down late to breakfast specifically to avoid him after what happened last night.

He shut the door, locking it. He looked sober, but what was with the locked door? My palms grew sweaty, my mouth dry, and my heart was pounding out of my chest.

"I wanted to talk to you about last night," he said.

I nodded, drinking my coffee.

He leaned on the buffet, keeping a healthy distance between us. It was broadcasting what was coming before he even said a word. I'd had enough of these letdown conversations in the past to spot the signs.

"I'm sorry about last night. That shouldn't have happened. I drank more than I should've."

My face felt like it was a five-alarm fire. If he hadn't locked the door when he came in, or if my heart hadn't made a little leap when he had, maybe I wouldn't want to crawl under the table right now. If he hadn't blamed it on being drunk, as if he never would've touched me sober, maybe that would've softened the blow.

But he was drunk? That was what he blamed it on?

"It wasn't all your fault. I drank a little too much myself." If he was going to start throwing around drunken excuse apologies, then I would too. "I would've stopped it sooner otherwise."

His eyes narrowed a hair. Oh, so he didn't like being considered a mistake either? Yeah, it wasn't fun.

He didn't move. In fact, he kept leaning there, watching me.

"Was there something else? Because last night is already forgotten, as far as I'm concerned." I sipped my coffee and then forced myself to eat my eggs, even though my appetite had died a fast and unpleasant death this morning.

The only thing making any of this better was the way he seemed to grip the buffet a little tighter as I told him it was already forgotten.

"There is something else. I saw you talking to Duncan. You need to be cautious about getting too friendly."

There was a snapping noise, and he let go of the buffet. I could see a crack in the wood.

So he didn't want me, but it seemed he *really* didn't want me with Duncan.

"What if I like him?" I dropped that little bomb and then sipped my coffee again.

"You can't. You don't even know him." His voice nearly reverberated through the room.

I shrugged and waved. "Some people click like that."

"You shouldn't get involved with him. I won't let you mess up our situation for some meaningless flirting."

"Do you plan on being celibate as well? Or am I the only one with the rules?" I licked my lips, and he became transfixed on them.

"Have you seen me with anyone?"

"Recently? No, but that doesn't mean you aren't. And you won't be telling me what I can do, either. We're partners in this, and that's where it ends." I got up and walked over to the buffet where he was leaning, making a show of refilling my coffee when, in truth, I just wanted to see his reaction to my nearness. "If I want to kiss Duncan, sleep with Duncan, do all sorts of unmentionable things with Duncan, I will."

He spun fast. My back was to the buffet, and he had a hand resting on either side of me. His eyes were on my lips, but he dragged them upward. "This isn't a game. I can't have you getting distracted."

He wanted me, and I needed him to admit it without having an excuse to fall back on. I needed it for myself. The idea that I could want him this badly, with this burning need, and have him say he was drunk? It was one blow too many to an ego that had already taken too many hits.

He looked nearly feral. One more push, the right incentive, he might crack.

"Now, if you'll get out of my way, I have plans to line up for tonight," I said.

I could see him snap, and a wanton greed exploded

inside of me. He sank his hand into my hair, grasping a hank of it as he angled my head.

His length pressed into me, and if I'd doubted his attraction, there was the proof. His mouth collided with mine, and a hunger even stronger than last night seemed to take hold of us both.

Someone was rattling the door.

"Did you lock this?" Soleil asked someone, and then there was a jingling of keys.

Kaden broke the kiss. "I'm in here," he said loud enough to be heard on the other side of the door.

"Sorry," Soleil said, and then we heard the sound of steps retreating.

Kaden was still only a hair away from me, still looking at my lips, and I could see him struggling to rein his control in, until he finally took a step away.

"I'm sure you'd love to apologize again, but it'll have to wait. I have things to do before tonight," I said, then turned and left before he had the opportunity to walk out on me.

I WAS LOOKING over the dress I was supposed to wear tonight when I felt a strange pull to go downstairs. I opened the door, almost expecting someone to be there. The hall was empty, but the pull grew stronger, almost as if I were being physically tugged somewhere.

I walked farther down the hall. I should be fighting the pull, but I didn't want to.

This place is a fortress. No threat can make it in.

The thought popped into my head as if someone had planted it there. I continued walking and making my way toward whatever was calling me. The upper hall was empty, along with the stairs. There weren't even servants buzzing about. It was as if the place was suddenly abandoned except for Farrow standing beside the stairs that led to the cellar, alone and waiting.

I walked closer to him, noticing a strange symbiotic feeling between us.

I glanced around again, expecting someone to walk into the hall and ask what we were doing. No one did. Had he done something to repel them, while luring me? That should concern me, and yet it didn't.

"We need to speak in private," he said, his eyes resting on my hair.

I didn't like this man, nor did I trust him. Yet there was something about his stare, our connection, that had me motion toward the door to the cellar. He might be luring me somewhere private to kill me, and I didn't seem to worry about that either. I didn't feel drunk, but something wasn't working right with my brain.

Even as I knew it, I couldn't seem to drum up a care. I grabbed one of the lit torches along the wall and went below. Suddenly all the horror movies made sense. Sometimes people did do stupid shit, like I probably was right now.

I got downstairs and managed to keep my hold on the torch, my one weapon, as I turned toward him. Or he was allowing me to?

"What are you doing to me?" I asked.

"Compelling you because we need to speak. Do you truly realize what's happening to you?" he asked.

I nodded. "I'm becoming one of your kind."

"You're not only transitioning, but you're truly turning into one of us." He reached forward, touching my hair and then taking a moment to stare into my eyes, examining me.

"I don't feel any different," I said, allowing him liberties that I wouldn't have in my right mind.

"Slower grows stronger. Only the strongest of Kradix get black or platinum hair. Your hair is a reflection of the power building within you." He lifted a lock, staring at it as if it were the finest of jewels. "I'd nearly given up hope that it would happen. I thought he was wasting his power with you, but now this."

He dropped the lock of hair, and the haze of compliance lifted like a fog from my brain.

"Don't *ever* do that to me again," I said, shaking with rage now that I was in my right mind. I was torn between leaving him here and hitting him with the torch.

"Hear me out. I have something else important to tell you," he said, waiting patiently, as if he knew I would.

"Why don't you just force me to keep listening as you forced me to come?" I asked, my dislike of him shining as clear as his of me. I should have walked away, but felt a compulsion to hear him out. This one came from my gut, not a spell.

"I need you to have a clarity of mind for what I need to tell you. Our race is dying out. There are no strong females of our kind left. We are a race that needs balance to survive. There is no light without dark, no moon without the sun's reflection." He shook his head. "Do you know why I've aged? I gave some of what I am, the way Kaden did for you, over and over, and couldn't accomplish what he did accidentally.

"Now it's up to you. Will you become one of us and help change the course of our people, or will you take the gift he's given and squander it?"

"I can't transition completely," I said, repeating what Kaden had told me, slightly grateful at the moment. I didn't want to be the link that either held a race together or doomed them.

I was supposed to be an accountant. Not the savior of some race I'd never heard of! No. No. No. This was not the way my life was going to go.

"You can transition fully, but you'll need this." He dug into his pocket and pulled out a small sack. "It's a seed from the Life Tree that only grows in our most sacred places. If you eat this seed, and you want to transition, this will complete it. Don't tell anyone about it, not even Kaden. There aren't many."

"Why are you doing this? You hate me. Why would you want me as one of your kind?" I'd never take anything this man ever gave me. He was trying to trick me. I'd pop this thing and die. That made a lot more sense than his savior bullshit. "Kaden doesn't want me to transition. Why would I do it against his will when he's the one who gave me this gift in the first place? You're telling me I can save the world and he doesn't want me to?" I swung my arms out, as if encompassing everything.

"Not the world. Just us. And it doesn't matter what he wants. He gave you a gift that can help. You have the responsibility to do it."

He held the small sack out to me.

I didn't take it. He placed it on the ground in front of me.

"When one is given the choice to become a god, you do not walk away. Choose wisely." He bowed his head to me, as if I were already on the way to becoming the god he spoke of, and then left.

If he was speaking the truth, I didn't want this responsibility. Kaden had saved my life by giving me something crucial to him, and now he'd have less to try again. Maybe it wouldn't work with someone else. What if he ended up like Farrow after trying again and again?

I picked up the small sack, having no idea what to do with it.

TWENTY-NINE

I walked into the night's festivities with two people on top of my list to avoid: Farrow and Kaden.

I didn't want to hear anything else about my responsibilities to the Kradix race for at least a day. And Kaden? I wasn't ready to deal with anything about that relationship as of yet. I needed to make it through another night of the vultures first.

Neither seemed to be an issue, as Farrow appeared to be keeping his distance, along with Kaden. Cookie, Dice, and Connor were rotating in and out, as if by orders, and acting as buffers this evening. They seemed to swarm over whenever someone who must've been tagged as undesirable got too close. Duncan must be at the top of that list, because all three swarmed when he neared.

There was no getting rid of them, either. I had more success getting gum out of my hair than losing the three of them.

They went to a lot of trouble for nothing. I wasn't

looking to have much of a conversation with anyone. Between my encounter with Kaden this morning and Farrow in the afternoon, I was too raw. I was almost as sore emotionally as I had been physically after taking the beating that nearly killed me.

Even now at dinner, I was drinking a little harder than normal, but I craved some extra numbing if I were going to sit here with everyone, eat, laugh, and act merry.

The only salve to my wounds was that his edges seemed a lot sharper as well. If I was raw, he was brittle.

I refilled my glass of wine and downed it, glancing over at Kaden. He was tilting his glass back as well, not that I was trying to notice. It seemed the more I wanted to ignore him, the more glances I stole.

I needed to put him out of my mind, but that was nearly impossible the way he seemed to monopolize all the attention in the room. Even when I did manage to forget about him for a second, someone would call his name, laugh at his joke, vie for his attention.

The second course was coming out as I turned my attention toward the other end of the monstrous table, where Farrow sat. It seemed as if he couldn't stop looking at me, unless that was my own paranoia. It was as if his judgment of a decision I hadn't made yet was already suffocating me. He'd look my way, and I could feel it.

Luckily he became distracted as someone's assistant showed up, looking more frayed than I was. The assistant ran over to one of the people I'd been introduced to but couldn't name. The man whispered in the ear of the elegant woman in black.

She stood immediately and made her way to Kaden. She smiled as she talked, looking as if she were making her excuses to leave.

A minute later, murmurs of her leaving for an emergency at home trickled down the table. I'd barely taken a bite of the second course when another assistant appeared. They walked over to a couple, and it was a rinse and repeat, with them walking over to Kaden and then departing.

"Something weird is going on," Cookie whispered from one side.

"This is weird," Dice whispered on my other side.

I'd begun to think the same, but not knowing the parameters of how things worked here, my instinct for odd meant nothing.

I shot a glance down the table to where Kaden was sitting. He leaned back, sipping his wine. He glanced my way, and that single look told me he wasn't relaxed at all. He was waiting for things to go badly.

The arrival of the third assistant started a chain reaction. Two people at different ends of the table got up and made their excuses without the preemptive visit from their assistant. That turned into four, and then eight, until the entire party had emptied out in a mass exodus.

Duncan stopped beside me during the mayhem. "I'll reach out to you soon, but I need to get home and make sure everything is okay. Something is obviously afoot."

I nodded, not being able to disagree even if I couldn't figure out what the problem was.

Within fifteen minutes, the fortress had cleared out.

All the guests were gone but Farrow. He was readying to leave as well but had taken his time, waiting until Cookie, Dice, and Kaden were all in other places.

"You need to make a choice before there isn't one to be made," Farrow said, then left.

Kaden walked in the door, glancing with a curious eye at Farrow as he left, before coming to me. Dice, Connor, and Cookie all made their way over as well.

"They're all clearing out of the cottages," Dice said.

Cookie and Connor nodded.

"What just happened? How have we gone from a full dinner party to this?" I asked.

Kaden walked closer to the window, as if he were expecting something. "Someone stirred up trouble in a few different places until everyone here was afraid they were going to get hit. We're being sent a message about how vulnerable we are."

"Are we?" I asked, feeling like the place was growing chilly.

"I'm not sure," he said, watching something out the window before going to the front door and opening it.

There, on the night breeze, flapped the wings of another silver butterfly.

Kaden looked over at me, and then so did Cookie and the guys. I walked out onto the stoop, lifting my hand. The butterfly landed on my palm.

. . .

MEET me at the same place. We need to talk. It's urgent. We might be the only two who can fix this. Come alone. I guarantee your safety.

I WAS HOLDING the note as Kaden read it over my shoulder.

Cookie grabbed it, glancing at it before passing it along to Dice and Connor.

"Absolutely not," she said. "This is not safe." She tugged me back inside and shut the door, making it clear she'd blockade it with her body if needed.

"Whatever you think of my grandmother, she won't hurt me." That was about the only thing left I was sure of. Anything else was up for grabs.

"What if she uses you?" Cookie said.

Kaden wasn't signaling any emotion at all. Connor and Dice were staring at me skeptically. No one believed this was going to work out, and if I were to be honest, that included me. But she was still my grandmother, and I was going to meet her and hear her out.

"I have to meet her before things spin further out of control. If I can head off a war... If I can help everyone come to terms..."

Cookie waved her hands. "No, no, no. That would be crazy." She spun, looking at Kaden. "Why aren't you saying something? You can't *agree* with this."

I didn't want to look at Kaden, knowing he could physically stop me if he wanted. This had to be done. I was beginning to understand too much, to know where things were headed. I couldn't get Farrow's warnings out of my mind. I didn't want to be the last thing standing between the destruction of a race. If I could negotiate a truce with Gram and this Herrick person...

The silence dragged out, and I finally looked at Kaden.

"You want to do this?"

"Yes. I have to," I said, trying to sound a lot more convinced than I felt. In truth, it seemed like a long shot. But it might be the only shot before a possible war.

He took in a deep breath before he nodded. He finally said, "Then you have to go."

"Thank you," I said, knowing how much more difficult he could've made this.

"This is crazy!" Cookie said. "Are you both out of your minds?"

"It's not crazy," Kaden told her. "I marked her. They can't sever that bond unless she and I are both willing. Even if they tried to take her, which would be very difficult, I'd be able to find her."

Connor whistled.

Dice said, "It's taken that well?"

Even Cookie was stunned into silence for a few seconds before she gasped. "The blonde hair..."

Kaden nodded.

"When I went to meet Gram that night, had it taken effect enough then?" I asked.

"I never imagined it was going to be a factor." The line of muscle that ran from his shoulder to his neck tensed the tiniest bit, and the answer was clear even before he spoke. It was strange how well I was beginning to know this man.

"It did," I said, making it easy for him.

How many other things were going to happen? I'd ask, but not now. It was going to have to wait. I had a meeting with Gram to get to.

GRAM WAS WAITING in the same place as last time, standing beside the fire.

"I knew you'd come," she said, smiling and taking me in a hug.

A few months ago, before I'd learned about Nowhere, before any of this happened, I would've let her hug me as long as she wanted to.

But I pulled out of her embrace. "What's going on? Are your people getting ready to make a move on Kaden and Nowhere? Did they kill someone named Larken?"

"Things are escalating quicker than I expected. You—"

"Oh no, they did. They, right? Not you. Tell me it wasn't you." I didn't know this woman in front of me. I'd tried to convince myself it was only the way she looked that was different, but she had changed since I'd known her in Nowhere. Or maybe she'd always been like this.

"It's him or you. You have to help me deliver him to them, or they'll kill you instead. They don't want you together." She grabbed my shoulders, trying to impart the importance.

I pulled away from her. "Why is that a problem for them?"

"Because it makes him stronger. Herrick isn't someone you can go against. You need to give him what he wants." She reached for me again.

"What if I won't help you or him?" I backed up as she followed me, looking crazed.

"That's your only option."

"No, I don't think it is."

She stopped chasing, looking almost frightening as determination came into her eyes. "I won't fight them, not even for you. I can't. It'll mean death for both of us. Herrick is stronger than you realize, and he wants Nowhere. He gets what he wants. He's more ruthless than that man of yours. And my own granddaughter, turning against me for some man you just met."

"That's not what I'm doing. It's not for a man. I'm doing what I think is right."

"You mean like taking care of your mother? How good did that feel? You need to save yourself by handing him over."

"I'm not doing it. I won't."

She looked over my shoulder and nodded. My stomach dropped, and I went cold in a flash.

She'd set me up. This was a trap.

I looked behind me, and there were people walking out of the forest in my direction.

"Gram, who are they? What did you do?"

"I'm doing what's best for you. I'm protecting you. It

was this or death, and I won't let you die." She looked behind me and nodded.

I spun, getting ready to fight, or run, or anything I could do.

I didn't make it more than a few feet before both my arms were grabbed.

"We're going to have to knock you out now. It's for the best. I know he's got you magically linked to this place, and if you're awake, what we have to do to cross you is going to be too painful to bear."

"Don't do this to me. Please, Gram. I'm begging you not to do this. Let's talk this out and see if—"

"Billie, you need to trust me. This is the way it has to be."

Someone hit me over the head. I fell to the ground.

THIRTY

I woke up in a room with a luxurious bed, expensive furnishings, and lush drapes. There was a pile of books and a reading light on the nightstand. It might be deemed luxurious if not for the bars on the window. It was a glorified jail cell.

I got up, feeling sluggish, as if I had the worst flu imaginable, but that didn't stop me. I dragged a chair to the window and opened it. There was a sun shining and rolling hills. I wasn't in Nowhere anymore. Kaden had said we'd be connected, that he could find me, but here? I didn't know where I was. There'd surely be a limit to his ability to track me.

I opened the window and grabbed the bars, trying to rattle them. They weren't going anywhere, unless I had a blowtorch or a backhoe.

The door swung open and Gram walked in. "They said you were up." She smiled at me, watching as I climbed down from the window.

"What have you done?"

"You should thank me for what I've done. I'm keeping you alive. It's the only way. It was you or him, and I'm not letting it be you."

"I don't want to be here. You need to get me out of here."

"That's not going to happen."

I went to cross the room, planning on grabbing her shoulders and shaking some sense into her if I needed. After all, this wasn't my frail gram anymore, but a femme fatale that had kidnapped me.

Only problem with that plan was I couldn't get to her. I had to stop and lean on the bed before I made it to where she stood.

"You need to conserve your energy," Gram said.

"What's wrong with me?"

"It's that." She pointed at the thin metal chain around my wrist. "We need to suppress what you're becoming, just until we get things settled. Then Herrick will take it off."

I grabbed at the chain on my wrist that didn't have a clasp. It was so slight it was barely visible, and yet I couldn't budge it.

"It was the only way we could get you out of there. Otherwise your bond with him would've caused us a problem."

"I'm not staying here. You have to let me out."

"You can try, but there are guards at the door. You'll never get past them. Now you need to listen to me so I can help you."

"Why? Why is it me or him?"

She walked over and picked up a lock of my hair. It was the first time in my life that I didn't want her to touch me.

"This is why." She stared at my hair as if it were a different entity. "You're becoming one of them, and Herrick will never allow you to be alive and with *him*."

I wouldn't tell her that what Kaden had done for me made him weaker. Not now, after what I'd seen.

"I'm not strong, so how is that possible?" I asked, hoping my doubts about that didn't show in my eyes. All I could think of was what Farrow had said.

"You're still a horrible liar, Billie. Now, Herrick is here, and he wants to meet you. You need to watch what you say. Just because you're here doesn't guarantee that he won't change his mind."

"And kill me?" I asked, watching as she walked over to a pile of clothing on a table.

"Yes." She held up a black, slinky dress with slits up to the hip on both sides. "He likes beautiful women, so it won't hurt for you to look your best. He expects to see you in an hour."

"Gram, what happens if they try to kill me?"

Our eyes met, and for the first time, I saw fear. She didn't know what she was doing. She'd dragged me into a mess and had no idea how to get me out. I might be walking to my death in an hour, and with the chain on my wrist, how weak I was feeling, I didn't have any faith left that my bond with Kaden would keep me alive.

"It'll work out," she said, shrugging off the emotion I'd already seen.

She had no idea if it would work out. She was flying blind and dragging me along with her into a hell of a mess, and now might get me killed.

Gram looked as if she were attempting to smile but failed. She patted me on the arm. "I'll send someone to help you get ready and be back for you soon."

She left me, and I looked about the room, knowing I was probably being monitored somehow. I pretended I was rubbing my chest, as if I were sick, while I tried to feel the burning-pulsing connection I had with Kaden. It was still there, but barely.

I LOOKED at the dress mindlessly, as my thoughts were already consumed elsewhere. The reality of the situation was finally becoming clear. She *had* been there the night I was attacked. She might've called Kaden, but if he hadn't come? She'd have left me to die.

If things had been reversed, I would've taken the beating with her, and risked death to save her. That didn't go both ways. She'd save me—up until a point.

My entire life, I'd looked to her. I'd counted on her. I would've given my life for her. I wanted to crawl onto the bed and sob my heart out for the perceived loss of something I'd never really had, but I wanted to survive more. That meant showing no more weaknesses that they could use. If I needed to look good in order to survive, I'd do it. I'd do whatever I had to in order to get out of here.

Two women with pure white skin, lavender hair, and silver eyes came in and nodded toward me but didn't seem to want to make eye contact.

They both had what appeared to be brands on their cheeks, making me think they were slaves of some sort. They weren't going to be any help. They couldn't help themselves.

They dressed me and then brushed out my hair and applied makeup. I sat there as they finished, thinking of all the wasted time at Kaden's. I should've tried harder to learn, to fight. I wasn't ready for this. Not even close. I might have power inside me, but I didn't know how to use it.

The women left, and I scanned the room again, looking for anything that could be used as a weapon. The heat of Kaden's mark in my chest warmed slightly, as if he were somehow reaching out to me from afar.

It was a naïve notion. I'd left the fortress to meet my grandmother and never returned. What were the odds he'd think I'd been dragged away against my will? Especially as I'd defended her right until the last moment, in spite of my fears.

My grandmother returned all too soon, and I stood in front of her as she took in my appearance.

"Herrick is waiting."

She took my arm in hers. I resisted the urge to pull away. It wouldn't do me any good to have her know my inner feelings right now. She was the only quasi-ally I had, and there was no room to alienate anyone at this point.

We walked out into the hall, and four guards were waiting, complete with armor. They fell into step with us as we walked, and I again held back, not asking why they'd imagine I needed this kind of guard.

The place might be larger than the fortress, but with stone walls instead of polished black stone. My grandmother didn't say much as we walked. I didn't ask a thing, positive every word would be reported back to Herrick.

My grandmother dropped her grasp on my arm, another reminder of how badly I'd misjudged our relationship, as we entered a main hall that was brimming with potted marigolds. The place was bustling with people eating. Every single set of eyes turned toward me as we walked, and none of them appeared friendly. Finding allies here was going to be hard to impossible.

Herrick was a large man, with thick red hair, sitting at the center of the dais on a throne of twisted, barbed metal. He stood, proving to be even larger than I'd imagined.

"This is her?" he asked.

"Yes," my grandmother said.

His eyes took a long, slow trip over every inch of me, stalling longer at certain parts. When he was finished, he nodded approvingly in my grandmother's direction.

My stomach turned as she beamed in response.

"How long have you been changing for?" he asked me. "What can you do?"

I clenched my hands together, trying to think of an answer that wouldn't give anything away. It was hard to do when you didn't know what would be helpful.

"I was a tinker. I still am, I—"

"No," he barked, filling the hall with his booming voice. "When did he mark you? How long have you been changing into one of them?"

I touched my hair, knowing it was a dead giveaway. Since I wasn't sure what answer would serve me better, I said, "A few weeks."

"Do you have any of their powers?" he asked. "Before you answer, know there's ways you can be tested."

"Not that I've been able to access yet." Every question was making me feel more desperate. Every glance around the room, searching for a glimpse of compassion, nailed home how bad this situation was.

He stared at me, as if assessing my honesty.

"I'll keep her for a bit, as long as she seems useful and doesn't play any games," he said to my grandmother.

He tilted his head, and the guards who'd accompanied me grabbed an arm each to march me back to my room.

———

I WAS LYING on the bed, looking at the dents I'd made with my nail on the wood of the table beside me. Seven days I'd been here, and each one had felt worse than the last.

I'd started to wonder if they were drugging me in addition to whatever the chain was doing, or plain old poisoning me. But why drag it out? If they wanted me dead, they could kill me easily at this point. The burning I used to feel in my chest was long gone.

There was a knock at the door, and Gram walked in. She walked over to the bed, laying her hand on my head. If I had the strength, I would've knocked it off. So many things I'd do differently. I was so sure of her that I hadn't wanted to hear anything else. I'd let her convince me she hadn't been there for my beating.

"How's my girl doing?" she asked, as if we were the same as we had been years ago.

"There's something wrong. Something is making me sicker every day. Whatever you're doing, you need to stop it, or I'm going to die." Even as I told her, my faith that she'd help me was gone. The only reason I said anything was because I'd promised myself that I wouldn't quit, no matter what.

"No, no, don't talk like that," she said, again running her hand over my head.

A tear drifted down my cheek.

"Don't cry, Billie. It'll be okay. Everything will be fixed soon," she said, sounding like a distant echo of the Gram I'd thought I knew.

She thought I was crying because I was ill, but they were tears of frustration. I wanted to rip her hands off me, but I was too weak. I wanted to scream my anger, but she was the only one who still might help me. I swallowed back more tears, not wanting her to have any reason to stay here with me.

"The chain will come off. As soon as Herrick strikes a deal, it'll be worked out."

"It's killing me," I said matter-of-factly, so there would be no delusions about it.

"You're stronger than you know. You'll be okay for a little while longer."

A little while? How many days did I have left before I *wasn't* okay?

She sat on the edge of the bed, as if she were going to get settled in.

"You should go," I said. "It's for the best if Herrick doesn't think your loyalties are torn."

"You're right. Staying in here too long could be an issue for us. See? Now you're getting the hang of things," she said, smiling and patting my arm.

I returned the smile, only caring that she left.

THIRTY-ONE

The knock came as the sun was setting, and the women entered.

"Time to get ready," they said as they walked over and helped me out of the bed where I spent all my time.

"I'm dying," I said.

"I'm sure things will work out soon enough," one of them said, but neither of them would meet my stare.

"If I do, and someone comes here to avenge me, please tell him I'm sorry and that I made a mistake," I said. "Tell him I cared for him."

I wasn't planning on dying, but as of this moment, I didn't see how I'd be escaping. If I did, I needed to know my message would be delivered.

Neither of them spoke.

"You don't have to say anything. But please do this for me."

One slave grabbed my hand and gave it the briefest of

squeezes. I didn't dare even thank her, or acknowledge what she did, in case her companion betrayed her.

They did my hair and makeup, fixing me like I was a lifeless doll. I was wearing the latest dress supplied for me. This time it was sheer black and fitted, with beading over the bare minimum, claiming the smallest amount of modesty possible.

My guards escorted me down the hall, each of them supporting some of my weight.

"How are you all this evening?" I asked, as I did every night.

They ignored me, as they usually did. I'd ask again tomorrow, and the night after that, and continue until I found a chink in the armor, a path forward, or was dead.

And after I was escorted back to my room tonight, I'd lie in my bed and focus on the warmth in my chest, focus on growing that back to what it had once been, fueling it, building it. At some point, I'd find an opportunity, and I'd be ready when it presented itself.

My guards escorted me into the great hall, and my arrival got less attention than it initially had. They placed me in a seat beside Herrick, where I would watch him eat and drink his dinner, until I would be brought back to my room again and fed with help.

Herrick looked me over, and then went back to eating. That was the most attention he would pay me all night. There had to be a purpose to this, but it was never spoken of, at least in front of me.

My grandmother sat at the end of the long table, but

we hadn't spoken since I'd warned her off coming to my room. Now I merely glanced at her across the hall.

The hours rolled by, and instead of being escorted out after dinner, I was left to sit there through dessert, and then more wine. Slowly the hall emptied out, and yet I remained.

The only ones left were a handful of Herrick's top people at the dais, including my grandmother at the very end of the table. She was making a concerted effort to not look my way tonight, but I caught her glancing at me every so often.

Something was coming.

Fifteen minutes later, my grandmother got up and approached Herrick. "You will uphold your promise?"

He looked at her as if she were a slug that just crawled out of the muck. "I said I would consider it. Don't press me. You won't like the outcome."

"I'm sorry." She nodded rapidly, taking a step back, then returned to her chair with hurried steps, as if hoping he'd forget she'd said anything. Once again I was reminded of the night of the beating. How naïve I'd truly been.

The clock kept ticking by. Herrick continued to drink as we all waited for something.

A guard stepped inside the door, approaching the dais. "He's here."

"Alone?" Herrick asked.

"Yes, sir."

"Then bring him in," Herrick said, sounding almost gleeful. It wasn't a tone the large man typically used.

I stared at the door, gripping the arms of my chair, terrified I'd see Kaden walking in, alone. This was a trap. It had to be.

Before anyone entered, Herrick reached over and pulled me in front of him. The hulking man wrapped an arm around my torso so tight it was like a vise. If he squeezed any harder, I wouldn't be able to breathe.

And then there he was, and it took everything left in me not to cry. I didn't want to see him die.

Kaden walked in looking like a dark prince, dressed in black with a cloak flowing around him. I'd thought I'd seen Kaden angry before, but the pure, cold rage in his gaze now was chilling. All I wanted to do was scream at him to get out of this place, away from these people. Tell him I was so wrong.

"Kaden. It's been a while," Herrick said, pulling me back toward his chest so I was partially on his lap.

Kaden took another step toward us, eyeing me and my captor.

"Take another step toward her and I'll break her neck, Kradix." Herrick's other hand wrapped around my neck.

"What do you want?" Kaden growled.

"What do you think? We've got your girl. It's time to give up."

"I'm not his girl. He doesn't care about me." I stared at Kaden, hoping he knew me well enough to read my thoughts. I wanted to scream: *Go. Save yourself.*

Herrick ignored me.

"What do you want?" Kaden asked.

"You know what I want. Control of Nowhere," Herrick said, standing, dangling my body in front of him as he carried me with him.

Kaden scoffed, averting his gaze from me and forcing his eyes to look only at Herrick. "You overestimate me. I can't single-handedly give you Nowhere. I'm not the only one who doesn't want you to take control."

"You mean the group you're gathering? They'll roll over as soon as you tell them to, and we all know it."

Herrick was right. Even I knew it. Kaden was the only one capable of holding any of that group together, if it were possible at all.

"I know no such thing," Kaden said.

"After they hear what happened here, what you agreed to, they will. You don't have a choice if you want her alive. Do what I want and you get her back. You can even stay in Nowhere. No one will bother either of you. We won't need to." Herrick laughed.

"Then I'll die, because he won't give up Nowhere for me," I said. I'd go out fighting until the last breath and accept the cost. My life wasn't worth that place.

Everyone was quiet. I looked at Kaden. "You need to leave," I said, meaning it, even as I knew it sealed my fate. As soon as he walked out of this room, I was dead. I'd fight with whatever I had left, but I was a lost cause if I'd ever seen one.

Kaden wasn't walking out, though. He was standing there, staring at me.

"What do you want to seal the deal?" he asked.

"You know what I want," Herrick replied.

I could feel him tense, his breathing quicken.

"Don't—" My words were choked off by Herrick's grasp on my throat.

"You hurt her, you get nothing," Kaden said through a clenched jaw.

The pressure on my neck eased, and I dragged in a deep breath.

Herrick nodded to his guards. Minutes later, they carried in some sort of strange, limp octopus-looking thing. Kaden unbuttoned his shirt as a guard waited beside him with one of the limbs of the animal.

"You'll have to bring her closer to me if you want this to work," Kaden said.

"Not acceptable," Herrick replied.

"She's been marked by me. I can't drain what you want without her close and making flesh-to-flesh contact —unless you know how Kradixes work better than I do? We're connected."

Herrick lifted my arm. "That's been taken care of."

"That mutes our connection. Nothing else. If it didn't, she'd be dead already." Kaden stared at the chain on my wrist as if he wanted to rip someone into shreds.

"Prove it," Herrick yelled.

"Take it off and you'll see yourself."

"Bring her to him, but stay close." Herrick held me out to his guards.

They approached me, grabbed an arm each, and then marched me closer to Kaden. My feet barely grazed the floor.

Kaden closed the remaining distance, wrapping an arm around my waist.

"Don't do it," I whispered. "Whatever happens happens, but don't do this. Don't give him what I think you're going to. Please don't." Tears began to roll down my cheeks in spite of my promising myself I wouldn't cry again in front of any of these people.

"What is she saying? No talking," Herrick yelled from his throne, but keeping his distance.

"I don't care. I'm just going to do it," Kaden said, repeating almost exactly what I'd said to him the day in the cellar before he marked me. He had a plan, and I was pretty sure it wasn't going to be pleasant for anyone.

Kaden looked to the guard holding the octopus thing. "I'll need to try to connect to her mark. Once I do, when I nod, you can place the sucker on me and take what you want."

The guards kept a hold of my arms as Kaden embraced me with both arms.

"You need to be open. This is it," he said in my ear, and then there was a boom, as if an explosion went off, with us at its core. We were suddenly in the center of a tornado, and it felt like one wrong move and we'd be torn apart. The guards were ripped from me, and things were flowing all around. I could hear screaming and yelling in the distance. The energy flowing around us was palpable, almost as if we were in the center of Chaos, but not.

The dread I'd come to associate with it wasn't there.

All I felt was *Kaden*.

He was slowly moving with me, step by step,

toward the door. I could see through the haze of wind and debris as people tried to reach us but were unable to.

"They're shutting the doors," I yelled, not sure he could hear me over the noise of the wind surrounding us.

He didn't respond, but as we got closer, the doors quickly flew off. Kaden continued to move us out of the building as we remained in the center of the cyclone.

He grabbed my wrist with the chain and brought it to his mouth. There was a graze of something sharp, and then the chain fell to the ground. It felt as if a thousand cinder blocks were lifted off me.

The cyclone around us didn't stop until we were fifty feet or so from the castle, and there, a lone soul was following us.

My grandmother.

Kaden was standing beside me, looking almost as weak as the day he'd marked me, as she rushed toward us, seeming to be the only one who could. Behind her, the door to the castle was barricaded by debris.

"Billie, Herrick won't quit. He didn't win. You need to come with me. I'll make all the excuses. I'll take some of the blame and tell them I misled you and that you didn't understand what was going on. That should be enough to smooth the waters, but the game is over. You need to grab him while he's weak and come with me. It'll prove your loyalty."

She moved to grab Kaden, and I took a step in front of him.

"No. You're not taking him anywhere."

"What are you missing here? There isn't a choice. You have to come with me."

"I don't want what you want, or what your people want. We're leaving." I wrapped an arm around Kaden, dragging him a step back with me.

I took another step back, my skin covered in goose-flesh as the possibilities of where this would end grew. Another step back and she followed me, her approach keeping pace with my retreat.

"Gram, I'm not coming with you."

"Billie, you have to. I'm not giving you a choice."

"And then what? Use me? No. You're not controlling me. No one is."

Her hands were on me, and suddenly it felt like she was doing the same thing the chain had done.

Kaden surged forward with what appeared to be his last burst of energy, about to pull her off me, when I shoved her.

The second I did, it was as if all that power Kaden had given me sprang to life.

I barely registered what was happening. The moves Kaden had been trying to drill into me over and over again set my body in motion. Instead of my just pushing her off, a burst of energy leapt out of my hands and she went flying ten feet away before falling limp on the ground.

I ran to where my grandmother was lying on the ground. She wasn't breathing. Her chest wasn't moving.

Kaden was beside me a moment later. "We have to get out of here. They'll get through my barricade soon."

I knelt there, numb. This was the second time I'd seen my grandmother dead, and it was worse than the first time. If someone had told me then it could be more painful, I wouldn't have believed them. But I'd never imagined I'd be the one to kill her.

Kaden grabbed me. "We have to go."

"I can't leave her here like this."

"She's gone, and they'll want to do the same to you next."

There was a loud crashing noise as they blasted through the barricade Kaden's magic had formed.

I was too numb to think clearly, but I wouldn't go back in there. My legs barely moved as he grabbed my arm, pulling me to him.

"We need to get out of here, and I need some of your strength to do it. I'm too weak." He wrapped his arms around me. "You need to trust me, let me in, or we're going to die."

"Do it." I could feel his power joining with the piece of me deep inside, the thing he'd given me that had finally woken up.

And then there was another storm brewing around us, but this time it didn't only feel like him. It felt like me as well.

It carried us up on a current of air. We didn't have wings, but we were flying.

THIRTY-TWO

It was an hour or so later when our feet touched the ground at the opening of a cave, halfway up a mountain.

"We need to stop for the night," Kaden said. "We can't use any of the established openings to Nowhere to leave because they'll be watching them. I can't force one open here, either. They'll sense it too fast and be waiting for it."

"Then how are we going to leave this place?"

"Hank is going to be waiting for us in six hours. He had instructions to be at a different location every day for the next month."

Kaden held my hand as we walked into the dark cave. He rustled around with something, and then a small blue light appeared. He walked us farther back and placed the light on the ground.

"We can't risk anything brighter because they'll be out looking for us."

I knelt, clinging to its small circle of light, which

seemed to stop as if there was an invisible wall around it so it wouldn't bleed out of the cave opening.

He brought a bag over and dug things out, obviously having scoped this place out ahead of time. He handed me a canteen.

"Thanks," I said before taking a swig of water. I waved off the jerky. My appetite was well and truly gone.

He was watching me, even as he pretended not to.

"Try to get some rest. There'll be time to talk when we get back," he said, as if he could feel my aversion to speaking at the moment.

I nodded and curled onto my side, staring at the light, afraid of the images my mind would produce if I closed them. It didn't take long to realize it didn't matter, light or dark. All I could see was her body lying there.

Cookie had told me not to go. Kaden hadn't wanted me to either. I'd been the one to meet her, in spite of all the warnings. Of all the horrors I'd thought to see, feared, the one I'd executed was the worst.

I turned on my other side, wanting the darkness to hide the despair that was written all over my face. I curled up on my side.

A shiver shot down my body as my brain tried to relay the message to the rest of me that disaster had struck. Then another, until I was lying there shaking.

Kaden sat down beside me and pulled me onto his lap. I didn't even fight, craving the warmth.

He held tight, cradling my body to his.

"You're in shock. Being cold on top of it will make it worse. We still need to get back," he said.

Hard. Cold. Logic. I could handle that. It wasn't pity or sympathy or some emotion that would dredge up *more* emotion. It was survival.

He wrapped his cloak around me as I lay there, trying not to think. We had to get back home. That was all that I could focus on at the moment. Nothing else. Nothing. *Don't let thoughts intrude.* I had to keep it together until we got back.

I shuddered again, as if my body were fighting against the idea of anything besides total loss of control. My soul wanted its piece of flesh for the crime I'd committed.

Kaden ran a hand over my hair and sang softly. It wasn't just any song. It was the song that had been stuck in my head ever since the beating. It was the song that had haunted me for weeks. It was his song. He was where I'd heard it. He sang in a strange language I didn't recognize, and some of the tension eased from my body, as if it held some special magic.

"What is that song?" I asked only after he'd paused.

"It's an ancient Kradix song," he said, running his hand over my back.

"What do the words mean?"

"There isn't a perfect translation, but it's something along the lines of 'calm your heart, still your soul, all will be well in the end.'"

"It's like a lullaby or something?" I asked.

"Yes, something like that. It's been passed down for longer than I can remember." He went back to softly singing.

How many times had he sung it to me? I'd thought he

abandoned me after he brought me to his house, but he must've sat with me, singing this song to try to calm me. How many times? It couldn't have been only once or twice. It felt as if that song had been carved into my soul.

I WOKE up in a bubble of warmth. The sickness that had been dragging me down since that chain was placed on my wrist was now gone completely.

Kaden was still holding me.

"It's time to leave."

I sat up, stretching, realizing I'd had his cloak wrapped around me. I stood, handing it back to him.

"You keep it. I'm fine. How do you feel?" he asked, looking me over in the rays of dawn light that trickled into the cave.

"I'm okay," I said, trying to sound as if I was, even if I still couldn't get the picture of my grandmother lying there dead out of my mind.

He nodded, not looking sure if that was the truth but not pressing.

We walked to the edge of the cave. The sun rose in the distance over a picturesque landscape, spotted with fields and forests. It was a beautiful land, such a contrast to its inhabitants.

"Do you need me to do anything?" I asked.

"No. I'm good now."

He looked back to his normal self, with a healthy glow to his skin, his eyes sharp.

He wrapped an arm around me and then flew us

deep into a forest until we reached a swampy area with a small, dry island in the center of it.

I didn't notice anything until we were a few feet from the spot, but suddenly there was the glittering outline of a door. A minute later the door swung open and Hank was smiling at us. Beyond him? The countryside of Nowhere, and in the distance, Kaden's black fortress rose.

"Good to see your faces," he said, not quite smiling but sounding about as jovial as he got.

We walked back into the fortress and were surrounded immediately.

"I was so worried," Cookie said. "He wouldn't let us come."

"We've been waiting here on pins and needles," Dice added.

"We're back and good," I said, trying to sound happy, or at least reassuring.

Their faces told me it hadn't worked.

"Billie, why don't you go take a minute? I can fill them in," Kaden said.

I was standing there, feeling like even the stairs in front of me were an insurmountable task, when I realized there was no one left around me but Kaden.

"Is there anything I can do?" he asked, suddenly looking as though if he touched me, I might break.

"No. I'm..." I shook my head, and then it kept shaking it, as if I couldn't stop it.

What were you supposed to say when your grandmother had betrayed you? The only member of your family you thought you could trust had tried to trap you, and then it had gotten so bad you killed her? There were no easy words for this occasion, and the night had been too hard for anything else.

"You're going to get past this. That might sound impossible now, but you will."

I nodded. It was easier than arguing with him about how it would never get better. She had been my rock, the one person who'd loved me unconditionally—except she hadn't. Maybe it wasn't everyone else. It was me. I was the problem. They saw something in me that wasn't deserving of love.

"Billie—"

"I'm really tired." I moved to the stairs. I couldn't handle a talk from anyone about how it wasn't me.

THIRTY-THREE

As the adrenaline of getting away from my grandmother and Herrick wore off, a stampede of misery followed in its wake. I didn't want to get out of bed, yet I couldn't sleep. I still didn't understand how it had all come to pass. How had I ended up in a place where I was kneeling over my grandmother's dead body? How was I still alive?

The fortress was quiet, everyone sleeping as I made my way to the balcony, knowing that was where I'd find him.

He was leaning on the rail and glanced over at me, as if he'd been expecting me.

"Why did you do that? Why did you save me?"

I grabbed the back of the lounge chair, too agitated to sit but too weary to stand and needing the feel of something solid in my hands. Something to keep me here, in this world, when nothing felt real anymore.

He looked nearly as weary as I felt, except he hadn't killed his family, so how was that possible?

"I don't know. I could lie and say I do, but I don't," he said.

"It could've cost everything—this place, the world...*worlds*." I couldn't help but look up, to all the galaxies swirling above and linked to Nowhere.

"I'm aware." There was a gravity in his voice that was so heavy it defied the laws of physics. He knew he'd put more than one world in jeopardy.

"I just need to understand why you took that risk." He didn't want me to transition or use me to save his people. It wasn't as if he wanted me, either. Every time he touched me, he buried me in apologies over how it was a mistake.

"I can't give you an explanation," he said, sounding edgier than me.

Whatever his reasons, he wasn't going to tell me. I stood there for a few more minutes, hoping he'd change his mind, but he didn't say anything else on the subject.

It was time to move on down the list to the rest of my questions, of which there were many.

"How did you get us out? It was almost like we were in the center of Chaos, but it didn't feel terrifying. It felt like you." I had already formed my own assumptions, but this was something I needed spelled out.

He nodded. "Chaos is connected to Nowhere. That's where it gets its strength, and so do I. It creates similarities." He shrugged, as if it were as simple as that.

"Are you saying you're linked to Chaos?" I asked.

"In a loose sort of way, yes." He turned to look directly at me, as if waiting for the connections to sink in.

"And now I am as well?" I asked.

He nodded again, watching as if he wondered whether I was going to lose my mind or reject the idea out of hand.

I dropped onto the lounge next to him, my world reeling—again. I'd suspected as much, but hearing it...

"Can it kill you?" I asked, wondering if there was a silver lining in this situation.

"No."

"Those times you'd run from it with me..." We'd hidden in the club, run from the motor vehicle—he'd created a tear in the universe to get us away from it.

"I was afraid it would kill you," he said.

I nodded, numbly. So I was intricately linked to the thing that kept everything in balance. It felt like my life was spiraling into madness, and there was nothing showing up to clean up this mess.

At least our escape made a little more sense—mostly.

"How was Gram able to get to us when no one else could? Was it something I did? Is she connected to Chaos as well somehow?" I rubbed my face, and my brain felt like it wanted to break out of my skull from overload.

"No, she's not. That was my fault. I carved out the area around her to not hurt her."

Her sworn enemy had protected her. I'd been the one to kill her. Somehow that made it worse—not that I'd tell him.

"So using it makes you weak?"

"No. Protecting her did. It's harder to control the power at that level than to let it do what it wants. Unfortunately, you might have to learn that too, depending on how strong you get."

Like Chaos, his power could cause utter destruction. I might be able to cause utter destruction as well.

Actually, I already had.

Gram might've made some bad choices, maybe insane ones, but I'd killed her. I'd lashed out, and instead of using the magic I had to save myself, I'd slaughtered her. Kaden had weakened himself to protect her.

If I'd done that with the beginnings of power I had now, what would happen as it built?

The door creaked open, and Cookie peeked her head out.

"Got a minute?" she asked.

"Of course." Even if I didn't have any words left in me, I'd barely spoken to her since I got back. I owed her as much as anyone. She wanted to talk? We'd talk.

Kaden got up, giving me a nod before he left us.

Cookie walked over and then dropped down on Kaden's abandoned lounge. "You okay?" She threw up a hand. "No, don't answer. I know you aren't."

"I'm trying?" That was about all I could lay claim to when every time I closed my eyes I relived the horror of what I'd done.

"Look, you're a mess. What you went through would do that to anyone, but you'll come out the other side stronger and tougher. You're just in the middle of becoming a better you."

She spoke with so much confidence, and yet here I was, without a single sign of waking up any better tomorrow. I couldn't sleep; I could barely eat. At this rate I'd be dead before this metamorphosis occurred.

"What if I don't come out of this better? What if I get worse? What if I become a basket case instead?"

She looked at me and shook her head, that confidence still shining in her eyes, as if there was no doubt.

"Nah, you would've cracked already. You'll be fine. Trust me, I've seen enough people to be able to spot the ones who are going to break. You're solid.

"Look, no one is born perfect. You have to work at becoming a badass. When you came here, you were a sketch, an outline of who you're going to be. Everything that happens layers on another touch of wisdom, another bit of strength. This is how life goes. Someday, a very long time from now, you might approach being as awesome as I am." She lightly punched my arm.

Instead of telling her she was crazy, that she couldn't see inside my head, or that she wasn't a psychologist, I found myself asking, "You're sure about this?"

"Yes. Now stop all that worrying about your sanity. A bud is beautiful and fresh, but nothing like a full bloom. Sometimes you gotta crack open in order to spread out and become who you're meant to be."

I nodded, letting Cookie, one of the craziest people I'd met, assure me that I was perfectly sane.

I was a moth in the middle of a hurricane, grasping a blade of grass. But that blade was sitting on a little mole-hill and rooted a lot better than me. Sometimes when everything was falling apart, you had to cling to whatever you could to make it through the storm.

"I killed her," I said. "I could've pushed her away, but I killed her. Maybe I was so mad at her that I did it on purpose? I don't even know."

For some reason I was able to speak to Cookie like I spoke to almost no one else. Maybe it was her abruptness that allowed me to speak frankly. I didn't know or care. It felt like a relief to lay it out there in all its horrific glory.

"You think she would've stopped if it had been a simple push? I've known her for hundreds of years." Her eyes opened wide as she leaned forward, putting a hand on my arm. "She would've kept going. You did what you had to do to survive."

I wish I was as sure as she was. I dropped my head back on the lounge, covering my face with my hands as her words spun around and around, until they felt like they were going to burst out.

No matter what I did, that moment wouldn't stop replaying, and the worst were the doubts that echoed. They'd started on the way back as I'd lain in that cave, and hadn't stopped building.

My grandmother hadn't sent me to Kaden's outpost because she thought it was some safe haven or because he was handsome. She'd sent me to set him up. Somehow, she'd known it would come to this. That I'd weaken him. Had she used me for her own ends, for Herrick's ends? I'd been nothing but a pawn. And now? I couldn't even confront her because I'd killed her, and I wasn't entirely sure it was an accident on my part.

I'd live with these doubts forever, but at least I'd live. Her life was gone, and nothing would ever make it right.

THIRTY-FOUR

Every morning for the last week, I'd gotten up and gone to breakfast. I smiled and tried to pretend I was part of the conversations going on. I pretended to listen to the strategy talks. How they needed to gather more people and where the next attack would come from. I'd occasionally force myself to comment on something.

They'd look at me and agree and then go back to talking. They'd stare without staring, looking at me like I was barely hanging on.

They were right. Something had to change.

I could barely focus on anything beyond my grandmother flying in the air and then lying limp and dead. That thought turned into how I could have done it. Which led me to the beating I'd taken, how she'd kidnapped me for Herrick. How she couldn't have loved me. Of all the times in my life I'd come up short. How I could feel power churning inside of me more and more every day, and it was beginning to terrify me. I couldn't seem to break the cycle of thoughts that was beginning to debilitate me.

I'd leave breakfast with some sort of excuse of things I needed to do, or that I was still feeling tired. And like the day before, they all watched me leave with helpless looks.

I walked back to my room and sat on the bed, accepting that life as I knew it was truly over. The last connection I'd had to my past in Nowhere was severed when I killed my grandmother. Whatever strange thing I was becoming, there was no going back.

Soleil tapped on the door before entering without an answer, because she knew I wouldn't. "Can I bring you anything? Something warm?"

"No. I'm okay. Thanks."

She nodded, as if she was *trying* to believe me, and began to back out of the room.

"Actually, can I ask you a question?"

She swung the door open again, as if excited I'd said more than a few words. "Of course."

"When I first came here, and I was hurt, how often did Kaden sit with me?" I asked.

She smiled, as if she were a teacher and her lagging pupil was finally learning to ask the right questions. "Many times and for many hours. You might feel alone at this moment, but you are anything but."

I smiled as much as I could muster. It took the sting out of the loneliness, but not the rest of the swirling pit of despair I couldn't seem to pull myself out of.

"Thanks," I said.

"Of course."

The door closed, and I sat there, staring at the dresser, thinking about what I'd hidden within it.

I might be damaged beyond repair, but there was still some good that could come from my life. It was the only thing that made me want to keep going, keep fighting. When I thought of Herrick, what he wanted to do, what he'd dragged my grandmother into, a rage that could take out an entire planet—or felt like it could—boiled my blood. But I didn't need it to take out a whole planet, just a handful of people.

In order to do that, I had to either use everything at my disposal or give up. There wasn't anyone else that would give my grandmother vengeance for what they'd dragged her into. If Farrow was right, I might be the only one who could help save Kaden and the people in this fortress. It was time to either embrace this world, what I could be, or let the depths of depression consume me.

I got up, walked to the dresser, and dug out the small sack I'd buried in the back of the drawer, hidden in the pocket of a pair of pants.

I opened it, and a small seed dropped out onto my palm. It was perfectly round and black. I wasn't sure what Kaden was capable of, but it surpassed my abilities for sure.

I turned my head to the squeaking noise of a mouse. It was standing on its hind legs beside the dresser.

"I'm sorry. I don't have any croissants up here," I said.

I looked down at my hands and nearly jumped out of

my skin when I heard a man say, "I'm sorry. I didn't want to interrupt."

The mouse was gone, and there, in front of me, was a naked man.

I would've screamed except for two things: he'd angled himself partially behind the dresser to hide his private parts, so it didn't feel like he was trying to threaten me. And second? I'd seen him before. This was the man that had been in my room the first day after the beating, when Kaden was painting my skin with grease.

Somehow I'd completely forgotten about his existence until this very moment.

Or someone had made sure I had.

I looked at the floor, where the little mouse had been standing, and then back at the man.

"You're..."

"A shifter. Yes."

My mouth gaped open. There'd been a little mouse the night I talked to Gram. The night I'd had it out with Kaden.

I got to my feet, ready to do battle. This man was the one who'd misled Kaden into thinking I'd betrayed him.

"Were you the one—"

He held up his hands. "Yes, but please hear me out. I relayed the entire conversation you had with your gram, not just the end. He knew you didn't betray him."

"What? That doesn't make sense. If that was true, why did he kick me out?" It had to be a lie. But Kaden wasn't a fool, and he'd trusted this person. I could tell, even from that small interaction.

"I don't know his mind, so I can only guess, but perhaps he feared you were being used to get to him? He was trying to distance himself so that you wouldn't be used?" He was posing it as a question, trying to act unsure, but he knew exactly what had happened.

It was true. My grandmother had tried to use me, and Kaden had known. How many warnings had I not heeded? How many things had I tried to ignore? I was listening to everyone now.

"You've heard a lot, haven't you?"

He lifted a shoulder, a coy smile on his face. "I've heard some."

"And the beating. It would force his hand. That was why she couldn't step in. They were forcing Kaden to do it?" I asked, taking a step closer to the mouse man, afraid he'd take off before I could get the rest of my answers.

"That's certainly the conclusion I came to. I mean, even going back with Antoinette couldn't throw them off the scent. They knew you were important."

"What do you mean?"

"He went back with her for you. He was upfront about it to her—not that she cared. She'd take any chance to be with him." He looked bashfully at the ground. "He might not know I heard some of those conversations."

I looked at the seed in my hand, knowing what I had to do.

"That looks mighty tasty, if you ask me." He lifted his head, looking at the seed as well.

"This is the only way." It was no longer a question as

I stared at it. It was just a matter of taking action. "Will I remember you tomorrow?" I asked.

"If you say nothing, I would imagine so." He winked.

But if I told Kaden, I'd forget. I nodded, fully understanding. "I'll remember you."

"I think that's wise." He gave me a sheepish grin and then turned to open the window. In a flash, he was gone, a large white bird flapping its wings where he'd been. It turned and flew out the window.

Once upon a time, I'd wanted to spend my life punching numbers and staring at data. I'd only had the occasional glass of wine and never smoked cigarettes, let alone tried something harder. I'd been cautious my entire life, probably from the fear of watching all the crazy people around me spinning out of control.

Well, it was time for me to lose control, because that was the only way I'd survive this world. I didn't hesitate another moment before I popped it into my mouth. It was time to break in order to bloom.

Whatever came from this would come. I'd either survive and be strong enough to kill my enemies, or I might as well give up. Because killing them was the only thing that might bring me some peace—and maybe not even then, because there would still be my guilt staring back at me every day. I wasn't sure I'd be able to ever shake it.

I didn't have to wait long. I could feel the power surging, pulsing through my veins. I held up my hand and almost imagined I could see a halo of power surrounding my flesh.

I sat for hours as it built, coming to terms with what I'd done. I sat there all night, not sleeping at all.

Everyone was gathered around, having breakfast, when I finally emerged from my room. Kaden's gaze was on me, the questions there, and if we were alone, he would've asked. He sensed something was off. He *knew*.

Cookie and the guys were all smiling, as if I hadn't been in hiding since yesterday's breakfast. I poured some coffee, grabbed a croissant, and took a seat at the table with them.

"You look...better," Cookie said, sensing something. She squinted her eyes, trying to nail it down.

"I am, I think," I said.

Connor smiled, and Dice leaned over, giving me a pat on the back.

"We knew you'd bounce back," Connor said.

I nodded. I wasn't sure if that was how I'd describe my current situation, but I *was* better. I had a purpose. I was going to kill Herrick and all his people. Maybe after that was done, I'd collapse in tears, throw myself against the rocks because I couldn't live with the guilt. I wasn't sure, and it didn't matter. That was another day's problem.

"We still don't have enough people, even if that trio can be swayed," Dice said, continuing a conversation from before I'd come down.

"Then we get more," Cookie said, being true to her ride-or-die style.

"How many do you think?" Dice asked.

"I'll have to do a fresh count," Cookie said.

Kaden wasn't paying any attention to them as they continued, his focus on me alone.

They continued for a few more minutes before Kaden said, "Why don't we regroup tomorrow?" He shot them a glance, and the room emptied but for us.

His gaze ran the length of me, and his perusal ignited every wanton cell. Whatever changes were occurring, they were lighting my libido up with a blowtorch.

Hopefully this would be a short-term side effect and I'd return to wanting him as much as I had before. Still uncomfortable, but more bearable.

His hand shot out, wrapping around my wrist, and I could feel the sizzle of our connection, much stronger than it had ever been in the past.

"How?" he asked.

His stare nailed me to the seat. Kaden was an intense man by nature, but the look on his face now, the heat that seemed to be igniting the air around us, made me fear standing, because my knees might give out.

He was so overwhelming that I found myself waffling on the answer instead of blurting it out like I'd planned. "What do you mean?"

"I know what you did. What I don't know is how. You would've needed help. Was it Farrow?"

"Yes." It was hard to concentrate wholly on what he was saying when I wanted to jump into his lap and maul him with my mouth. What the hell was wrong with me?

"Did he tell you everything that it's going to do to you? To us? What comes along with fully transitioning? Because I can't believe you chose this." He dropped his grasp, almost as if the connection were too much for him as well.

"Of course. Or mostly." *Wait. Us?* "What do you mean? I'm the one who is fully transitioning. Why would there be a cost to you?"

He shook his head, then got up and headed toward the door.

"What are you doing? Aren't you going to explain?" I yelled after him.

"Why? You didn't care to ask before, and now it's already done. You'll have to live with the consequences. Both of us will."

"That's it? You're going to leave me without explaining?" I asked.

"You'll figure it out soon enough," he said.

He left me in the room alone.

He was wrong. I'd agreed to pay the price, and there would be no regrets, at least not on my end, whatever the consequences.

WATCH FOR GOING NOWHERE #3 LATER THIS YEAR.

Use this QR code to sign up for new release notices from Donna Augustine. Don't worry! I won't flood your email box. You're more likely to wonder if you signed up correctly. Two emails in one month is my record.

Or, follow me on one of these platforms:

https://www.facebook.com/ groups/2231805984868 78/

http://www.donnaaugustine.com

https://www.bookbub.com/authors/donna-augustine

https://twitter.com/DonnAugustine

ACKNOWLEDGMENTS

Thank you to Arran at Editing720 for your amazing editing and accepting that I can't seem to ever send in a file on schedule. Donna, Camillia, Lisa, Ashleigh and Lori, I know my books wouldn't be the same without your inputs.

ALSO BY DONNA AUGUSTINE

Born Wild (Wilds Spinoff)

Wild One

Savage One

Wyrd Blood

Wyrd Blood

Full Blood

Blood Binds

Torn Worlds (Paranormal Romance)

Gut Deep

Visceral Reaction

River of Luck

.